Blissful Encounters

J.F. Ruffin

Dedication

DEDICATION

To my friends and family, who thought of me enough to tell me to follow my dreams. You'll always be my light, my loves, my everything. Thank you.

To my Parents. Thank you for allowing me to dream without limits.

To Shirley, Chanie, George, and Bill. Who are immortal in my heart.

WARNING

THE CONTENTS INSIDE THIS BOOK ARE NO BASED ON THE LIKNESS OF NAY ACTUAL PEOPLE. ALL CHARACTERS AND SITUATIONS ARE COMPLETE LY FICTIIOUS. DOMESTIC VIOLENCE AND OTHER SENSITIVE TOPPICS ARE DISCUSSED IN THIS NOVEL. READER DISCRETION IS ADVISED.

Contents

BLISSFUL
Encounters

PLAY*List*

1

The Christmas Party

The Christmas party at Hall and Bell was ones that Poppi didn't fit into. It was her husband's sleek brokerage firm. Everyone there looked as if they had stepped out of the Golden Age of Hollywood. Almost as if headshots had to be attached to the resume, and her husband Mitchell Baxter fit the bill perfectly.

With thick and healthy chocolate brown hair, golden and glowing tan skin, a dazzling confident smile, and a perfectly chiseled jaw. His headshot would have flown him in the door. It didn't hurt that he had the body of a Greek god and eyes of hazel that sparkled like diamonds.

Once upon a time, he was her prince charming. Willing to take a chance on the crazy loser. Or at least that is how her mother put it on her wedding day. Only now his charming features had turned mean and hurtful. Sometimes Poppi wondered if he still loved her, even as he paraded her around the party.

"Thanks for coming tonight, babe." He kissed her cheek. "I like the dress, really compliments your figure. Nothing like the stuff you wear when you're with your friends."

Those were his compliments now, backhanded. Poppi hadn't had the best confidence since she graduated college and threw herself into being the best lawyer she possibly could. She'd gained weight that wouldn't budge, and when she went out with her friends, dressing in baggy clothes so that she wouldn't feel massive beside her pole-dancing besties. It never helped he never said anything nice or encouraging about the way that she looked.

This year, she promised herself that she would do whatever it took to get into shape. She would make herself happy with her look. She even spoke to her best friend Roxanna about taking some classes with her.

She would work harder at being his perfect wife. She would work to be more like the women he adored. Including Roxanna, her drop-dead gorgeous Blackrose modeling, exotic dancing best friend. She was married to Mitchell's best friend Alton. They were the couple she envied. Alton treated Roxanna so well that it would make Gomez feel like he needed to step his game up.

"Thank you for bringing me." Poppi gripped his hand with a smile.

"I know you don't like to be social but–"

"Babe, c'mon, it's fine." She reassured him. "I wouldn't miss the night you win broker of the year."

"I love when you say things like that." He smiled "You're an amazing wife."

"Only because of you babe." She looped her arm in his and let him lead her around to mingle some more.

After meeting Cindy, the blonde bombshell secretary, Olivia Foucher the doppelganger for Angela Lansbury who was the financial coordinator, and a beautiful woman with deep onyx skin and breathtaking blue eyes who introduced herself as the CEO Frederick Bell's wife Claudia Bell. They ran into a man who was middle-aged and boring as watching a professor talk about the art of the percentage of time on paint drying. Poppi's confidence, and social battery had begun to wear thin.

"Are you okay?" Mitchell asked leading her back to the table.

"I'm going to get some air. I need a little bit of time to process everything I've learned about how amazing you are." She kissed his cheek. "Be back in a tick." She grabbed her coat with her cigarette case in it. As she was walking out of the door, she felt the eyes burning into her. She turned and Cindy waved to her while a brunette gave her an icy grin and muttered something that looked like a 'fat cow' and judging by Cindy's eye roll and stroll away. She might've been right. 'Confidence Nichols' She thought as she walked through the double doors. 'Confidence.'

POPPI moved away from all the other smokers who were laughing and gossiping. She walked to the corner of the area that was dimly lit and fully abandoned. She pulled out her cigarette case and traced the L on it the way she often did when she missed Lydia. She hated these things as much as Poppi did. They deserved to not be at them together instead of Poppi suffering at them alone.

She pulled out a small cigar filled with marijuana and sparked it. She was grateful for this. She was even happier she got it from her sister, and it wasn't going to bring attention to her. She let the warm smoke fill her throat and lungs. She took a deep breath of the crisp cold air and exhaled the cool fog of her breath and the slow steady smoke. Letting herself lean against the pole.

"Isn't that illegal?"

"It's herbs."

"Right. Isn't that illegal?" The deep smooth voice asked again.

"It's medicinal, if I don't have this then a real pretty brunette is gonna have a real ugly time."

"Yikes, I'd hate to be her."

"I'm just being silly." She muttered. "The woman doesn't know me, and I just don't like being called a fat cow across the room with a glare and a snicker. I got that enough in college."

"Where did you go to college?"

"Harvard." She answered turning to talk to the man who decided he wanted to strike up a conversation with the isolated stranger.

He was a foot and a half taller than her in a deep green suit and looked like he pulled cars and ran across the world for a workout. In the dark, she could tell his eyes were lighter than hers, but the light was hazy, and she couldn't tell the color. He smelled like Green Irish Tweed and sweet tobacco. He looked like he belonged inside, like everyone else. Perfect.

"Harvard must've been your parents' idea. They must've told you first Harvard then 1600 Pennsylvania Ave or the supreme court. You know whichever you prefer." He took a puff from his cigarette and then put it in the ashtray. "A rose that grows in adversity is the most beautiful or however the saying goes?"

"I like being the best, so I wanted to go to the best school. I had to be Ivy League. I graduated with honors, and I got a good job, not supreme court, but it will do. I think I like it more than that anyway."

"What do you do?" He asked looking at her as she handed him the blunt. He took it from her without question and inhaled as she answered.

"I'm a lawyer." She replied. "Mostly contract, but I'm qualified for a few things." She looked at him. "What about you?"

"I work here. I just got a promotion and transferred here actually so I don't really know anyone other than family that live in the area."

"It's tough not having friends and being in a new place so close to the holidays I'm glad you've got some family here."

"All of the ones who matter anyway." He smiled. "My brother and his husband moved up here after they had kids, and my parents have always called this place home. What about you? Do you have people here?"

"My sister just moved here, she and her husband just got divorced. And my husband is inside." She answered. "What about friends? Have you made any since you got here?"

"My best friend owns Hallbrick Publishing, he lives about twenty minutes away, and I seemed to have made one, "he looked at her handing her the blunt back "if she'll have me."

"You don't know my name." She laughed. "You can't be friends with someone if you don't know their name."

"You're very right." He held out his hand. "I guess I should make a formal introduction, hello I'm Zander Bell."

"I'm Poppi Nichols-Baxter." She took his hand. "It's Poppi with an 'I.' I always have to make that clear."

"Well, Poppi with an I it was a pleasure to meet you." He sighed kissing her hand "I wish I could stay, but duty calls." He looked back. "If I'm honest I'm kind of nervous."

She scoffed. "You'll do fine." She waved a hand "You'll fit right in with those beautiful people."

"Yeah, but the most beautiful one isn't in the room, are they?" He smiled and walked into the building.

2
The Award

"And this year's top broker is..." The brunette from earlier cracked open the envelope. "Mitchell Baxter!"

Mitchell strutted up to the podium and she held up a mistletoe and the audience made the normal sitcom "OOOO". Poppi wasn't so excited about the kiss he gave her on the cheek, but she smiled when everyone cheered for his success, and Cindy looked at her with a small smile of sympathy and a thumbs up. As if she needed her to know she knew Poppi was his wife.

Poppi thought that she should be bothered by it. Jealous. Something. All she could think about was scanning the crowd for the man who kissed her hand in the haze of soft white lighting in the dull country club they chose to have the party at. She applauded thoughtlessly bringing back her focus when he began to speak.

"Thank you to everyone who saw my worth and commitment to making this company the best that we can make it. Thank you to my beautiful wife for putting up with my long days and longer nights, and still finding all of the ways to make our marriage count. Thank you to Mr. Hall and Mr. Bell and the rest of the partners for viewing me not only as an asset, but as a friend. Words can truly not express how grateful I am, and I will continue this upward trajectory with this company for as long as I am blessed to. Thank you so much."

While he walked through thunderous applause, Poppi had to remind herself that this was a show, that this was a display to prove that he was the total package. A man of complete perfection. Poppi wished the man who thanked her on stage and walked to their table kissing her while taking his photograph was the man she was really married to, but it wasn't. No matter how much she wanted to pretend it was.

"Congratulations my love!" She smiled wiping lipstick from his lips. "I am so proud of you! I knew you could do it."

"Thank you for believing in me." He took her hand. "C'mon we've got to go be congratulated by the Bells." He said and walked her over to the beautiful onyx skinned woman they met earlier and her almond skinned husband in a deep red suit. And their son. Zander.

"Ah there is our award winner!" Frederick bellowed. Frederick Bell was three or so inches taller than his son when they stood to greet the award winner and his wife. Frederick had a sharp salt and pepper fade with a very crisp and clean line up. His deep brown eyes were shielded by thick black ray ban glasses. His red suit was tailored to a man who took time to care about his body even in his age. He was what they meant when they used the term 'silver fox.'

"Congratulations on your award Mr. Baxter." Frederick continued; his voice reminded Poppi of Santa. Full and jubilant. As if he enjoyed life as much as he did work. "And who is this pretty little thing?"

"This is my wife, Poppi. Poppi this is my Boss Frederick Bell, his wife who we've met already Claudia, and their son our new V.P. Zander Bell."

"Hello Mrs. Baxter." Zander held out his hand once again with a small smile.

"Hello Mr. Bell." She returned the smile. This time it was only a handshake she was privy to, not the soft warmth of his lips on her hand. "Pleasure to meet you all."

"The pleasure is all ours dear! Though I must say in Mitchell's time with the company I've never seen you around." Claudia eyed her, "and I would have remembered seeing you. How long have you two been married?"

"Five years this spring Mrs. Bell." Mitchell had been with the company since he graduated college in the second year of their marriage. Mitchell rarely invited her to any of these events, but since he had to look his best tonight, he wanted to dust the best prop off, his wife.

"Wow, I never would have known. I thought your wife's name was Patricia." Claudia chuckled. "I always get people so mixed up! All that says is that we must get better acquainted dear." She took Poppi's hand "Frederick tells me your husband is a rising star at the company."

"I've seen the numbers and I'd have to agree." Zander nodded. "Mitchell, I think you and I have a lot to talk about."

"Why don't you all come to New Year's Eve dinner at our place? I know Christmas is reserved for family of course, but I think you're right. And I'd love to make you all a dinner you won't forget."

"Can she cook?" Claudia asked Mitchell.

"I'm not going hungry ma'am." Mitchell smiled "I promise it will be unforgettable."

"Then consider it a date." Claudia looked at Poppi "I look forward to being impressed."

"She's only this hard on you if she likes you." Zander nudged his mother. "She's trying to make sure you can take the heat from all those other stick in the mud wives that Mitch is gonna force you to deal with while he's climbing up the ladder." He looked at Mitchell. "We'll get the details together Monday?"

"Sounds like a plan. It was a pleasure to see you guys and happy holidays!" Mitchell walked Poppi toward the door. "Honey you were amazing."

"Just trying to help my man reach the top of that ladder."

"You're so hot when you say things like that." He kissed her head and wrapped his arms around her. Making her feel like the only girl in the world of glaring eyes.

3
Details

Z ander unpacked the last box in his office. He liked the layout of the office his father had picked for him. The desk was in the center with a couch by the wall of fancy art he'd picked up at a few galleries here and there. He had a shelf full of books that had to do with investing, and some were just for relaxing reads. His two large computer screens covered his desk and a television with CNBC muted running in the background.

He wasn't entirely sure of what this move meant when it came to his personal life. He had completely uprooted and left everything to come here. His office threw him a tearful goodbye party, his friends told him they'd come to visit, and he and Carmen had fought since he got the offer in October.

He missed his family. He'd missed Sawyer and Thea grow up for the past three years and he was glad he wouldn't be missing anymore. Even if it was putting a strain on his relationship.

He looked at the picture of him and Carmen he was used to sitting on his desk. He hadn't talked to her since she was filming her daytime show and her primetime series. The last time she spoke to him she suggested that they should take a break to see if this was really what they even wanted. Then she stopped taking his calls.

"Will she be coming with us to the Baxter's?" His father asked cutting into his thoughts.

"No, I don't think so." He shrugged. "She is busy making sure that the elderly and invested have their favorite villain on the soaps, but she said she'd try." He lied.

"Haven't you two been at this back and forth long enough?" His father asked, Zander hated talking about Carmen with his father, he knew that he would ask the hard questions Zander just didn't have answers to. "Don't you think it's about time you both figure out what you want?"

"We're at work Dad I don't want to talk about my love life. "

His father ignored him and snapped his fingers. "You know son, that Poppi is a nice girl, maybe she's got a friend." Frederick looked at him. "You know what they say. Nice girls run in packs, don't they?"

"I don't know Dad, and I don't want to talk about this. Carmen and I are fine." He assured him. Not wanting to think about Poppi either. She'd been making herself known in the back of his mind, making him curious about her, when he knew he shouldn't be.

"Knock knock." Mitchell peaked his head into the cracked door.

"Oh Mitchell, Good! Come in!" Zander motioned. "Ready to get to work?" He decided to pick Mitchell's brain on the best approach to a few new accounts that had come across his desk this morning. Before they came to him Mitchell had been running numbers on them for the previous VP.

"Poppi wanted me to hand deliver these to you two." He held a small red and green Chinese food box with a card taped to the top.

"What are these?" Frederick asked amused as he looked at it pulled off the envelope and opened the box.

Zander opened the envelope:

You're

invited

YOU'RE CORDIALLY INVITED TO A NEW
YEAR'S EVE DELIGHTFUL DINNER!
TIME: 7P
PLACE: 912 LAKESIDE ST TOWN
HOUSE 2
DRESS: SEMI FORMAL
PLEASE ONLY BRING A SMILE, AN
APPETITE, AND A NEED TO MINGLE!
EVERYTHING ELSE IS TAKEN CARE OF.

Zander looked at his father who was biting into a large tree-shaped chocolate chip cookie. "I hope you keep those here, if Rayden sniffs another baked good from another baker, he will never forgive you."

"I won't tell him if you don't." He chewed, "But if this is what we have got to look forward to, then I think my darling wife will be very impressed! Mitchell, please tell her thank you for me, would you?" Frederick looked at Mitchell. "I'm so glad that you're here." He picked up his things and looked at the young man. "I've decided to create a position called Directive vice president. I've got a few people in mind, it'll come with a 10% raise in salary, international clientele which means travel, and when the next Vice president position is opened if everything is in order, it will go to them. Are you interested?"

"Yes sir of course I'm interested!" He exclaimed. Shaking Frederick's hand.

"I've told Zander that he has to have his decision made by the new year. So hopefully you'll have news by then." He looked at them "I'll leave you fellas to it. See you at seven on the thirty-first."

"Yeah, I'm really looking forward to it." Zander watched his father go and moved the box that was hiding his and Carmen's picture.

Mitchell looked at it and then back at him. "You know Carmen Grace? I am a huge fan! She is the most beautiful woman on the planet!"

Zander agreed that Carmen was beautiful, but he found it odd he could call her the most beautiful woman on the planet when he was married to someone as stunning as Poppi. "She's, my girlfriend."

"I thought she was dating one of those famous for being rich guys... Someone with a K."

"I don't think you're as big of a fan as you say." Zander chuckled. "We've been together for two years." Not that Carmen made it national news, and Zander was having second thoughts about it himself. Mitchell didn't need to know that. The less he knew the better.

"Will she be coming to dinner?" Mitchell asked, "I'd love to meet her."

"Unfortunately, no, but the second she makes an appearance I'll be sure to let her know one of her biggest fans is in the building." He smiled. "Let's get to work."

4

Christmas Eve

"Come on Poppi you have to answer." Mitchell jokingly poked her.

"Is this really how you want to spend Christmas Eve? Playing twenty questions?"

"You're too invested in cooking to do what I want to do." He winked taking a muffin she baked earlier.

Poppi wasn't that busy, she just didn't want to spare the five minutes for a man she wasn't emotionally and barely physically attracted to anymore. Pretending to be busier than she had just better suit her than telling him the truth. "Fine. What was the question?"

"What is one gift you desire most."

She thought about it as she basted the turkey and poured two glasses of wine handing him one. "I'd want an all-expense paid vacation somewhere beautiful, somewhere I haven't been."

"You'd have to take off to get that Poppi."

"I have the vacation time I've been working like mad since I graduated."

"That's something to think about." He sipped on his wine. She knew he would forget. She knew her gift was something he quickly picked up on his way to get himself something really nice. She wasn't angry about it; it was nice to see him thinking about something she wanted for once.

Poppi looked at him as she took a small sip of wine. She wanted to ask him something hard, something that would solidify how she felt about their life together. "What do you love most about me?"

"You're the perfect wife for me. You balance work and home like the perfect little seal." He pinched her chin playfully.

Poppi didn't know what she wanted to hear, but that wasn't it. She forced a smile. "All for you, love."

"I have a spicy one for you."

"Only if you answer it first and you're reasoning."

"Okay, so the question is: If you could sleep with someone, we knew guilt free, who would it be?" He asked and then took a sip from his glass. "For me it would be Roxanna because she is a hot head-lining stripper, who has literally worked with like superstars in the sex industry. It'd be nice to be with someone experienced."

"That's an interesting question." She inhaled the savory aromas. "Let me think about it."

Poppi knew Roxanna would lie on glass and bathe in lemon juice before she would ever touch Mitchell, she's been told this numerous times during times it was fitting and just in passing. Still, she tried to picture it. She tried to imagine what Roxanna would look like having sex with her husband. Bored out of her mind. She doubted he could handle her "experience" since the first time Poppi ever tried something new, she got a broken nose.

"Are Alton and I wife swapping?" He chuckled playfully.

Poppi didn't think that was funny, she didn't understand how he could be so comfortable with having sex with his best friend's wife. She understood why, they were a gorgeous couple.

Alton Hampton was a dark-skinned tall slender man with a square jaw and dark eyes. He kept a clean haircut and made sure his wife kept him in the latest fashion. He was emotionally intelligent, and tender, and made Mitchell look like a complete brute.

Poppi knew that Alton would do it, he would even offer to make it the three-some of a lifetime, but she couldn't do it not even in her imagination. Even if it was guilt-free.

If had to be someone they both knew, she'd want it to be someone they didn't know well enough. But someone who was still attractive and would make her feel like Alton would, nonetheless. "Zander Bell." She finally replied. "Your new VP."

POPPI finished displaying the table with all the food she'd cooked for them and his parents. Mitchell stood in front of her making her jump as he looked down at her. "Jesus Mitchell!" She jumped. "You scared the hell out of me!"

"What about Zander Bell makes him the one you would risk your marriage for?"

"You said it was guilt-free." Poppi reminded him placing the macaroni and cheese on the table. "As in my marriage wouldn't be at risk." She walked past him to the kitchen to get the rest of the dishes putting them on the table. Lighting some festive candles as she went.

"What is it?" He repeated. "His position?"

"No, I'm not impressed with that, besides it'll be your title soon enough why on earth would I risk it for that?"

"His salary?"

"It's a guilt-free fling, and that's to assume it's one night, and unless he's paying me ten million to sleep with him, I don't think that matters too much."

"As if you're worth that much." He muttered. Poppi pretended not to hear him and kept busying herself washing the rest of her cooking dishes. "Is it his looks?"

"He's handsome." She agreed. "The only time I'll ever see him is at office family functions and dinners you invite me to or we're hosting. Which is rare, because as you pointed out earlier, I work all the time. I also believe that I pointed out when we talked about this before that the likelihood is so remotely small that anything would ever happen it was the perfect choice."

The doorbell rang, and she turned to go to the door "I'll get it."

Mitchell yanked her back by her wrist. "If you so much as show any indication of being attracted to him Saturday I will push you off the fucking balcony." He snapped.

"Go let your family in please." She inhaled tightly. "I have to use the restroom." He stared at her for what felt like hours. She could see the dark thoughts running through his head. Then he shoved her hand away.

Poppi quickly wiped her tears with the backs of her hands. She couldn't even have a fantasy based on a question he asked without him getting angry at her. She didn't even understand why.

She wished she could call Lydia, and tell Lydia that this terrible thing with this terrible person happened. But if Lydia was alive, they would be spending their holidays with Juniper and the kids in some foreign Disneyland. Just like they planned. Instead, she was here wrapping her freshly reinjured wrist.

"I'M glad you all could make it this year." Poppi looked down at the table. Mitchell's half-siblings Brantley and Sara smiled back at her. They were identical for being Irish twins.

Brantley was tall and looked like a replica of his father, Randall. He had a round face and a button nose. His skin was the color of creamy hazelnut coffee, and his eyes were the smooth and cool gray of his mother's. His lips were full, and they carried a warm smile on them. He kept his hair short, and his muscles were wrapped in a nice soft black sweater and black slacks.

Beside him sat his wife Patricia, a blonde bombshell with sepia skin and green eyes. She wore a pink dress and her make-up was professionally done. She and Mitchell had been in a secret drinking contest since she arrived.

Sara had long ginger locs and for tonight they were on top of her head like a crown even with gem embellishments. She wore a white sweater dress and knitted black tights. Her eyes were hazel like Mitchell's, unlike Mitchell's they were filled with bright kindness and love. "I am so glad to see you Poppi, I haven't seen you since our family vacation, I've missed you to bits."

"That makes two of us Pops." Her wife Alexandria nodded. Alexandria was a beautiful Samoan woman with deep black hair and a charming smile. She was a gynecologist with her own practice. Lydia would have made an amazing partner for her practice. "We were looking forward to seeing you at Thanksgiving, but we understand you were busy."

"Our girl has been *very* busy." Paulette smiled proudly. Paulette was Mitchell's maternal grandmother, who at 74 years old was ageless. Like she stopped the clock in her sixties. Her almond skin barely wrinkled, and where it was, they were dignified and brought an aged beauty to her heart-shaped face and silver cat-shaped eyes.

Her hair was silver by choice curled to perfection. She wore a designer suit with four-inch spiked heels. She was the powerhouse of their family. "You know when that son of a bitch left our Juni, she helped move her pregnant sister across the country by herself on Thanksgiving?"

"Why didn't you tell me Poppi?" Brantley looked at her "I would have helped you."

"Well, your brother was supposed to help, but something came up and he had to stay home." Paulette looked at Brant "With just too little time for her to call anyone else to help, almost as if she was being punished for going to help her pregnant sister move closer."

"She was fine grandmother." Mitchell spat. "Something came up, and as you can see, they all got here just fine."

"You could have been a little less damn selfish! At least called someone who wanted to help your wife and her sister. You could have for once been useful in your marriage!"

"Oh, really Paulette! You're always saying the meanest things about your own grandson!"

"So why didn't he go then Patricia since you seem to know everything?" She placed her fork on her plate and looked Patricia deep into her green eyes.

"I don't know what you mean Paulette." Patricia backtracked innocently.

"I'll make it clear for you then." Paulette folded her hands on the table staring at Patricia. "Why didn't my grandson go with his wife to help fly her pregnant sister and her two children out? And I know he took a flight that day so where did he go? And what exactly came up since his firm was closed the entire week? Where was he, Patricia? Since you seem to know everything about Mitchell."

"They're here now Mother," Sabrina interjected quickly. "No need to fuss."

"That's right." Poppi put a hand over hers. "And they are dying to see you tomorrow."

"Oh, I can't wait to see little Oli! I've got him something special!" Brantley exclaimed. "And I just know Daisy is gonna love the doll house I built her since she literally gave me her ideal schematics."

"Wonder where they got that from." Randall winked at Paulette who smiled brushing him off with a wave. "I've gotten them enrolled in BelHart and have gotten them in some very nice extracurricular programs."

"Randall, you didn't have to do that. You guys are going to spoil those kids."

"Are you kidding? I love my children, but those two, soon to be three, are the closest things to grandchildren I'm going to get. I'm going to spoil them rotten."

"Yeah, and we love being the rich aunties."

"Bit dramatic don't you think?" Mitchell rolled his eyes.

"I don't think so." Brantley smiled at Sara "Those kids are so easy to love. They are smart, funny, and they both have their own unique individual personalities that just make them so fascinating. I just love being their Uncle B."

Poppi smiled watching Brantley's face light up as he talked about the children. She knew he wanted to be a father, but she knew like herself, it wasn't in the cards for him.

"Brantley relax, will you? It's not like you even related to them. Hell, you're barely related to Poppi." His wife scolded.

"Patricia, I don't think you have very much room to talk about who is and isn't related to Poppi seeing as how you yourself like to blur the lines on relatives." Paulette chuckled. "Family is who you choose, and as long as I live those little angels will have a filthy rich gran in me and can have whatever they want."

"Well drop dead so I can have *whatever* I want," Mitchell muttered.

"Mitchell Jackson Baxter what the hell did you just say?!" Sabrina looked at her son in shock.

Sara shook her head. "You're such a fucking Pig Mitch!"

"Well, what did you expect coming from someone like him." Brantley spat looking at his brother with something in his eyes Poppi couldn't quite make out but didn't like it.

"What's that supposed to mean?" Mitchell looked at him.

"You know exactly what the hell I mean." Brantley spat. "If it weren't for my sisters and my mama and my Nan, I'd kick your ass right here right now. Maybe then you'd show these women who love you some damned respect!"

"Brantley darling, calm down." Paulette soothed. "No need in getting yourself worked up."

"Listen to your grandmother son." Randall looked at Mitchell. "Apologize."

"I was joking!" He searched the sea of faces. "C'mon you know I was joking."

"I'm going to get dessert." Poppi stood. "You need to lay off the wine."

"Don't tell me what to do Poppi." Mitchell rolled his eyes at her. "I'm a grown-ass man."

"You're acting like a damn child!" Sabrina scolded him "C'mon honey I'll help you get dessert."

SABRINA shook her head when they got in the kitchen. "I just don't know where I went wrong with that boy. He shouldn't have any memory of the man I made him with let alone act just like him." She sighed. "I thought I did everything right. I changed his name, went no contact with his paternal family and he still acts just like him."

"You can't blame yourself, Sabrina." Poppi cut the slices of black forest cake onto dessert plates. "He's a grown man who can think and say his own thoughts. And that was one he's had for Creator knows when."

"And you shouldn't have to make excuses for him. If he says that about his grandmother, what is he saying about you?" She asked.

"What do you mean by that?" She asked looking at her with her arms folded.

"I mean, is he treating you well? Is he making you happy? Are you still thinking about leaving him? If you are you know you have our full support."

"I'd never ask you to choose sides. And I'm not going anywhere, Sabrina." She promised. "I love Mitchell, and yeah, he has bad days, but I still love him very much. For better or for worse."

"Please don't stay for the worse." She looked at her. "I spent ten years of my life with the worse, and it never got better. He just died in a plane crash. And left me a son who just told my mother to drop dead." Sabrina took two plates and walked into the dining room.

5

It's a "Wonderful" Life

Zander woke up and looked at his clock. At least he slept in, he sat up and began to stretch. Maybe taking one day to himself wasn't exactly a terrible thing.

The Condo that Zander moved into had a pool, a gym, and plenty of privacy. It was communal, but no one made it a habit of meeting the neighbors unless it was in passing. Everyone who he met was kind enough, but none were memorable.

He went to the gym, and it was empty, of course it was no one works out on Christmas, they are all curled up with their families. His family didn't curl up together until they opened presents and ate dinner at sharply 4pm. And he was single this year which meant there was no one for him to laze around the house with watching his favorite movie. The Wiz.

Part of him wanted to call Carmen, tell her that she should come home. He missed her, and they should talk about moving in together again. Even if she did tell him that that would be "the worst mistake she could ever make" it didn't mean that forever, right? They could rethink it.

If she moved in, he could be a better partner. They could talk about all the things he needed to change and work on so that he could be the best for her. He would even do the half his time in California thing she wanted so they could be together more. Even if he wasn't sure about it.

Zander took a hot shower after his run. His mind began to wander. Making small trips back to the woman in the red dress. He wondered what Christmas would be like with someone like her. How would life be with someone like that constantly challenging you to be the best because she deserved it? He almost wished he could see her alone again.

He slid on a soft gray sweater with a pair of black jeans and started packing gifts into the car when his brother called. "Hello."

"Hello! Merry Christmas. I forgot dessert."

"You're a baker Rayden how did you forget dessert?"

"I have twins, I had fourteen cakes, two hundred cookies, and a six-foot-tall gingerbread castle to bake this week I've been busy."

"That's completely fair." He chuckled shutting his trunk. "I will get dessert."

"And that is why I told Mom and dad they could keep you when they got you from the stork. Love you, bye."

"Love you, bye." He hung up. "Where the fuck am I going to find dessert at two o'clock on Christmas?"

ZANDER walked into the only supermarket that didn't follow the on holidays we close policy. He stared at the bare display of Christmas cakes trying to decide between a Rudolph with a candy nose or a snowman that his mother would absolutely hate. Both were something that would make his snobby bakery brother critique his choices. Zander tried to focus as two voices duetted about finding love under the Yule tree.

He never understood why love had to be something that had to be in *every holiday* maybe some people didn't want love. Maybe some just wanted a reindeer cake with pretzel antlers. He sighed. Maybe it would look better out of the fluorescent lighting. He walked past the men who were scratching their heads muttering to themselves "What the hell is this?" Or "How many eggs?"

He envied them. He found himself wanting to do the mundane every-day things that came with marriage. He was envious of the men who actually got to do it. He was even becoming slightly envious of the dark-skinned man with round glasses talking to the small blank-faced cashier in a black and silver vest. Expressing to her that he needs cider, not juice, but cider. And gods help him if she can't help him.

His mind went back to Mrs. Nichols-Baxter, he wondered if Mitchell was the type who had to go out during Christmas for last-minute items. With Poppi though it seemed like she would be a real live Samantha Stephens. Just one twitch of that cute button nose of hers and his hideous reindeer cake that looked like it was made by a teenager who was rushing to clock out would be turned into something immaculate. Something his mother would love and not criticize until next Christmas.

Poppi was like a seed that had taken root in his mind, he couldn't help but think about her. What would her theme song for her own adorable sitcom be? How could he be her love interest in the said sitcom? How could he be it in real life?

The loud crash of two shopping buggies brought him back from his monochromatic fantasy. "I am so sorry!"

He looked up when he recognized her soft voice with southern af-flictions. "Wow." He was flabbergasted by her beauty, trying to ignore the sitcom laugh track that had begun to play in his head for his ten seconds of gawking at her. She was beautiful under the hazy and dim streetlights and then the pale white lights of the Christmas Party, but here she was breathtaking.

Her skin looked like raw honey seen through the setting summer sun, her eyes deep pools of chocolate with rich 24-carat gold flakes floating through them. Her soft ginger hair was straightened and pulled back, but she let a few of her curls hang by her ears for effect. Her face was heart-shaped, and her chipmunk cheeks were rosy and freckled.

Her body was curvy and full in her deep blue sweetheart Lamar swing dress. She wore a thin gold necklace with a rainbow moonstone resting above her cleavage.

"I'm sorry! I know I am a terrible driver." She blushed, making her look even sweeter to him as she shyly tucked a hair behind her ear.

"I meant wow, you look beautiful." He corrected.

"Oh." She looked up at him her eyes widened a bit, and a bright smile came to her face. "Thank you, Mr. Bell."

"Merry Christmas." He tried to recover from his unique reaction to her beauty. She was a marvel to look at. As if Venus herself had assisted in her creation.

"Merry Christmas to you too!"

"Was Santa kind to you?"

"He said I was getting Cole because I got my husband's boss high."

He chuckled "I think we will be forgiven if you tell me, you like my cake." He pointed to the cake in the basket.

Poppi looked down at it with a grimace. "Please don't tell me you're serving this to your mother! Bless your heart!" Poppi gave him a smile and giggle of sympathy. "She's gonna disown you."

"I'll take that as a no." He muttered leaning on the handle. "She'll forgive me, it was short notice, my brother was supposed to bring it, but he got busy, and I wanted to play hero," he slumped his shoulders "but you know what they say about good deeds."

She smiled "Luckily for you I also know what they say about super-heroes." She motioned to him. "I think I might have something for you."

THEY walked together to a black cross trek "Where's Mitchell?" He inquired looking around the dark parking lot.

"He spends Christmas with his father's side of the family." Sabrina tried to keep them from influencing him, but they'd grown close in college, and he spent the holidays that his mother's side wanted to spend with her niece and nephew with them. Since he was their only grandchild. "He and my sisters don't mesh."

"That's no good. I can understand. I was protective over my brother when he got married to my brother-in-law."

"How long have they been together?"

"About ten years."

"So, how'd you feel at the halfway mark?"

"I loved him, and by then they had the twins, so I was totally obsessed. It's one of the reasons I am glad I moved back. I get to be close to the four of them again." He held her groceries in his hands as she opened her trunk and began shifting things. He wondered if she was cold. Should he offer her his jacket? Would she think he was trying too hard if he offered it to her? He tried to stay on the subject with her. "Why don't your sisters like him?"

"They seem to think we're on different paths and he keeps changing my navigation."

"Is he?"

She looked down at her trunk and then took the groceries from his hands standing there looking at him for a moment. Zander wished this moment would freeze in time. Her hand softly touching his, looking into her sparkling eyes, and her beautiful heart-shaped lips fixing to open. "I know that Mitchell is a good man. And an even better broker and whatever my path, I'll get there."

Zander appreciated her dedication to someone who couldn't sacrifice a few hours of uncomfortably to be with her. He wondered if Mitchell knew how lucky he was to have such a beautiful, delightful woman in his corner. He wondered what it felt like to be so lucky in life.

"Poppi! There you are!" A male voice called. Zander turned to see a man holding a bag and strolling briskly to them clutching his black coat. "I got the damned cider!"

"Good! Roxanna will now spare your life!" She laughed. "Alton, this is Zander Bell he'll be joining us for the New Year's Eve dinner party, Zander," Poppi put her hand on her friend's leather-coated shoulder. "This is Dr. Alton Howard my husband's best friend and my best friend's husband."

"I prefer the last part more than the first." He held out a gloved hand. "How are you, man? Merry Christmas, or whatever holiday you celebrate."

"I'm good! I hope you're having a merry Christmas."

"I would if this woman would obey the doctor's orders!" Alton scoffed looking at Poppi who went back to struggling to pull a bag out of the car. "You're not supposed to be trying to lift things with your sprained wrist!" He scolded reaching for it.

"I've got it." Zander quickly lifted it for her. "I have a feeling it's for me anyway."

"You would be correct." She huffed glaring at Alton.

"Glare at me all you want to, but I'm not going to let you do any more damage." He folded his arm. "I'm not budging, and I think Juniper will agree."

"Bringing my sister into this is warfare mister and you know it!" She poked him.

Zander watched them wondering what it would be like to be in her inner circle. What it would be like to be able to fawn over her openly. Scolding her and making sure that she was taking care of herself. "What is this?" He asked looking at the loaded reusable grocery bag.

"It's a triple chocolate cake from scratch, a cheesecake pound-cake, one dozen ginger-doodles, hot chocolate fudge, and white chocolate fudge, with some kid-friendly treat bags."

"I need to give you money." He began pulling out his wallet.

"You carried my groceries to the car and were very much in need of a Christmas miracle, if Alton eats another piece of fudge he might explode and then my best friend will be angry with me."

"You're saving me from myself, truly." Alton smiled. "It's very addicting stuff."

Zander raised an eyebrow. How was she so good? What lab did they build her in? "What are you? A saint or something?"

"Goddess no! I just want to do my good deeds so I can get something good back one day. I have someone on the other side I want to make proud of me."

"I promise you she is Poppi." Alton gave her a comforting squeeze. He looked at Zander. "It was a pleasure meeting you Mr. Bell, but if I don't get her and this cider where they need to be I won't hear the end of it."

"Dr. Hampton I look forward to meeting the Mrs. and getting to know you both better on Saturday!" He shook his hand.

"Me too Zander. And please call me Alton. All my friends do."

"Mrs. Baxter, it's a pleasure to see you again, and thank you for saving me from holiday ridicule." He smiled at her.

"It's what friends do for each other." She closed her trunk. "Have a safe and wonderful holiday." She waved and slid into the car.

CLAUDIA curled beside her husband having another slice of the pound-cake that Poppi loaded in the bag. She even put in loaded gift bags with small toys that were very popular with Thea and Sawyer. Rayden chewed in approval of another piece of hot chocolate fudge.

"Rayden this is phenomenal! You have outdone yourself this year."

Rayden shook his head. "I didn't make this ma."

"I thought you were bringing dessert?"

"Zander had to, the Jacaris family called for a fucking dessert table, and that was a huge deal so we had to handle that at the last minute, and we couldn't do this dessert too."

"Zander can't cook." Claudia looked at the cake. "Carmen must have called in a favor. Where is she tonight?"

"She's busy." Zander shrugged. He hadn't spoken to her in the last two weeks ago the night of the Christmas party. "She said she sends her love."

"So where did you get this? I know you couldn't have gotten it from Alberts. There's not a ridiculous snowman or something on it."

Zander cracked a smile. "Poppi Baxter ran into me and told me that if I served you said ridiculously decorated dessert you would have my head, so she had this in the back of her trunk from her run through of some homeless shelters and she gave it to me."

"Well, isn't she kind?" Claudia looked at Frederick. "What is a kind girl like that doing with Mitchell's son?"

"Well honey, not everyone turns out like their family. I mean he's been dead for almost thirty years now."

Zander looked at them. "Mitchell is a junior?"

"Mitchell's father was a broker, one of the best in the game, we did a few deals together before you were born, and I think Sabrina was pregnant with Mitchell. He was a good broker, but he was a lousy man. He was a cheater, that's how he died, on a plane with his mistress to Hawaii." Frederick nodded.

"Shit." Crispin, Rayden's husband, coughed. "What a way to go."

"Sabrina was too strong for all of that. She did a great job making a life for herself and her son, she even changed their last name back from Kiperman to Baxter. She erased her whole life with that man." Claudia poked the cake with a fork. "I look forward to meeting her even more now."

"Zander said you were hard on her." Rayden looked at her with his royal brown eyes. Rayden favored their father more than Zander; Rayden was fit he never missed cardio, and he had to make sure he could run from kitchen to kitchen. "Were you?"

"Oh no! I just said I wanted to be impressed." She smirked. "And so far, she makes a pretty good cake."

"It's damn fine honey." Frederick took a bite. "Damn fine cake."

6

Hypothetical

The house was immaculately decorated, and smelled with heavenly aromas of Fried chicken, homemade collard greens, and her grandmother's "catch-a-man" mac and cheese. She knew Alton always wanted seafood on this holiday, so she made a seafood boil, homemade rolls, with appetizers of crab and spinach dip.

She set up two serving tables and one dining table so that everyone who wanted seafood could have seafood and everyone who wanted soul food could have soul food and no one had to cross contaminate in case of food allergies. She even made some soul food vegan options in case Roxanna didn't want to eat meat tonight.

Poppi got dressed in a black long sleeved pencil dress that her Aunt Peony had brought her for Christmas. She liked the way she looked in the warm glow of their over light. She wondered if Zander would look at her tonight and say 'wow.' She thought as she pulled out her pin curls and let them fall to her shoulders. The bathroom door suddenly swung open.

"The set-up downstairs looks like you worked all day on it. Did you?" He asked. He was dressed in a tailored suit, his hair freshly cut and combed, his skin glowing and fresh. He had been gone all day, and she had no idea where, she was kind of glad, she assumed he and Alton had spent the day together.

"I started at five this morning." She replied turning to him. "How do I look?"

"Fantastic." He smiled "Good enough to eat that's for sure."

"Thank you darling." She smiled, trying not to compare the compliment to that of a man seeing her and having wow be the only word he could say. She'd never had that happen before. It made her feel genuinely beautiful.

"You know honey I've been thinking."

"About?" She asked adjusting the amethyst earrings her niece made her for Christmas and applying a coat of gloss to her brown lined lips.

"The whole Zander thing?"

"This again?"

"I don't know why I was overreacting. He would never look at you that way." He scoffed "I think he still sees Carmen Grace; you know that gorgeous movie star? And he was also engaged to that singer that you like Cassandra. And then he was in a long relationship with like a brain surgeon bombshell and do not even get me started on the super-model. You are about the furthest thing from his type. Even in a silly hypothetical. You are just not his type of babe."

"Right." She attempted not to be insulted by what he said. Holding in their encounter at the supermarket. "You are right, besides. You are the only man I want." She smiled.

He took her hand. "And no other man will feel this way about you." He placed it on his hardened penis. He took a handful of her hair and pulled her down to her knees. "Will they my dirty little slut?"

"No Sir." She replied flatly unzipping his pants. "They won't." She opened her mouth and let his penis slide down her throat as she pretended to be anywhere else as she went into auto pilot. She wondered why she couldn't be associated with praise, why couldn't she be good in his eyes. Why couldn't she be his sexy little slut? Or his darling little whore? Why must she be associated with dirt? Or being dirty?

His penis tasted bitter and salty. It did not fit how she wanted it to. She wanted it to be full and wide. She wanted her full lips to be able to rest on the base and savor going up and down the shaft, but instead she had to suck in her lips.

She also had to act inexperienced. She could not enjoy dick sucking with him. She could not wiggle her tongue or lick or anything. She just had to sit there and let him face fuck her until he made that terrible hissing moan and spoke. "Oh, shit Poppi! Oh, Fuck yes! Shit."

She held her breath as he shot his seed down her throat. She thought about all the things she would taste tonight that would wash away the bitter harsh bile that was his semen. He pulled back from her and put his dick back in his pants. "You're getting better and better at that baby." He said and patted the top of her head walking out of the bathroom without a second look at her.

Poppi fixed her makeup and hair and brushed her teeth. She looked at herself in the mirror. Her eyes read misery. She took a deep breath. "Keep it together Nichols." She exhaled. "It will all be over soon."

"IF you're ever lost and you need me all you gotta do is call me, Nichols. And I am there. I will always be there for you, livin' or dead, 'cause you're my girl."

Poppi thought about Lydia's last words to her as she sat outside and smoked her blunt in silence trying to feel something other than the emptiness she felt from her husband. Poppi inhaled staring at the inky black night and the twinkling stars.

She thought about the first night they spent together. It was her freshman year in an all-girl boarding school, and their dormmates switched so that she and Lydia would be in the same room. They stayed up all night talking about things they wanted to do with their life, and now Poppi stood in the alleyway of a townhouse in Cole Harbor Maine and Lydia's final resting place was her family's mausoleum.

Dreams of what could have been brought tears to her eyes. She was never meant for this misery. She was even forced into this marriage under the terrible guise of someone caring for her. She knew she deserved better. She just wished she knew how to get to a place where she could enjoy it when happiness found her.

Poppi took a deep breath. She believed Lydia was just waiting for her in the afterlife. Waiting on her moment to prove to her that there was life after Lydia. Even if she had to be the one to give it a little push. "Lyds. I obviously don't know what I'm doing down here, I told you I'd never survive without you, and I'm slowly proving to be right... Please... Please send me my peace."

Poppi blew out more smoke. She felt silly. Lydia was at peace somewhere enjoying a grunge rock show with the greats who went before her. She had to be realistic. If she wanted her peace, her happiness, she was going to have to get it herself. But how?

"We have got to stop meeting like this."

Poppi let out a horrified yelp and jumped.

"I am so sorry!" Zander held out a harmless panicked hand and grabbed her waist steadying her from falling over a box and into the dumpster.

Poppi's heart pounded so loudly in her ears she could barely hear what she was saying as she blinked to focus on the man holding her tenderly and tightly to him. His hands fitting perfectly in the curve of her back. His cologne tingling in her nose. Her fingers brushed his broad chest as she gripped his sheepskin coat.

Her lace black panties were saturated with arousal. Something she hadn't felt in so long she was convinced her body stopped feeling it. Her head was clouded from smoking, but him holding her this way made it hazy with lustful thoughts. She wanted to kiss him. Feel what his full soft lips felt like on hers.

"Are you alright?" He asked.

'Fuck me and I might be.' She thought as she nodded taking a deep breath. "F–fine. I'm fine." She swallowed dryly.

"Would you like me to let you go? Or do you need me to keep you warm since you always seem to misplace a coat?" His grip slightly tightened causing her to bite the inside of her cheek to keep herself steady.

She looked up at him. He was looking at her with something that she couldn't place, but she was sure it was special. She wouldn't over think it. "You smell nice." She finally took a step away.

"Thank you, you smell like dessert, you have my whole family excited about tonight. My brother is a little intimidated by my new favorite secret weapon." He smiled.

PoppI looked at him with a melting smile. "Really?"

Zander nodded looking at her. "My brother owns midnight bakery, and he said if you ever wanna quit law, you two can go into business together."

"Get out! I love that place. I'll have to give that some serious thought." She smiled "I feel special."

"I don't ever think there was a question that you weren't." He passed the blunt back to Poppi.

Poppi's heart fluttered, an experience she only ever had once in her life. When she met Lydia. She knew that Lydia had nothing to do with Zander showing up in the alleyway unannounced, but if anyone were to push someone who made Poppi feel special into her life in a moment where she didn't, it would be Lydia.

Poppi looked up at him. Her smile was half faded. When she thought about what Mitchell said as she hit the cigar again. "I don't know, I doubt I'm as special as glamorous movie stars, brain surgeons or pop stars."

"What did you do?" He looked at her. "Look me up?"

"No... It's a lot weirder than that." She kicked a rock with her shoe. Trying not to play the heluations week she'd had dealing with Mitchell's insecurities.

"Well, I like weird." He looked at her. "Tell me."

"Hypothetically, what would you say if someone like me found some-one like you attractive?"

Zander took a puff. "Someone like you or you?"

"For the sake of the hypothetical," she looked at him nervously. "Me."

Zander looked down inching a step closer to her, a flirtatious grin spread across his cheek. "Then I'd say that those movie stars and brain surgeons better watch out."

Poppi's heart hammered in her chest. He was close enough for this to be dangerous. She could do everything she'd ever wanted to and stop being perfect for once.

"Poppi!" A call brought her back to reality. She turned and her pregnant sister was walking towards them. Zander fixed his posture and looked at her once more making her blush. "Hello." She looked at Zander. "Who is this?"

"I'm Zander Bell, Mitchell's dinner guest. Poppi's Christmas damsel." He chuckled.

"Oh! This is who made you late and caused Roxanna to have an entire panic attack over five minutes?" She looked him up and down "You were right. I would've done it too."

"Why don't you let me help you up the stairs?" Zander offered her his arm. "I want everyone to be jealous when I walk in with the prettiest single woman on my arm."

"I like you already!" Juniper looped her arm in his and they walked up the stairs.

7

New Year's Eve

C laudia and Fredrick Bell were a lovely power couple. Claudia wore a beautiful silver top and sleek black pants. Frederick wore a matching suit. They reminded her of her family back home. It made her miss her aunt and uncle. They reminded her how nice it was to have a love like that.

Claudia and Juniper were pleased to see each other. Poppi soon found out that Claudia was Juniper's doula. Frederick, Mitchell, and Alton talked about work and other things as Zander made a run to his car.

Roxanna kept Poppi company by bringing out the serving silverware. "You didn't tell me Zander was a hottie. I will forgive you for being late."

Poppi rolled her eyes. "You're being silly."

"Hell, you need to be silly too! Ask him if he's single." She nudged her.

"He is not, and neither am I!" She stirred the punch.

"Yes, but we can fix that with a shovel." She laughed. "You just look really sad, and no one would miss him. I'm sure Paulette will get us off."

"You are terrible Roxanna!" She tried to hide her smile.

"I bet Zander is fun in bed." Roxanna slid a spoon into the macaroni and cheese. "I bet he does foreplay five play..." She looked at Poppi deviously. "A little sixty-nine play."

"Roxanna Monique! I am going to send you to your room." She clenched her teeth to hide the laughter.

"Poppi."

"Zander." She turned to him holding a spray of white roses with small blue flowers and a golden masquerade mask on the top. It was breathtaking. "What is this?" She put her hand to her chest.

"It's supposed to represent new beginnings, and I figured since you're hosting the party to start them, that this would be a nice thank you for everything."

"Oh, Zander, thank you."

"I'll put them on the table!" Roxanna's face almost cracked from the smile formed grabbing the vase. "Zander these are breathtaking."

Poppi looked at him. He was a very handsome man. She studied his face for a moment. His smile was flawless, but his fingers were fidgeting. He was mindlessly rubbing his ring finger. "Class or wedding?" She looked at his hand.

"Class." He chuckled. "I've never been lucky enough to make it to wedding bells."

"Maybe Miss Grace will see how lucky she is."

"Maybe." He looked at her, "It is the year of new beginnings after all who knows what will happen."

Poppi watched anxiously as Claudia tried everything once. She'd chew and then look at her husband and mutter something. Poppi's palms were sweating. Why was she so nervous?

"Honey, are you alright?" Mitchell looked at her as she sliced through a lobster cake.

"Yes dear, I'm fine." She nodded. "Thank you."

"Sure honey." He kissed her hand. "I hope everything is to everyone's liking."

"Poppi, this is damn fine!" Federick approved. Poppi exhaled slightly, but he wasn't her critic. She wanted to impress Claudia. It had become severely important to her that she did. She wanted Claudia to like her. To find herself impressed.

"I hope you bring leftovers when you're working long nights with me as Directive Vice President Mitchell." Zander looked at him.

"What?" Mitchell looked up at him.

"I've been thinking about it for a while, but I think it's the best thing for our company. I've seen your numbers. You've invited me into your home and treated me as a friend when you and your family didn't have to. I think that kind of energy is what we need in Hall and Bell don't you agree Father?"

"Your mother will murder us for talking shop at the business table, but yes Mitchell I do agree with my son. I think you'd be fantastic."

Congratulations filled the table. Claudia was still making her way through her meal giving her nods of approval. Poppi studied her, she was regal. She was nothing like Poppi's mother. Perhaps that's why she wanted to impress her. She was like Sabrina and Paulette. Powerful, kind, beautiful woman she just wanted to fill a maternal hole in her heart with words of gratitude, but Claudia felt like a harder nut to crack.

Alton looked at Zander. "It was the fudge, wasn't it?" He chuckled.

"You weren't wrong it was very addictive. I thought my niece would disown me if I ate another piece of her favorite."

"Fudge?" Mitchell looked at Zander. "What fudge."

"My brother owns Midnight Bakery, and they got an important call so the baker of the family couldn't bake Christmas dessert and they expected me, the man who burns water, to get dessert. I went to Albert's, and I rushed to find something, but instead, I crashed right into Poppi, who took one look at my cake and took me to her car, and gave me a bag full of treats for my family. She figuratively and literally saved my life that day because as you can see, my mother can be very picky."

"She just knows what she likes son." Frederick defended his wife.

"You never told me this Poppi." Mitchell eyed Poppi darkly. His tone was a warning.

"It must have slipped my mind." Poppi flushed.

"She couldn't stop herself from talking about you, Mitch. She called you the best broker in Maine and said if I didn't recognize that I was insane."

"What can I say." Mitchell took her hand tightly. "She's got great taste."

"Poppi." Claudia finally spoke making Poppi take a deep breath. "Where are you from?"

"Colorado ma'am." She lied. Mitchell hated when she mentioned her 'hick family'. He hated being associated with the southern belle that she kept tucked deep inside of her. Another difference that he and Lydia shared. She would call her silly names from old movies and ask him to read her Shakespeare because she loved the way it sounded.

"You are not! You can't be!" Claudia squinted. "This doesn't taste like you're from Colorado. These are fatbacks in these collards, I haven't had greens like this since my Aunt Aggie died."

"You can thank my sister. She was raised in the South. I wasn't. But she taught me to cook."

Claudia looked at her. "Some things just can't be taught. There is something in this food. Chile you put your foot in it!"

Poppi inside was jubilant she was dancing and sighing with relief, but if she showed any indication, she knew what it meant Mitchell would have her head.

"I assure you Mrs. Bell both my wife's feet stayed on the ground." Mitchell chuckled.

"Tell me Poppi, Juniper, do you have any single cousins? Sisters? Maybe Poppi has a clone, I'd love to find one just like her for my Zander."

"I'm afraid things like that don't exist Mother. You know what they say." Zander shook his head his blue eyes locking with Poppi "Lightning never strikes the same place twice."

8

Cheesecake

"I am so sorry I have to leave like this!" Claudia rushed out. "But you know babies, they never want to miss the exciting stuff."

"You don't have to explain a thing to us." Mitchell smiled. "Babies are very important to some people. I mean just ask her." He handed Poppi his glass with a small kiss on the cheek. "Scotch, on the rocks, please."

Poppi blushed deeply and took his glass. "Sure honey." She felt Zander's eyes on her as she traveled to their bar.

Claudia looked at him. "You're very right. Tell your mother and grandmother I said hello! It was so nice to see you, Mitchell. You've grown into quite the young man. Your father would have been proud." She smiled.

"Are you sure you don't want me to drive you, sweetheart, I don't like you getting a cab at this hour."

"Honey it isn't late, and I'm fine. You stay and enjoy dessert I'm sure Poppi has whipped something delightful up and I want a piece to ring in the new year with."

"Don't worry about it, Mrs. Bell I'll make sure you get plenty."

Claudia smiled. "And I wanna see more of you missy! I think it's about time I finally have a wife in the circle I can tolerate." She winked. "Zander, behave."

"Of course, mother. Best behavior."

"It was lovely meeting y'all. Bye."

"I'll grab dessert can I get anyone anything else?" Poppi stood.

"No, but I'll help you clear the dishes." Roxanna pushed back her chair.

"I'll help you, honey." Juniper stood. "You're gonna need someone to help you pack up those leftovers you promised."

Zander and Alton got up and began to help Roxanna clear dishes from the table and take out the trash. Mitchell grabbed Poppi's hand. "Mr. Bell, why don't I show you my father's cigar collection? They told me you used to collect yourself."

"Still do, I'm even allowed one on special occasions." He chuckled. "Poppi are you sure there is nothing we can do?"

"She's fine Mr. Bell," Mitchell assured him. "She's a regular Holly Homemaker." He kissed her cheek. She tried to hide the flinch with a smile.

"He's right! You're a guest, please relax." She strolled to the kitchen holding her urge to eye-roll.

"WHAT is going on between you and Mitchell?" Juniper looked at her. "You barely touched your plate."

"I was just nervous is all."

"And hiding your roots? He can't strip everything original away from you." Juniper sighed. "All of your favorite memories come from summers with Gran and Auntie. It's not your personality sure, but it still means something to you."

Poppi pulled the cheesecake from the refrigerator "Mother said I would have to pick my roots or Mitchell, and I picked love."

"Against everyone in this room's will," Roxanna looked at her. "I objected remember?"

"Yes, I remember the very stern speech you gave that everyone thought was a comedy show. I remember my stepmother sobbing and calling out for me as security dragged her and my father from my wedding. It's a lovely memory for me."

Roxanna's face darkened with sadness. Poppi was forced to marry Mitchell three months after Lydia died. Roxanna didn't know the ugliness behind it. But she knew that her best friend was sobbing uncontrollably as her mother proudly walked her down the aisle. "I'm sorry Honey Pop. I didn't mean to bring that up."

"It's fine Roxi I'm fine." She sliced another piece of red velvet cheesecake.

"Where did you get the flowers on the table?" Juniper asked. "They are stunning."

"Well since she brought it up." Roxanna looked like she was about to explode with laughter. "How crazy is it that Zander picked out a bouquet with two of her favorite flowers in it?"

"He doesn't know they're my favorite."

"He may not know they are your favorite, but he thought about you at least. I think he thinks about you a lot. He seems very interested in what you think, how you feel, and how you look. He literally said you saved his life."

"Roxanna... Stop smokin' weed."

"She might be adding a little fairy dust for her to see at the hearts and stars she is seein'." Poppi laughed. "She's been like this about him all night. She's a bad influence."

"Say what you want Poppi Nichols, but that man likes you." Roxanna took two slices of cheesecake.

"Mitchell," Frederick held his bag of leftovers shaking his hand. "You have a damn fine wife and friends. I'm so glad that we could get to know each other this way. I look forward to working closer to you."

"Thank you, sir."

"Poppi?"

"Yes sir." She looked at him.

"You're a marvelous young woman, I'm looking for a new law firm to hold on retainer. I'll have my people call your people."

"Wow, thank you, Mr. Bell."

"Please, call me Frederick." He placed a gentle hand on her shoulder. "It was lovely meeting you Poppi." He walked out of the door. A weight lifted from Poppi's shoulders. Maybe she didn't do so badly after all.

Roxanna addresses her as only she could. "We're going to smoke. You're coming with us, yes?" Roxanna shrugged into her coat as Alton held it open. Zander was doing the same for her sister.

"I'll walk Juniper out and I'll join you and Mitch." Zander looked at Mitch who was pouring another drink.

"Actually, I'm going to borrow my wife for a minute or two."

"You get five minutes." Roxanna pointed at Mitchell. "And then I'm coming to get her."

"She'll be with you I promise." Mitchell smiled holding up his hands and looking at Zander. "I'm glad that someone else witnesses how they team up on me. With you around I might have a fighting chance."

"Don't be so sure about that Zander." Juniper chuckled.

"I'll see you Saturday, right? We'll meet at the gym then go have a drink?"

"Yeah, I'm looking forward to meeting Derrick Hallbrick he is one hell of a writer."

"I'll tell him you said that." Zander shook his hand. "I look forward to some competitive spirit amongst friends."

Poppi hugged her sister goodbye. Her sister held her a little tighter.

"I don't like this. You should let one of us stay in here with you. I am getting a weird feeling."

"I'm fine. I don't need a chaperone." Poppi rubbed her belly. "You gotta cut it with the hormones little one. You're making mommy paranoid." She kissed her belly. "Happy New Year. I can't wait to meet you."

"I'll get her to her car unharmed Mrs. Baxter. I promise."

She smiled. "Thank you."

He returned the smile "It's what friends do for each other." He nodded to Mitchell "Good night."

POPPI watched them all pile out and she wanted to hold every good feeling they gave her, but she knew that it was going to be taken away as soon as the door echoed it shut. She thought about running, just full going full speed to join them, but she knew a scene would just make it worse.

Before she could make her next move a sharp pain flung her to the floor. She was shocked, but not surprised. He wasn't the center of attention tonight. It was spread evenly. But the important people noticed her. Handsome men and beautiful women alike bid her compliments.

"I'm sorry sweetheart." He groaned. "You just made me a little jealous with all of that back and forth at dinner. I don't like how he was talking to you."

"Who?" She cried as he helped her up. "Zander? The man you said wasn't attracted to me. Mitchell, he was just being nice."

"You're no angel Poppi and you know that. If he was trying to be nice, he would have said something normal. He's just trying to see how far you'll go to further my career."

"Mitchell, you're being ridiculous." She tried to hold it together. "I value our marriage as much as you do. And you would never cheat on me? Would you?"

He shoved her against the wall by her throat. "What kind of fucking question is that?! What did Kandi say?!"

"Why would Kandi have anything to say about you?!" She struggled. She could smell the alcohol on his breath. She just wanted this terror to be over. "Please let go of me. You've been drinking and it's not the right time to talk about this."

"I don't want you around him Poppi! He's just trying to get another notch on his belt. And I will be damned if you embarrass me."

"It would be very embarrassing if he were to come back in here and see us like this because you can't keep your fucking hands to yourself." She broke his hold. "I'd never do anything to jeopardize my marriage." She looked at him. "I wish you could say the same." She grabbed the coat and walked out of the door.

9
Good Greif

Poppi laid in her lap. She only came to this memory when she needed to remind herself that love was real. It was too painful any other time. She looked up into Lydia's beautiful mossy green eyes. They exchanged a passionate kiss.

Her fawn skin was freckled and flawless. Her hair wavy and dark as the midnight sky. She held her hand. "You're my light Nichols. I love you. I can't wait to make you happy for the rest of my life."

"Poppi Hart does have a nice ring to it doesn't it?"

"When you agree to be my wife, we can set the date to make it a reality."
She slid the ring on her finger.

It was simple, sweet, and perfect. Their engagement. The happiest moment of her life, the eve of the end.

Poppi's mind was clearing, her tears were fading from her eyes, and it was dark enough no one would notice her makeup. She was curled into the shadows, and she knew she took longer than five minutes to collect herself.

It had been six years since Lydia's passing and she still found herself missing her more than the day before. She wore her moonstone on her neck since Mitchell destroyed her engagement ring. She wished she could be with Lydia anywhere on this planet, but instead, they were in different planes.

She heard the door open. "I'm coming Roxanna." She called. "I just... I got a little lost."

"I'm not Roxanna." He spoke out. "It's Zander." He lit his lighter. "I was sent to check if you were okay because Roxanna had to go to her car." He took a step closer. "Are you okay?"

"Fine!" She faked her best voice, but she knew she fell short of the change on his face.

"So why have you been crying?" He asked blowing out the flame. "If you're alright?"

"I'm still in that stage of grief where at the slightest inconvenience or holiday I burst into tears."

He sat at the bottom of the stairs. "I'm sorry that you're going through this." He looked at her. "Would you like me to tell them you need a moment? Or I can wait until you're ready. I hear talking about it always helps."

"You don't have to be so helpful you know; my husband likes you just fine."

"It's not your husband I'm worried about right now." He looked at her. "It's really the least I can do. You've helped me a few times."

"I miss my dead fiancé is all. She and I were supposed to be traveling the world and doing amazing things, but instead, she's dead and I'm..."

"You're stuck hosting dinner parties with stuffy men in suits and their parents for a husband who doesn't let you get a word in at dinner?"

She laughed. "Yeah, but I enjoyed your company, and your parents were delightful."

"Delightful." He looked at her. "My mother was right you are southern! Where are you from?"

"I was born in Virginia, and then my parents divorced, and my mother moved to Colorado Springs and my father moved to Aspen. My mother let me summer with my grandparents and my aunt in Georgia, and my dad would let my sisters join, but I was mostly in private schools around the border of the north."

"Wow, must have been lonely."

"I met Roxanna when I was ten at my first one, and we always stayed in touch. She even went to school in Boston to be close to me. We've been friends my entire formative life. And I met Lydia when I was a freshman. My whole life changed then."

"Oh?"

"Yeah, we spent our entire high school career together, got into Harvard together, and got an apartment together our sophomore year. But then she died the day after our engagement and my life hasn't been the same since."

Zander nodded. "I'm sorry for your loss, you two sounded like you had a lot to do together."

She smiled. "Yeah, we did, but you don't have to be sorry. It's not like you knew her."

"If she was anything like you. She was a force of nature that couldn't be reckoned with." He stood. "I'd like to think Roxanna won't kill me if I don't present you, but I'm very afraid of that woman. I saw Alton have an argument with a woman in a store over cider in the name of this woman, I'd hate to see what she'd do if I didn't turn up with her best friend." He held out his hand.

"We wouldn't want that." She took his hand. "Thank you."

"It was absolutely my pleasure. It's what I'm here for. Just do me a favor?"

"Sure."

"Don't tell my mother your lineage, she'll be convinced to try cloning and I like the original just fine."

10

Resolution

Zander walked to the alleyway hand in hand with Poppi. Her hand fit perfectly with his. She was the perfect size coming up to his collar bone. She smelled sweet, like a fresh morning's dew, fresh cut flowers, and juicy ripe fruit. Bringing the idea of spring and freshness to the crisp chilling frigid winter.

She was magnificent. He loved listening to her talk; at dinner she was passionate when she got the chance to be. He thought about how intelligent she was. It had to be so interesting to have conversations with her all the time. He wished he got the chance to experience it, but she had someone who got to do that, and he had Carmen. Someone who couldn't be bothered joining him.

"Mitchell doesn't think that we should be friends because you're single and I'm married."

"I can understand, I'm not exactly single, but I also wasn't being subtle about how fantastic I think you are."

"You were just being kind."

"Poppi you deserve only the upmost kindness, but hypothetically." He looked at her thumbing over her soft knuckles. "What if I were attracted to someone like you."

"Is it someone like me or just me?" She asked with a coy grin.

"I think you know the answer to that." He chuckled. "Would you want to be friends with me then."

"You are just sayin' things you think I wanna hear 'cause you think I'm sad." She chuckled. "I know after five minutes of just you and I you'd be bored out of your mind. I'm really quite boring. I just want to hang out with my niece and nephew, watch cozy murder dramas from the

80s and work. You're dating an actress. I'm sure you're all about glitz and glamour when it comes down to it. And that's something I'll never be."

Her accent was heavy, Zander could tell it happened when she got flustered. And it was making him salivate. He wanted to hear her talk for hours about anything. She turned to walk away, but he pulled her in, closing the gap between them.

Zander wanted to lean in and kiss her. He wanted to show her how wrong she was. How he couldn't wait to have play dates with their siblings' children and thinking about cozying up to her in any aspect was exciting to him.

"For the record." He whispered huskily. "I love cozy murder mysteries and cuddles."

"Good! You found her!" Roxanna walked up to her. "I thought I was going to have to commit homicide."

Zander stepped away. "No! No need for murder." He chuckled. "I found her in one piece."

"Yeah, he was just being a real friend, and lending me an ear." Her voice became refined and posh. Her entire face changed into one of happy and hopeful expression from the one of melancholy and sadness.

"Are you joining us?" Roxanna asked him, looping her arm into Poppi's. Poppi's eyes had not left his.

"I wish I could, but I've got a phone call to make before I go to bed tonight, Goodnight, ladies. Happy New Year."

"Happy New Year." They repeated in unison and walked toward the alley.

Zander watched them. *If she looks back,* He thought *I'm not the only one who felt the spark. There is something there.* Poppi turned her head and locked eyes with him smiling shyly and giving a small wave before turning into the alleyway.

ZANDER walked into the darkness and emptiness of his Condo. He turned on the light and looked around. Other than his furniture the place was bare. No photographs, barely any paintings. He didn't have much inspiration to do anything. He was hoping this would just be a seed.

He'd once hoped he would be planting his roots in a nice home with Carmen, but when he brought it up to her, she said she'd rather die than be stuck in a small town barefoot and pregnant. It saddened him that she thought of him like that. He would never want to domesticate someone who didn't want to be. He just wanted to be close to his family. He wanted to make a home. He walked to his bar, maybe one day he would.

His phone rang and he picked it up quickly. "Hello?"

"Hi, honey I just wanted to tell you I made it home. And I wasn't sure if you made it to your place yet."

"Oh, hey ma! How did the delivery go?"

"Flawless. Mama did perfectly."

"That's a lovely mom! Juniper is really excited to get to enjoy the Bell baby experience."

"I'm glad I got to meet her sister. She talks a great deal about her, and Roxanna and they seem like very lovely people. That Poppi knows her way around a kitchen I'll give her that, but... I don't like her makeup."

"I thought she looked fine."

"Your father said the same thing about Mitchell's mother when we were younger. I had this same feeling, and he barely let her speak tonight. She directed everything to Mitchell in some way."

"Mother I think you might be overthinking. I thought you enjoyed yourself."

"I did." She defended. "I'm just a worry wort is all. Have you spoken with Carmen? I thought we'd see her tonight."

"She is busy, but I'm sure she'll be joining us soon." He deflected.

"Funny, that is the same thing you said to us when you moved here alone. You don't have to cover if you two have broken up Zander, we won't judge. And I'll make sure Crispin doesn't celebrate too loudly."

Zander laughed. "We're fine mother. She's just busy."

"Honey," Claudia's voice was filled with motherly concern. "Maybe you should take this year and really think about the things you want, the things you need. Be a little selfish, since she seems to do a fine job doing it."

"Mother c'mon. She is doing the best she can she has a very exhausting career."

"And you do too, but you make time for her, I'm sure."

"Listen Ma, I'm getting another call. I've to go, I'll see ya later."

"I love you, honey." She sighed. "I'm sorry if I've upset you."

"No, I'm not upset. Just..."

"I get it, darling. Sometimes it's hard saying goodbye to something that's comfortable to try something new."

"Yeah exactly." He sighed. "I love you."

"Always honey." She hung up.

Zander got on the treadmill and began to jog. No better way to ring in the New Year than burning off a few calories from the best dinner he'd had in a while. Zander let music fill his head as he let his mind find its own path to wander.

"You're dating an actress. I'm sure you're all about glitz and glamour when it comes down to it. And that's something I'll never be." He replayed it in his head over and over. Was he dating an actress? Did he want to be after tonight? He knew that he liked the way Poppi looked at him. He liked the way her hand felt in his. How her voice sounded like a melody.

He thought about his parents, how loving and caring they were towards each other. His father worked hard when he was a child, but the moment he began to become a life-changing version of wealthy he took all the time he could to spend with his wife and children. He was dedicated and caring to his wife. Zander watched his father go above and beyond for his mother and he wanted to do the same for his person.

ZANDER stepped into the shower. He thought about the events that happened at the party. Poppi was a special woman, and she had a special defense team around her that always made Mitchell look like he was a spectacular husband, and he wasn't.

She surrounded herself with the most interesting people. Roxanna and Juniper worked in very different fields, but their stories were both interesting and funny. Poppi would add things, but then she would put the conversation back towards Mitchell so that she didn't have too much of the spotlight when she deserved most of it. She was the funny one, the bright one, the one who could hold a conversation. Mitchell wasn't exactly someone he'd like to sit down alone with. He was sure he'd be bored before the meal was over.

He had to clear the air with Carmen. He thought as he finished his shower. He would call her and tell her that he's met someone he has an interest in, and he'd like to take some time to himself to figure out what he wanted. She would be angry, but at least she'd never have to step foot in Maine. It was the thing she complained about the most.

He stepped out of the shower and picked up the ringing phone. "Hello, this is Zander Bell."

"Hi, babes! I'm so glad you're home!" She laughed. "Where else would you be?"

"I had a dinner party tonight, Carmen, don't you remember I invited you when we talked last week."

"That was tonight?! Damn! I'm sorry honey. I mean I guess this makes up for you missing my red-carpet last month."

"I had my family's Christmas party that night, in another state, you know where I moved?"

"Speaking of that. I've put it in the calendar, but I'm coming to spend some time in Maine with you, I want to see if I like it enough to make it a permanent thing."

"Carmen you don't have to do that. I know what you said, and I don't think it would be fair to make you do something you don't want to do."

"Who said I didn't want to move to Maine?"

"You did! You said moving to Maine would be a terrible decision and that you didn't want to be lost in a boring sleepy town barefoot and pregnant, you said being married and starting a family would be career suicide and you never wanted to do it. I respected that."

"Zander that isn't what I said." She laughed. "No silly! I said that motherhood just isn't a hat I want to wear. I know you want to be a dad, but you also said you were fine with being childless and that's great. Maybe me being in a nice small town and coming to Cali when I need to film isn't a bad idea."

Zander listened to her, not knowing what to say about her completely different tone. "Carmen, there is something else... I've met someone I've taken an interest in, and it's very complicated." He admitted. He waited for her to say something.

Instead, she burst into laughter. "Someone else? You? Zander, you're loyal like a golden retriever, and more boring than my 90-year-old great-grandfather. Where on earth would you meet someone? Your office? You think I'm going to believe some frumpy secretary has caught your eye when you've been committed to *me* for two and a half years." She cackled. "You're funny."

Zander swallowed his next statement. "It's kind of hard to tell if you're joking, I haven't seen you in two and a half months."

"And now you'll see me in less than a week." She sucked her teeth. "I think it's very cruel of you to make up some silly woman to make me jealous. I've got to go. I love you, see you later." She hung up.

Zander tossed his phone on the bed. Maybe it was better having her around, Mitchell wouldn't feel so intimidated by their friendship then.

He would work on being the best him he could be the man who deserved a woman like his lightning bolt.

11

New Year, New You

P oppi had made a lot of change in the few days after her successful dinner party. She met with her sister Lavender and opened a bank account in an elite bank that only Lavender had clearance to get her into. She put five thousand dollars she'd been saving in a shoebox in the guest room and moved it in the account.

Roxanna told her that Kandi, their baby sister friend, had messed her shoulder and wrist up badly during a fall from the top of the pole at Lucky's and she was out for seven weeks. Roxanna was down a partner, and Poppi volunteered.

Poppi didn't need to work in a strip club, but she wanted to. She wanted to enjoy the freedom that came with making money Mitchell would never suspect and have it tucked away for when she could finally get a judge to hear her conservatorship case.

Maybe without the weight of knowing that they can put her away whenever they noticed she wasn't being their perfect little doll. She could take the first steps of freedom. Poppi was slowly coming to terms that her marriage was in shambles, and she was trying to revive something that didn't need it. Mitchell would be happier without her. She was sure of it.

While she lie in wait for her daring escape, she would get her body to her liking and practice, preform, and perfect pole dancing. She walked into Roxanna's gym Top Paid Performance.

"Holy shit." Roxanna walked up to her. "You're here! I thought you were bullshitin' me!"

"Nope I'm here and I'm ready."

"Oh my God, you came! I'm so glad to see you!" Kandi wrapped her free arm around her. Poppi hugged her back. Her mind went back to Mitchell. Why would she accuse him of being unfaithful?

"Well, no time to spare honeypop! We are on a crunch so we gotta work and work fast and hard. I need you to show me what you've got.

AFTER learning, so many different holds and swings Poppi was sat in a smoothie bar feeling alive, free, and for once happy that she was doing something for herself. Kandi danced her straw around her smoothie. She had been distant for a while and stopped coming around them, she even declined her invitation to the New Year's Eve dinner, and now she barely spoke to Poppi. Something was up to her, and she was worried. "How was your New Year's Eve?"

"We missed having you there." Poppi took a sip of her drink. "You have been off the radar for a bit. I miss you."

"I miss you too Popsicle, Freda and I broke up and I've just been so out of it about it you know, I just I've been to myself. And then duty called on the night of your dinner."

"If duty hadn't called. You wouldn't have fucked yourself up." Roxanna nudged Kandi who smiled weakly. "How have you been since New Year's Eve Poppi?"

"I'm dealing." Poppi decided she'd be more honest with her friends this year as a resolution. "He has been very prickly since our dinner, he hasn't spoken to me, and when he does it isn't pleasant."

"Why is he acting like this now, first it was something weird that happened at the Halloween party, and now this?! What is going on with him?" Roxanna wondered.

Poppi watched Kandi's face turn sour at the mention of Halloween. "Are you okay Kandi? You look like you swallowed a bug."

She scrunched her lips to the side. "I'm fine babes, just trying to figure out what's got your dumb ass husband's taint in a twist. Why don't you fill me in and maybe we can figure it out together?"

"Why don't you?" Poppi looked at her. "You've been sitting on something for months and I want to know what it is."

Kandi looked at her. Her eyes were wide from Poppi's accusation. "What the fuck Pops?"

"She's not lying you've been acting kinda weird Kandi." Roxanna looked at her.

"Oh! So, we're tag teaming?" Kandi folded her arms."

"I wanna know why my husband thinks that I've spoken to you about him being unfaithful."

Roxanna looked at her. "What?"

Kandi looked at Poppi. "Why would he say something like that? I'm under an NDA I can't say anything about anything for the next two years."

"From?"

"I think that's enough." Poppi swallowed the lump in her throat. Kandi said everything and nothing. "I mean no one wants to get into trouble."

"Poppi, please... I'm so sorry." She looked at her. "We broke up like the night of, and then–"

"Kandi stop." Poppi held her hand up. "I don't want you getting in trouble."

"Well, can't you just know how sorry I am?"

Poppi sighed. "I know." She wiped a tear away. "I just wish it still didn't hurt so bad after everything he's put me through. I wish I could do something about it."

"Like guilt-free and no one would know about it?" Roxanna grinned. "You know I bet he'd be up to something like that."

"Roxanna please quit it he would not!"

"Who?"

"Zander, Mitchell's super nova hot boss. And he's interested in Poppi. Like real interested."

"She's exaggerating." Poppi scoffed. "He is just someone who has been nice to me more than once. And Roxanna's trying to run with it."

"You know since she's working at Lucky's for Eros night why don't you just invite him? You can both settle this debate." Kandi looked at them. "And since it's mostly fantasy, it'd be considered guilt-free."

"Kandi you're brilliant!" Roxanna squealed "And you'll make so much fucking dough that night you can leave for real!"

Poppi heard them both talk about Eros's night. The most intoxicating night of the year. The year when all the Cherub fae shed their skin and just allow their way of passion, lust, and love to flow through the club. It gave different effects on different people, but it was a very elite group who got to experience it. And there was almost always someone from the legion there.

She thought about being able to feel Zander's deepest desires. She knew she wasn't privy to the information but to be desired like that, even for a moment would be the luckiest thing in the world.

"Poppi, what do you think?"

She looked down at her smoothie. "On New Year's Eve, I asked Mitchell if he valued our marriage, and he never said yes. He just screamed about you. So, I figured that was my answer. And he doesn't value it. I'm tired of putting value into something he views as worthless. It'd be nice to be desired for once."

12
Lucky's

Z ander had a blast playing basketball with his friends and Mitchell. Alton and Derrick hit it off extremely well. They even agreed to taking a cooking class together that they saw in the community center they went to. Mitchell told them there was no need for him to do the class since he had Poppi, but Alton had Roxanna and almost seemed excited to take the weight from her.

Zander was glad he'd be able to learn how to do something in the kitchen that might impress Carmen when she was home. She showed up two days ago and left the same night after a few rounds of sex.

The sex didn't feel great. It felt mechanical. Like he knew he had to because he was with her, but she didn't make him feel like he was wanted, just the way he got her off. Zander shook the thoughts as he walked through the beautiful glitzy burlesque club. Women walked around in masks with black lingerie as a uniform.

Zander looked at the performance going on the main stage. The women were tangled beautifully twirling around the pole together as raining confetti covered their masked faces. "Wow. That one in the gold is beautiful."

"She's too fat for my taste." Mitchell sneered his nose. "Her body could use a surgery or two. Then she could look like her partner."

Derrick looked at her. "Man, you don't know how to handle a real woman and it shows. She's thicker than duck butter!" Derrick put his hand on Zander's shoulder. "And the girls got talent."

Alton chuckled. "C'mon let's go order drinks and we'll find a table." Alton led them to the bar. A short dark skinned curvy young woman with a pink bunny mask covering her face, and only showing her black sparkling lipstick. Her eyes were neon pink and her lingerie matched.

"Hi Alton!"

"Fella's this is Roxanna, and Poppi's faux little sister Kandi. Kandi this is Derrick, and this is Zander."

Kandi looked at them. "Hello, boys. A pleasure to meet you."

"Careful you two she can smell out a dollar from a man in another state." Mitchell chuckled. "You know what they say about her type."

Zander looked at Mitchell. Why would he say something like that about his wife's best friend? He looked at Derrick who was studying the beautiful woman in the pink bunny mask. He could tell Derrick's jaw was clenched.

Derrick looked at Mitchell. "I don't. Why don't you tell me." He leaned on the bar.

"She's only into felons, high-risk rappers, you know the type! Look at where she works."

"It's where your best friend's wife works are you insulting her as well?" Derrick looked at him. "Just because a woman is liberated in her skin enough to bless us with a small glance does not mean that she is only into a certain type of man, woman, or non-binary being. It's truly up to her. And I think you're angry."

"Me angry? Why?"

"You couldn't satisfy any woman in this club, and it shows. It shows that your wife has been settling for a mediocre man for ages and I'm sure is becoming bored. I'm willing to bet you tear her and any other woman down for that matter so you can feel better about how you know deep down in your tiny man complex she deserves better than a bitter he-man woman hater."

Mitchell looked at none of the men coming to his aide. "Fuck you, man. I was joking. You're just being sensitive."

"There's nothing sensitive about a woman's mood visibly changing when you open your mouth." Derrick looked at him. "Apologize to the lady."

Mitchell looked at Alton. "Will you tell him that I'm joking!"

"Are you?" Zander asked. "I mean you did call that woman fat, and she looked about the same size as your wife. Do you think she's not your taste?" Zander inquired casually.

Mitchell looked at him. "I appreciate your friendship. But don't ask about my wife and my fucking taste." He looked at Kandi.

"Look I'm sorry alright. Obviously, there was a misunderstanding. Can I have a Vodka soda please I'm going to the table." He put his money on the bar and walked toward the empty table in the back.

"You pissed him off. I like that." Kandi grinned watching him walk away. "I guess that means I'm buyin' you a drink."

Derrick looked at Zander. "Did you hear that? My future wife wants to buy me a drink."

ZANDER stood outside smoking a cigarette. He tried to call Carmen, but it went directly to voicemail. He stood looking at his phone and found himself wishing that he could call Poppi. He sighed which was unreasonable. He knew better than to want something like that. Mitchell made it clear he didn't want him around her. He would have to respect that.

"You're not inside having fun? That is very weird Zander Bell." Roxanna walked out in a black sweatsuit.

He turned to her. "How so?"

"The women are giving lap dances to Alton and Mitchell; Derrick has politely declined and you're out here. Do you not enjoy the dances?"

"No, I just have some things on my mind." He looked at her.

"I heard you were into the routine; did you really like it?"

"Was that you when we first came in?" He asked looking at her. "You were great. Your friend was wonderful too!"

"Would you believe that was her first time in front of an actual audience?"

"Really? She was flawless." Zander rubbed his ring finger subconsciously. "What are you doing out here?"

"I had to get away from Derrick and Kandi for a minute. They are... Gross."

Zander chuckled. "I know you're not talking about my emotionally detached workaholic best friend Derrick."

"Not unless he's the same one who is fawning over Kandi like she is the only girl in the strip club."

Zander furrowed his brow. "Really?"

"Yes." Roxanna laughed. "He hasn't moved from the spot you guys left him in. He's been so sweet to her; I think they're even going to Tony's after. Which reminds me I better get some food. It looks like Alton wants to spend the night at Mitch's and I'll be crashing with Poppi, but I need junk food."

"I know a guy. I can get you some. On me of course." Zander offered.

"I knew I liked you! I like you so much that there is some money I want to invest in a few little things, and I think you'd be the perfect fit for me. And to show you I'm serious I'm giving you this." She handed him a heavy red envelope.

"What is this?"

"An invite to the most elite night of the year. You're going to be rubbing elbows with some of the most beautiful women and successful men this side of Tristate." She smirked.

He tucked the envelope away. "I take it Mitchell isn't going?"

"God no! He would never survive." She laughed. "You can't be a pig and enjoy this night."

"Does Poppi know that all of her friends hate her husband?"

"Believe it or not we don't enjoy hating him, and we do our best to fake it for her sake, we know she's stuck, so we make the most of it. We don't hate him on purpose. That's for sure."

"I see." He looked at her. Zander wanted to ask her things; things he knew she couldn't answer. "How is she?"

Roxanna smiled. "She's fine, in fact, you just missed her. She had to drop something off for Kandi."

"Of course, I did." He looked at her. "Come by my office Monday and we'll start talking business."

"Don't worry I'll tell her you said hello." Roxanna put out her cigarette. "I like you, Zander." She eyed him. "Don't fuck that up."

13

Slumber Party

Poppi made it home before anyone saw her. She was showered and lounging on the couch when Roxanna let herself in and put two large pizzas with a salad on the table and kissed Poppi on the head. Then she made her way upstairs to shower.

Poppi missed this ritual with Lydia they'd sit on the floor of their apartment and talk for hours while sharing a pizza laughing at each other and telling each other about their goals for their lives. They had big dreams, and one day Lydia would get to see Poppi fulfill some of them.

Roxanna laid her legs across her thighs and stretched out on the couch placing the box on her thighs. "Glad to see you made it home Clark Kent." She smirked.

She laughed pulling a salad to her "I don't think I could change in a phone booth."

"I think I know a guy or two who would pay to see to see you try." Roxanna swallowed her bite of pizza "Did you know Zander and Mitch were coming to the club tonight?"

"Obviously not, but when I recognized Alton, I figured my exit should be hasty."

"You were very correct because Mitchell saw you on the pole. Not that he'd ever believe it was you, but I can say if you're serious about Eros night it will be a success."

Poppi rolled her eyes. "And why do you say that? What happened?"

"All second hand of course, but apparently Mitchell called you fat. And Derrick, Zander's childhood best friend and Kandi's newest victim told him he couldn't handle a real woman. But Zander was drooling over you. Allegedly she said he didn't stop watching the show until you left."

"Something else happened, didn't it?"

"Okay, you pulled my leg!" Roxanna giggled. "He asked about you! He wanted me to tell you hi. I'm telling you Poppi I think he genuinely likes you."

"You're being ridiculous." She rolled her eyes. "Maybe he was being nice."

"Maybe he was wondering how you were because he cared! Poppi, I know you're with someone who doesn't give a damn if you eat sleep, or breathe right now, but there are men out there who not only care, but they will also call you a good girl and give you treats when you actually do the stuff that you're supposed to do. I should know I married one."

Poppi smiled thinking about how Alton feeds Roxanna her gummy vitamins from the palm of his hand and calls her 'my princess.' Alton even sliced her steak for her. If she didn't want to, she'd probably never have to lift a finger, but he also respected her independence. He was beyond supportive. He would even give her scene partners suggestions so that her films were the absolute best and won her as many AVAs as she could.

Their relationship was tender and unique. They even had other part-ners and respected each other enough to talk about their feelings and go to therapy together when they couldn't find a resolution. She would never be that lucky. Zander was no knight in shining armor to her. He was someone else's prince charming.

"Not everyone can be as lucky as you are Roxanna, some people just get stuck with toads."

IT had been a few episodes since Roxanna and Poppi had gotten quiet deeply watching television while casually making a comment about one of the reality stars. "I bet you she's going to be pregnant."

"I've just never seen a woman take a pregnancy test while smoking a Newport on national television." Poppi heard the doorbell. She looked at Roxanna in her baggy flannel pajamas. "Did you call something in?"

"No. but I'd kill for something sweet." Roxanna looked at her. "What do you have left over?"

"Nothing. I got rid of all the sweets a week ago." She stood. "I didn't want to be tempted." Poppi walked to the door and a man stood with a large black box and Kandi leaning on his arm. "Uh... Hello." She looked at him.

"Hi, I'm Derrick Kandi's- "

"Boyfriend. He's, my boyfriend." She giggled.

"I'm her boyfriend." The handsome well moisturized light medium skinned man smiled. His smile was just as dazzling. "And these are from Zander, he and the boys are going to grab something greasy to fight their hangover. Well, Mitch's hangover. He figured you ladies might have a sweet tooth."

Isn't he just the sweetest?!" She looked at Derrick. "I'll call you when I get home tomorrow, and you can take me on that hike you promised."

"Sounds great! I'll see you then." He kissed her on her head. "It was a pleasure meeting you, Mrs. Baxter."

"Please call me Poppi, you make me feel like you're dropping my little sister off from a date." She took the box. "Tell Zander I said thank you."

"Yeah of course." He smiled. "Bye Angel."

"Bye D." She grinned and watched him walk out of their view. "I'm so in love with him my heart and vagina are about to explode." She took Poppi's hand and walked into the door.

"What the hell is going on Popsicle?" Roxanna asked as she sat up. "When the hell did, she get here?"

"Just now with her boyfriend?"

Roxanna burst into laughter as Poppi placed the box on the table. And Kandi sat across from her. "You swore off men two years ago. You said you would never date another man ever. And now you have a boyfriend since when?"

"Since he asked me..." Kandi got a smile on her face that made her look like the black Brittney Murphy. "Over waffles."

"You're gross. That's gross. I want to hear everything!" Roxanna opened the box "Did he bring these?"

"He did." Kandi looked at Poppi. "Only they're from Zander. He met us at the diner after picking them up for us. He said he wanted to measure you had something sweet."

Roxanna opened the box and there was an array of snacks. Different brownies, cookies, cake pops. She looked at Poppi. "You didn't even have this one." She winked.

14

Investment

"Sign here, and initial here. If you want, we can make sure your lawyers approve or we can get ours to go over the strategy and send it to you."

"I think Poppi will want to see the paperwork." Roxanna looked at her. "She knows this stuff better than anyone and she's, my lawyer."

"Did you all have fun Saturday?" Zander put the papers in the folder and handed them to her.

"Did you know that Derrick and Kandi are an item?"

"My workaholic, pessimistic, antiromantic best friend? And the bright bubbly pink dancer?"

"Yeah, the one who hasn't dated a man in two years." Roxanna looked at him. "And Derrick didn't sound so antiromantic when she talked about him. Which she hasn't been able to stop."

Zander smiled. "He asked her to be his girlfriend?"

"Over waffles." Roxanna gagged playfully. "It was almost as disgusting as your little run in with Poppi."

Zander looked at her. "I don't know what you mean." He tried to busy himself. Thinking of Poppi was something he had forbidden himself to do since Saturday. He didn't want to get too invested. He knew the rules and he didn't want to fly too close to the sun.

He enjoyed his time with Juniper, Daisy, and Oliver. And he didn't want them to think he was doing it to get to her. He wanted everything to be organic. He wanted his own friendships, and if they were mutual with hers maybe they'd run into each other, but he knew he wouldn't be inappropriate.

She looked at him. "Yeah, I guess you don't." She smiled coyly. "She liked the cookies by the way. She said they were a very sweet gesture."

His office door burst open and Carmen, his tall deep brown skinned long legged beautiful girlfriend walked in. Her smile faded when she saw Zander sitting across from Roxanna. Roxanna wore a deep black V-neck sweater and tight black jeans with combat boots. Her locs were pinned up on her head and she only wore gloss on her full lips. The rest of her skin was naturally flawless.

"Who is this?" She pointed at her.

"You're dating Carmen Grace!" Roxanna spoke as if she had figured out some equation that she had been working on. "Okay! That would explain that. Hi! I'm Roxanna your man's new client." She stood and held out her hand.

Carmen took it with a bright smile. "Hello."

"I'm Roxi Blake." She smiled. "Such a pleasure to meet you in person! I've heard a lot about you. I've worked with Keres Abraxas a few times at the AVAs. He's a great host."

"Who is Keres Abraxas?" Zander looked up from putting things away on his desk.

"Nobody babe." Carmen looked at him. "Just a work friend."

Roxanna's face visibly changed to one of confusion before she hid the knowledge behind a smile. She looked at Carmen. "I loved your new character arch in Passions! Oh, it is so good! If I knew Delta was such a bad bitch I would have auditioned."

"Well, she could always use a side kick." She giggled.

"Maybe more of a friendly rival." Roxanna smiled cheekily. "I always like stirring the pot."

"Zander I have those-"Mitchell investigated the room. "Oh, I didn't know you were busy. Hello, Miss Grace, so nice to see you!" Mitchell walked over and kissed her hand.

Zander wanted to roll his eyes, but he kissed Poppi's h and the first time he met her. He couldn't be too jealous. He watched as Carmen giggled bashfully. He didn't even acknowledge Roxanna. "Thank you." He took the files from Mitchell.

"Miss Grace, please forgive me for saying this but you are the most stunning woman I have ever laid eyes on. The screen does not do you justice."

"Oh, Mitchell you are too much." She giggled playfully tapping his chest. "You think so?"

"Yes ma'am. Mr. Bell is a very lucky man to have you." He looked at Zander. "I think I've told him that a time or two."

"Finally, someone who gets it." Carmen looked at Zander, but Roxanna noticeably rolled her eyes. "Zander here forgot we were doing lunch and works over."

Roxanna walked over to a painting she had been eyeing their entire meeting. The bright and vivid blues and greens slashed across the hands breaking apart. "This is beautiful! Who painted it?"

"I didn't forget." Zander turned to Roxanna "I did, do you like it really?"

"It's lovely. Glad to know I have a broker of many talents." She smiled.

"Yes, he's very talented, but we're going to be late for our reservation." Carmen hastily looked at her watch. "I'm sure you all can chitchat about art some other time."

"Why don't I keep you company while he walks his client down to the elevator? I don't mind."

"I'm sure you don't." Roxanna muttered and looked at Mitchell. "Be sure to tell your wife I said hello."

"My who?" He looked back at her. "Oh sure. And you do the same for your husband or whomever." He turned his attention to Carmen.

Zander walked Roxanna to the elevator. He didn't want to speak on a matter that he knew nothing about. Something he knew for sure was that Poppi was unforgettable, and Mitchell playing dumb like that was annoying to him. He watched as Roxanna stormed to the elevator. "I'm supposed to be walking you, remember?" He tried to act calm and casual, but he could understand her anger.

"Did you see that fucking shit! Just gonna flirt with the movie star in front of us like we're not fucking standing here?!" She sighed "I wish I could say I was shocked, but he's always making a damned fool of her."

"He said he was a huge fan, maybe he was just excited. Don't think too much into it Roxanna." He sighed. "You know people are around celebrities."

"You barely spoke to her." Roxanna argued. "I've seen you look at someone like that and it was no superstar." She tilted her head. "She doesn't believe me you know. I've told her several times I've seen the way you look at her. She doesn't believe me... It's because she doesn't believe she deserves to get looked at that way, and I just wish once, someone would prove her wrong."

The elevator opened and Roxanna stepped in. "Have a great afternoon, Zander. One of us deserves too."

Zander walked back to his office and Carmen was cozy speaking to Mitch. He cleared his throat and they straightened themselves. "Are you ready for lunch?" He asked.

"Can we bring him along?" Carmen wrapped her arm in Mitch's. "He's so funny! I love him!" She smiled widely.

"Sure." Zander looked at Mitchell who was eating it up. "The more the merrier."

15

The Meeting

"**M**s. Nichols has been a wonderful asset to our team." Lorna Hopkins the lead partner of the meeting spoke. Lorna was a tall woman with Onyx skin and a platinum blond bob. She wore a red power suit, and her partner Delona Hart wore a blue one. Her skin was a deep almond color, and her cheek bones were sharp and as intense as her light brown eyes. Her curly honey blonde hair was in a slicked back ponytail.

"With an 89% success rate with being such a fresh lawyer I would say so. I've also heard about the large amount of pro-bono cases she has done for families who can't afford lawyers. Not to mention the charity work this firm does for the houseless, LGBTQI plus, and women."

Zander looked at Poppi who sat between them. Her shit was black, but she wore a silk burgundy shirt under it that was V-neck and the same moonstone from each time he saw her laid on her chest. "Some of her cases don't even make to court from what I've heard."

"You've heard correctly." Delona looked at Poppi. "She's truly phenomenal, and I can't believe she's brought the Bells into our law firm. What do we owe the pleasure?"

"I'd like to bring in a team of attorney's who aren't jaded and will let things slide, lately we've seen some disloyalties with one firm that we once viewed as family. It's believed by our accountants they may've embezzled from us, and I can't even bring myself to believe it. But the time has come for us to split ways."

"I'm sorry to hear that." Miss Hopkins replied looking at him. "Are you shopping around? Would you like to know what our rates are?"

"You may not be able to afford us." Ms. Hart chuckled looking at them. "After all we're not exactly most male lead companies speed."

"You're just what we want. This firm stands for something." Zander looked at Delona. "I've spoken with my father about this numerous times, and I think an entire female lead law firm that looks like us sends the exact message we want."

"You flatter us."

"And it will get you everywhere," Delona smirked. "So, what is this like a trial or is this a serious retainer."

"Son, will you grab me a coffee, I forgot mine and I am a bit parched."

"Sure, where is it?"

"Poppi will show you." Lorna nodded. "She has spoiled us with a fabulous coffee bar. And this morning she brought in scones!"

"Well, this is going to be a good day then." Frederick smiled excitedly.

ZANDER followed her walking down the hallway. Her body moved to its own beat, but it was hypnotic to watch. He looked at her. "How are you? How have you been?"

"I've been fine, thank you, and yourself?"

"I've been thinking about Roxanna's contract, is I to your liking?"

"If you'd like after the meeting you can come to my office, and we can talk about it. I don't see anything wrong, but I can give you your copies with some of the things I've worked out with Lorna. I think you'll find some of them to your liking." She handed him a scone as he fixed the coffee.

"You're going to spoil my family. Carmen doesn't like to cook, but my mother has been bragging about how her son's special friend is making dessert for her upcoming luncheon."

"Your mother isn't entirely wrong." Poppi grabbed her cup. "I'm your friend, and I find you pretty special." She smiled and walked out with Zander behind her.

"I LOOK forward to working with you ladies." Frederick smiled shaking hands with the three women. "And you're sure this is acceptable and fair?"

"This is more than fair; we really can't ask for anything else."

"Poppi I'm glad that you'll be consulting. I know you're weary because of Mitchell, but I can assure you, you will only be working with me, and if Zander has to sit in on a negotiation."

"I appreciate you thinking so highly of me."

"Of course, Ms. Nichols." Frederick shook her hand. "And should you ever need anything you let me know and I'll be here for you."

"Let us walk you out." Lorna cleared up the papers. Attorney Hart began to lead them out. She turned to Poppi. "You have just fast-tracked yourself to fucking partner Nichols. I'm so goddamn proud of you, my girl!"

Poppi tried to hide her smile as she walked to her office. She couldn't believe that she just got her firm the biggest client they'd ever had, and it was because of her. They never even mentioned the connection between her and her husband. This was her win.

She closed the door and turned on her favorite song and started dancing to celebrate. She could use the burn of carbs. Her body allowed the music to let her shed her corporate skin and let herself go for a moment. "Go Poppi! Go Poppi! Get Busy!" She cheered.

"Yes, go Poppi indeed," Zander smirked.

"Geez!" She straightened herself up. "Do you have to always sneak up on me?! You're going to give me a heart attack!"

He held up his hands. "I'm sorry, but you did say that you were open to talking about Roxanna's investment portfolio."

She huffed out a laugh. "You're very right I did say that." She put her hands on her hips. "Let me grab the files."

"If it makes any difference, I think you fully deserve to celebrate. You are amazing Ms. Nichols."

"Thank you, Mr. Bell, now let's get to business."

After a few minutes of corrections and signatures, Zander was shaking Poppi's hand. "I'd ask for my own private dance party, but I feel like that would be unprofessional."

"A dance party is never unprofessional." Poppi smiled tucking a hair behind her ear.

He looked at her thinking for a minute and a soft blush came across his deep onyx skin. "Yeah, but I'd get greedy." He shook his head. "I should go, congratulations." He took the file and left her there wishing for Eros night more than she had ever before.

16

Playdate

Zander and Juniper sat together at the Play Palace a place where children could play their hearts out in different terrains for hours. Today the children chose the trampoline park. Thea and Daisy had gotten along well, so well they called each other every night and watched their favorite tv shows together.

Oliver and Sawyer were slower to get to know each other, but there was always a sullen look when it was time to say goodbye to each other. Zander and the children spent a lot of time with Juniper and hers. He'd gotten off early a few times and they'd have dinner together. He'd even met Poppi's brother-in-law Brantley when he'd come to join them.

"Here." Juniper handed him a nice grocery tote bag. "This is for your mother, who my sister thinks is Mary Berri."

Zander laughed. "Why do you say that?"

"Something has happened with my sister; she's gotten this over-whelming need to make your mother love her. And I truly cannot express to you how much the two of them go on about each other when the other isn't in a room, but my sister felt the need to make your mother all of her favorite desserts, she's been baking for two days, and she's made her small samples and an actual cake. I think she thinks she's in a competition."

Zander could feel by the weight of the bag that she wasn't joking. "My mother thinks the world of her, I mean she calls her my special friend. She's so excited for the luncheon she has told all her friends about how good she is. I really think she's fine."

"Claudia reminds me a lot of our Aunt Peony. Poppi and she used to spend entire summers together. She even met Lydia. They loved her so much they wanted to adopt her, my father wasn't too keen on the idea, but she would have been closer, and they never would have cut him out of her life, but my mother is a bitter woman who didn't want that girl to know happiness for some reason." Juniper sighed. "Maybe that's why she's trying so hard to get approval from this woman she barely knows, because she feels like it will fix some mistake."

"What mistake?"

"She and everyone she loves to have been on the outs for five and half years. Since her wedding."

"Oh, I'm so sorry to hear that."

"My aunt came to Christmas this year and they celebrated together for the first time and there were more tears than laughter. All in love of course. They sat together for hours. Her, my aunt, her mother and grandmother-in-law all sat around sharing stories of what a darling child Poppi used to be. When she wasn't in boarding school." Juniper looked at Thea and Daisy holding hands and jumping together. "Thea reminds me a lot of Poppi actually."

"She does?"

Juniper nodded with a small smile. "Poppi used to be a small shy smart bookworm much like Thea and our sister Lavender used to be like Daisy. Where you saw one you saw the other during the summer, and any other time. Then when Poppi met Lydia, they were quite the trio for a while. Poppi was even talking about following her dreams and becoming a dancer. But then Lydia died, and Mitchell came around."

"I've noticed there seems to be that same consensus when Mitchell is mentioned."

"Zander, you have to work with this man, so I won't say everything I want, but I think we're friends."

"My niece and nephew call you Mama Junie, my brother is buying baby clothes out of the wazoo because he's now known a moments peace because of you, you and I are practically related." He joked.

She smiled sadly. "Then I can trust this won't go any further than us?"

"Of course, Juniper." Zander face turned serious his brows furrowed. "What's going on?"

"Mitchell had been looming over Poppi, Roxanna, and Lydia for a while. Lydia had called me and told me that she was getting a weird vibe from him. She expressed her worries to Poppi, and Poppi tried to keep her distance, but whenever she did, he would just, make it harder for her. Lydia died in December, a few days after she called and told me that she and my sister were going to transfer and move to California."

"Did she say why?"

"My mother had been coming to campus more, she'd been forcing Poppi to go to lunch with her and Mitchell, she would say she invited Lydia, and she never did, things like that."

"That's weird."

"Very, and then she just up and dies of a drug overdose, Lydia had been an avid cannabis user, Poppi is, she has all the trauma she needs to be medically licensed to have it. But she never took hard drugs they killed her brother, her parents were devastated, they wanted to bring Poppi home, they begged her, but my mother would have none of it. My sister mourned herself into losing fifty pounds."

"What did they do then?" He asked looking at her "Where was Mitchell when all of this was happening?"

"Playing the hero of course, he made it look like he was helping her, but I don't think he was. About six weeks later Mitchell announced they were an item. Then on Valentine's Day they were engaged."

"That seems very fast. Like they didn't really know each other fast."

"You're not the only one who thought that, and Roxanna made it very vocal, but my sister just said it's what needed to happen." Juniper shrugged. "She was in a car accident a week after that, she broke bones and almost was paralyzed because of a fracture in the J2 and J3 vertebrae, but she was lucky."

"What happened?"

"The jury is still out. If you ask her now, she'll say it was raining and she thought she saw someone in the road and tried to stop but over corrected." Juniper waved at Sawyer who was waving at them.

"What do you think happened?"

"I'll tell you what I know, and you can make your own choices." Juniper watched the children play, but her face looked like it was being transported through time. He felt terrible for making her have to relieve this event.

"Poppi called me that evening, I was in the UK because I had a conference. She told me that she was flying home to be with the kids and that she couldn't do it. She couldn't go through with the wedding; she knew he didn't really love her, and she wanted to be with people who did."

Zander listened as she told the story, he tried to imagine what Poppi was like then, how strong she had to be to pick herself up every day as she had to continue living without the love of her life. How brave she was.

"My mother put her in a private hospital, and she couldn't have visitors, the next thing I know she and Mitchell are getting married in this big event on my mother's birthday. She even wore white and walked Poppi down the aisle. My father and stepmother screamed and begged for her to run to them, but she didn't budge. They told her if she did this, they couldn't look at her anymore, they couldn't watch their baby girl be miserable for the rest of her life. She had to watch them be roughed up and dragged from the wedding. My daddy even tried yanking her off that alter." Juniper tried to smile thinking about it. "I think she would have gone."

"What stopped her?"

Juniper looked at him. "Sometimes Zander, genies are forced into bottles for no other reason than people want to dim their magic or kill their color."

Zander looked at Juniper, she watched the children with a sadness, he felt terrible for making her relive memories that made her think of her sister in that light. He took her hand. "Juniper, you forget one thing."

She looked at him. "And what is that?"

"All genies can be saved with the right wish." He smiled.

17

Lunch

It had been a week since the meeting between their firms. She hadn't stopped thinking about Zander since. How he bragged on her to her own boss, the way his broad muscular frame was wrapped in an expensive suit made her knees weak. The way he smiled at her when he caught her dancing in the office made her heart flutter. She'd never been smiled at like that before, like she was the cutest thing in the world. Like she was being enjoyed.

Poppi remembered the warmth in Zander's eyes for comfort when her nights with Mitchell were cold. Which had been more often than not. He would work late hours and go out with clients more often than normal now and she barely saw him most days. And when they did see each other, it wasn't always pleasant. He'd insult her weight or tell her he wasn't exactly attracted to frumpy women anymore.

She walked into the elevator that led her to the upper level of Hall and Bell. She looked at herself in the mirrored door. She sculpted her body today with a white corset blouse, black pencil skirt suit, and red stiletto platform heels. Since pole dancing, she'd found more confidence in her body, even if Mitchell hated it there were people paying to see it.

She looked behind her and everyone busied themselves. She looked ahead and Mr. Fredrick Bell was walking out of her husband's office. "Mrs. Nichols! What a pleasure to see you!" Frederick shook her hand. "Claudia is going to be mighty disappointed she missed you. I like your curls, not that my opinion matters, but your natural hair looks lovely."

"Oh!" She subconsciously touched her hair. "Thank you, Mr. Bell."

"Your New Year's resolution is paying off by the way." He smiled "You look great! You've trimmed down a bit too."

"Well," Poppi blushed, she wasn't used to men complimenting her, but lately it was becoming more familiar. "It isn't hard to see where your son gets his charm from. Give Claudia my love, maybe we should do lunch or something?"

"I think that would be wonderful. I'll check with Claudia when we're free. You take care of yourself." He smiled and walked back toward his office.

Poppi supermodel strutted into the office and leaned over his desk showing him her cleavage. "Hello my sexy husband. I've come to take you out for dessert, and maybe some lunch." She winked.

"Zander you remember my wife." Mitchell replied without looking up from his papers. "Hello dear."

"I'm so sorry! I saw Mr. Bell leave and I thought you were alone!" She looked over at Zander. "I'm sorry! I hope I wasn't interrupting."

"No worries Ms. Nichols!" Zander replied smoothly standing in front of her holding his hand out. "I wasn't aware you two had lunch plans, we can always pick this up later." He held her hand in his for a moment longer as they made eye contact.

"Baxter. It's Mrs. Baxter, Zander." Mitchell wrapped his hand around his wife's waist. "She's dropping the hyphenation so it's less confusing." He kissed her cheek "I wasn't aware we had lunch plans darling."

"I wanted it to be a surprise." She looked at Mitchell. "I know that you've been working so hard lately we barely see each other."

"My fault again." Zander chuckled, "I should leave you two crazy kids to it. Enjoy dessert." He and Poppi locked eyes for a moment, and he walked out closing the door behind him. Her body was buzzing with arousal.

"You could stand to miss a dessert or two. Couldn't you?" He moved away from her.

"Mitchell!" She blinked stunned at his response. Her blood suddenly running cold.

"Listen I've got calls to make. I'm not hungry, and even less so now since you decided to come in here like a cat in fucking heat."

Poppi stood there shocked at how he spoke to her. "Aren't you tired of speaking to your wife like this?"

"I didn't say anything wrong. You came in here acting as if you were in a porno Poppi! You know that isn't your style you're not some sort of sex kitten. You're a wife. And you need to act like it."

"I thought that wanting to see my husband was me acting like a wife."

"You're dressing like a high-priced whore, and you expect me to believe that this is you acting like a wife and not you trying to prove some stupid point. Yes Poppi, Zander looked at your fat ass are you happy? He's a man. That's all you'll get from him." He led her to the door.

"Mitchell- "

"Maybe if you have dinner on the stove like a good little thing, I might give you the attention you're dying for okay, but this is a place of business honey. And I think we both know I don't want to see you naked under fluorescents, right?"

Poppi slid through the crack of the elevator door that was just closing so that she could avoid any more embarrassment. She prayed she just missed it and fell down the elevator shaft so she could just end being around Mitchell forever.

"You and Mitch in a race?" Zander asked behind her.

"Mitchell got a call just as we were about to go, and he said it looked like a long one, so I told him we could have dinner." She straightened herself up swallowing the bucket of tears from her throat.

"I'm sorry, Carmen just canceled on me. She has to take a last-minute flight to California for some reshoots, so I don't have anything to do for lunch. Why don't you join me?"

"Oh no Zander I couldn't." She shook her head folding her arms. "I don't want to intrude on your you time."

"Actually," he looked at her. "I could use this time to pick your brain a little. Oliver will be joining me and Sawyer for jujitsu tonight, and I'd like to know a little bit more about him. I'll buy."

She remembered Juniper mentioning Oliver taking jujitsu, but never with who. She smiled. "If it's about my two favorite humans in the whole world, how can I say no?"

THEY walked down the block to a small hole in the wall called Trips. "I haven't been here in ages." She looked around the Hollywood memorabilia-decorated restaurant. "Roxanna and I used to meet Mitch and Alton for lunch here sometimes. I always loved their bacon cheddar fries. Too bad I'm on a diet."

"What if I got the bacon cheddar fries and turned my plate towards you? Then you can say you didn't order them, but I ordered so much that you just had to take a few."

"Now who's being the bad influence?" She ordered a lemonade to drink, and their eyes met, a relaxed smile came over Zander's face that put Poppi at ease. Everything cold and hurtful Mitchell said to her was melting with the brightness of his smile. "I have heard so much about the playdate and the many that followed. I'm sad that I missed them. Did you have fun?"

"I loved every second of them. Your sister is delightful. The only thing that was missing was you."

Poppi smiled trying to hide the blush. "My sister isn't always fond of men, other than my amazing brother-in-law, but it's a very thin ice they skate on, you've seemed to make it with her."

"Brantley is your brother-in-law, right?"

"How do you know about Brantley?" Poppi asked curiously.

"I've had dinner with them a few times, they've invited the kids over and my brother couldn't make it, so they call good old uncle Zander, but Uncle Brantley has stopped in a few times too. He's a pretty good guy. He's crazy about the kids, and your sister."

"Yeah, they have this cute little crush on each other, but he's married and she's very pregnant, not that I think her being pregnant would matter."

"He speaks very highly of you too; he calls you his little sister and his actual brother the guy you married. But what about your sister-in-law?" He asked. "I thought he was married."

"I could care less about what my sister-in-law wants." Poppi twirled her straw in her cup. "She isn't very nice to Brant. She doesn't really deserve him. He deserves someone who looks at him the way my sister does. Like he's the most wonderful thing in the world. Even the children love him."

"You can say that again, they're crazy about him." Zander chuckled. "Oliver is very close to him. He also doesn't seem very fond of men. He was a little prickly to me the first few times. I'm glad we can get together a few days a week."

"He's prickly toward new people, he's been a little more overprotective since he found out he was going to be a big brother again. Maybe a little before then, he's always wanting to be attached at the hip. I've been spending a few nights a week with him, mainly since Mitchell works super late."

"They don't stay with you guys?"

"Mitchell isn't big on children, if I wanted to have slumber parties at my place, I'd have to have my own place." She shook her head trying not to allow the possibility to run rampant.

"What would it look like? Casa de la Poppi's?" He asked after they ordered their lunch.

"I always wanted a little reading nook in my living room with a burgundy bubble chair for me to curl up and read in, Lydia said she would put it across from her couch because she likes being near the window, and she knew how much I liked the sound of rain." She sighed.

"I like the sound of rain myself." He smiled "I guess we're kinda in the right place."

"I'd want to have a vanity in my walk-in closet so that I could get ready at my own pace and not have anyone rush me. And I want a blackout canopy bed."

"That sounds interesting, would you like a star projector?" He followed. "So, you can have a nice light show when you're decompressing."

"I hadn't thought about it." She smiled "It doesn't sound like a bad idea. Maybe if he's nice enough a certain artist can commission a mural in my bedroom."

Zander looked at her. "I'm not an artist."

"Roxanna told me about your painting. She said it was beautiful, and I can't help but believe her. In her spare time, she collects art."

He smiled at her. "You're much too kind to me, I painted that a few years ago, I don't paint anymore."

"Why?" She looked at him.

"Not much inspiration, I guess. Carmen and I used to argue over it a lot and I just gave it up altogether."

"Why did you argue?"

"I was enjoying it, painting, I even sold a few. She said I was letting my hobby overtake my relationship when I preferred nights in, to nights clubbing."

"I think you can still do it, we should do it together sometime, paint together. We can even bring the kids it would be so much fun!" She picked up a bacon cheddar fry from the plate he put between them.

"You'd want to do that?" He looked at her. "Really?"

"I'd love to! It would be so much fun! I'd love to see you do something you enjoy with the kids!"

"So, if I'm going to paint does that mean you're going to dance? I heard you used to be a dancer. And I've seen your moves."

Juniper must have been talking her up again. Poppi didn't always enjoy thinking about her dance life. It always was a reminder that she could have had a different life. "A long time ago when those kinds of things were in my plan."

"What was your plan?" Zander asked.

"Lydia and I were going to California two days after she proposed to me. I had an audition for the Jacarius dance studio. I was so excited. She was excited. But instead, I woke up beside the love of my being dead. I still wanted to go, but then I got into a car accident that really fucked me up and I couldn't dance for a while, now I just dance in my office."

"You're still a superstar to me Nichols." He smiled. "Don't ever forget that."

Something warm burned in her soul. She hadn't been called Nichols in 6 years, and it felt good. It felt good to hear it be said attached to something so sweet. It was perfect. She couldn't imagine being this lucky twice. She didn't want to fly to close to the sun, but she had to try. She scribbled her number down on a napkin with a pen. "Here."

"What's this?" He looked at her. "Are you sure? I don't want you getting into any squabble because of me."

"I heard Daisy and Thea talking they want to take dance; I think that we should have each other's numbers since we'll obviously be seeing each other, right?"

He smiled. "I won't abuse this. I'll only think about calling you when it's unimportant."

"When you call it's always important." She finished her salad. "We should get back, right?"

Zander looked at her. Their hands touched and his eyes gazed into hers. "I wish no was the right answer."

18

Carnival

"Hello?" Zander answered his phone walking up the stairs to his brothers. One of his clients gave him tickets to a Jacarius show in New York and he gave them to his brothers, but that left him with Thea and Sawyer with nothing to do.

"What are you doing today?" Juniper asked "I have three extra tickets to that huge winter carnival in Alp Springs and I was wondering if you wanted to bring Thea and Sawyer. I know Daisy has been dying for some hang out time."

"What is it with you and Poppi knowing when I'm in distress?" He laughed. "It's almost like I emit a signal."

"Not to me, maybe to Poppi. She's the one who won the tickets and suggest you bring the kids; I thought that Carmen had come in this week, so I didn't think you'd be interested."

"Nope, she said she had a party to go to in New York and was gonna take the train, I am free, and I'm only my way."

Zander stood at the door of Juniper's beautiful colonel house with a painted blue door. The children's, Poppi, Lavender, and Juniper's handprints decorated the door with their name painted above it. 'The Nichols'. Zander hadn't taken time to notice and with the sun not being visible at five pm he barely saw it, but today he got full view. He smiled to himself. One day he wanted to do the same thing with his family. Since he suddenly had the inspiration to paint again.

The door opened and Poppi stood in front of him wearing a burgundy sweater tucked into her dark blue skinny jeans and black combat boots to top the look. Her hair was in two space buns and her make up kept the theme.

"You look fantastic." He smiled. "I'm so glad to see you." He instinctively wrapped his arms around her in a hug. She smelled divine. Her small hands wrapped around his shoulders. He pulled away. "Kids, this is Mama Juni's sister Poppi."

Thea hugged her tightly. "Daisy told me you were my aunt too since we're sisters now, I hope that's okay."

Poppi smiled widely. "It's more than okay, in fact why don't you guys go upstairs and get them. They will be so excited to see you!" She hugged tightly to Thea and smiled at Sawyer who shyly hid behind his uncle. "Let me grab my jacket." She smiled. "Can I get you anything?"

"No, thank you." He smiled looking at Sawyer. As she walked to the back. "Are you okay bud?"

"She looks like the pretty ladies from the Wiz. She's so pretty."

Zander smiled. "She had that same effect on me too." He chuckled. "I guess it's a good thing that all the pretty ones are good then huh?"

"Miss Carmen isn't very good uncle Zander." Sawyer looked at him. "She called Thea a brat."

"Sawyer!" Daisy called.

"Daisy!" Sawyer ran to the group. Hugging Daisy and walking into the playroom. Zander watched them go and Juniper slowly walking up the walkway.

"Hello." He smiled. "How is the tiny overlord."

"Hangry and cramped." She smiled. "How are you?" She asked.

"I feel like I shouldn't leave you alone." Zander looked at her. "Should I take the kids and let Poppi stay with you?"

"Goodness no! I have a babysitter for the evening, I want you two to go and enjoy yourselves."

"Ah Brant is coming by?"

Juniper smiled. "Mind your business, Zander." She grinned as Poppi walked into the foyer. "Here." She handed her the keys. "Take the minivan and have a good time. Bring me back some snacks."

"Yes ma'am." Zander smiled.

"C'mon kids." Poppi called. All four of them walked out. Oliver stopped at the door. "Does everyone have everything? Daisy, do you have your phone and inhaler in case we get separated?"

"Yes Oli."

"Thea, you know the safe word, right? If you feel uncomfortable, what do you say?"

"Gigabyte."

"I hope the Ropeman twins aren't there today but if they are I don't want you anywhere near them."

"Who are the Ropeman twins?"

"Kids from our school, they aren't very nice to me." Thea played with her soft yellow sweater. "Sawyer does what he can, but since I'm in different classes Deidra and Dexter aren't exactly friendly."

"Well, we're with you today, and if you have any problems you can come to us."

"See Ollie it's okay, we can have fun today, you don't have to protect everyone." Sawyer wrapped his arm around him. "Besides we've got level fifty to beat in Crashing Kingdoms."

"I think the drive should give you enough time if you've leveled everything up like I told you boys to." Zander smiled.

"I did Uncle Zander." Oliver smiled. "C'mon guys let's go!"

"You've been promoted." Juniper folded her arms watching the boys run to the car with their sisters in tow. "My own brother-in-law is still called Mr. Baxter."

"I'll try to live up to the hype." Zander held out his arm for Poppi. "Shall we?"

She looped her arm into his. "We shall." They walked to the car.

AS they drove the radio played soft R&B. Poppi hummed along. Zander enjoyed her humming; he drummed his fingers on the wheel. He looked at her from the occasion and she was staring out of the window watching the scenery deep in thought. He turned up the radio when an old Prince song came on.

He noticed her smile when he began to sing the opening verse off-key. She looked at him. "You know this is technically a duet." He smirked.

"Do you want your eardrums to bleed?" She laughed.

"C'mon, we're supposed to be having fun." He looked at her. "What's more enjoyable than karaoke?"

Poppi sang the female part of the song and Zander took up the rest. The kids joined in with pretend instruments and by the end of the song, the entire car was filled with laughter and singing. Zander liked the way Poppi sang she used her 'true voice' to sing. It was soft and comforting, slow and sweet.

"My eardrums aren't bleeding Nichols, you're not as bad at it as you think." He winked at her.

"You're not so bad yourself Mr. Bell, you might be on lullaby duty when the baby comes."

Zander liked how that sounded, more time with the people he'd grown extremely fond of. He couldn't think of anything better.

THE carnival was a beautifully decorated field with games, food trucks, bright lights, photo stands, and fake snow falling from the sky. After an array of photos in different booths, a carriage ride, and a fire dancer show. Zander and the boys played all the games they could while the girls went to the petting zoo and got their faces painted.

The boys worked desperately to win their sisters two of the newest rainbow monkey toys that they had, and they fought a victorious battle. When Sawyer ran off to find their sisters and Poppi. Oliver chose to stay behind with Zander.

"Are you having fun?" Zander asked holding his own prize of an overstuffed care bear.

"Yeah! I'm having a really fun time Uncle Zander thank you for bringing us!"

"Your Aunt Poppi is more responsible for it than me." He admitted. "She usually is the one with the ideas."

"Yeah, but I'm glad we get to have fun with her now, Mr. Baxter never let her have any fun when we went on vacation, he was a real jerk to her and everything. He pushed her."

"He did what?" Zander asked trying to remain calm. "When?"

"We were on vacation, he pushed her down, and I couldn't stop him. I went to help her and he... he locked me in a closet."

Zander looked at Oliver with a soft smile and got on his knees. "You know you're safe now though, right? You know that if anything like that ever happens again you can call me day or night no matter when and I'll come to you don't you?"

He looked up at him. "Do you mean that?"

"If you're gonna call me Uncle, I'm gonna act like one, I know we haven't known each other for a long time, but you do mean a lot to me kid, you, your sister, your mom."

"What about my Aunt Poppi?"

Zander smiled. "Your aunt means the world to me."

"Then can't you two get married? Can't you just tell Mr. Baxter to go away?!"

He laughed. "Life is a lot more complex than that kiddo."

"Oli! Look at my face." Daisy had a pink rainbow monkey on her left cheek, Thea ran behind her with a yellow one on the right.

"It matches your surprise." Oli smiled widely hiding all of the sadness and bother in his face, much like his aunt he was an expert at it. Zander looked at Poppi who stood behind them.

"Uncle Zander, can we go to the kids club down there?"

"Sure, I don't see why not. We're going to get snacks for Mama Juni. And then I think we're going to call it a day we've been here for hours."

"Okay! C'mon, guys."

Zander made his way over to her watching them run off together. "They're cute."

"You can say that again." She smiled looking at him. "What were you and Oli talking about?"

"I just wanted to make sure he was having a good time." Zander decided to not mention the grievances her nephew had with her husband.

"Is he?" She asked kicking a blade of grass with her boot. She looked beautiful with the fake snowflakes in her hair. Her face sullen but joyful.

"Are you?" He asked holding out the bear to her. "Or are you just being grumpy?" He made a fake cartoon voice that made her crack a smile.

"You're kind of a dork." She giggled looking up at him taking the bear. "Thank you."

"You're welcome." Zander's smile turned quizzical when he noticed as she was holding her grumpy bear, she wasn't wearing her wedding ring.

STADING in the line Zander tried not to look at her hand too often to cause attention, but he was curious. How long had she not been wearing it? Her arm was behind the door when she opened it, she was holding one of the children's the entirety of their walking together. Or they were tucked in her pockets. He never saw it.

He didn't want to ask, he was still in a relationship with Carmen, and there was nothing he could do if there was something happening on her side. She was doing this for her, and he didn't need to pry.

"Are you alright?" Poppi asked looking at him. "You seem distracted."

"Are you aware your niece and nephew call your husband Mr. Baxter?"

"He doesn't make them feel comfortable for them to call him anything else, and I think my nephew called him the devil one too many times, so we asked that they call him Mr. Baxter."

"Oliver has some strong feelings about him." Zander looked over where Oliver and Thea were going into the funhouse.

"I wish I could fix that, but Mitchell hates children and he married someone who loves them. Who wants them."

"Is that why he made that comment at dinner? Because you want children?"

"I haven't talked about it in years. I don't even think about children if they aren't those two, well now five if you count those two and the baby, but he just had to make sure I knew he didn't want them." She shrugged. "I don't mind being childless honestly."

"I'd like to be a father one day, Carmen is heavily against it, and I don't disrespect her choices, but I think it's a reason that we aren't serious."

"You and Carmen aren't serious?" She looked at him "Why do you say that?"

He shrugged. "We want different things. I want to sit at home on a Friday night order takeout and watch Quantum Leap or Star Trek for the fortieth time. Hers isn't, and I don't think it ever will be, so why should I force her to be? She is going through something and using me to get through it, and I'm letting her because I enjoy the punishment. I'm lonely, and I'm developing feelings for someone I can't have." He admitted.

Poppi's finger wrapped around his. "Zander I-" She looked behind them and there was a commotion coming from where the children were. "What is going on over there?!"

"You stay here, I'll go see what's going on, Juniper might be angrier if we don't have snacks.

"You make a good point." She smiled. "No use in her blowing the roof off angry. And I'd never forgive myself if I denied my future niece or nephew the beauty that is carnival food."

"I'll be right back." He smiled and rushed to see what was going on.

19

Fight

"Gigabyte!" Daisy shouted. "Let me go!"

"I'm coming Daisy!" Oliver decked a red-headed freckled face boy in his nose so hard it began to gush blood. "Don't touch my sister. Sawyer you get Thea, I'll handle them."

"Not without me you won't." Daisy threw a clean right hook and hit a red headed little girl who had pigtails. "Make fun of her now Deidra! Can't do it with a busted lip can you?! What'd you call her?"

Dexter tried to run back at him, but a tall broad man picked him up midair. "Now just what the hell is going on here young man! You can't just go around bloodying people's noses."

"And he can't just go around shoving little girls!" Oliver lunged back at him, and Zander scooped him up.

"What do you mean he shoved a little girl."

"He shoved Thea in the haunted house, and she scrapped her knee on a board she coulda got really hurt Uncle Zander! So, I chased him out here, but Daisy and Deidra were already fighting."

"It's not my fault!" The little girl wailed.

"Shut up before I punch you again!" Daisy spat. "It is your fault you mean rotten Raggedy Anne doll! You tried to hit Sawyer and take Thea's Monkey and you called him a lab rat! What the heck does that mean?"

"It means he has two daddies, and he can't have two daddies and be a real boy! He's a robot, my mommy said so, and she also said that you're not a real witch. That your mommy is just a delusional person who doesn't kno-"POW. Daisy slung her fist right into the girl's stomach. She went down with a gurgle. "You say one more thing about my brother and sister and I'll do it again." She looked at the man. "Who are you anyway?!"

"I'm their father young lady."

"And you let them talk like that?"

"What I do with my children is none of your business."

"It's mine." Poppi stood behind Daisy. "And I think she's within her rights to ask her why on earth a nine-year-old is spewing such hateful rhetoric!"

"Your children probably started it!" He spat. "She's probably just defending herself."

"Against what exactly? My nephew who is over there with my sobbing niece does indeed have mud on his shirt, and she's crying and there is blood on her jeans. How did it get there?" Poppi looked at him sternly.

"She probably slipped hell you see she's got glasses on those fun houses are hard to see."

"Hold my bag please." She held it out and Zander took it. She looked at Thea. "Come here honey. It's okay." She cooed. Thea limped over to her. "So, what's your name Mr. Ropeman?"

"Harold."

"Harold. Dexter. Deirdra. Did I get that right?" She asked pulling a first aid kit from her backpack purse. "This looks nasty sweet girl. Are you okay?"

Thea shook her head. "It really hurts."

"I bet it does, this looks painful." Poppi cleaned the wound. "Dexter did you know that Thea's favorite color is yellow?"

"Wh-What?" He cried. "Why do I care?"

"I think I saw you and your family at the basketball game with the rainbow monkeys. You were watching the boys, I got to see that before it was my turn to get my face painted." She slid a band aid on her knee.

"Ma'am I don't see what that has to do with anything we lost fair and square."

"Right, but my boys didn't. No, my boys won two. In their sisters' favorite colors, no less! Isn't that funny?" She looked at Dexter. "Tell me

Dexter, do you the like the chocolate double decker nachos that Spaced out snacks sells? They are really tasty. Every child's dream, I'm sure."

"No, I don't like them."

"Then why did I spend ten bucks on a tray?!"

"Oh, he liked them just fine Mr. Ropeman, I assure you, but what I'd like to know is why you felt the need to use my niece here as a napkin?" Poppi pulled off her yellow sweater turning it to reveal two chocolate handprints on her back. She looked at Harold. "I think this corroborates Oliver story. Don't you?"

"Dexter, you apologize to that young lady right now!" He scolded.

"Sorry." He muttered. "But she was still beating up my Deirdra dad!"

"And I'd do it again! You don't talk about people I love that way and not expect consequence Dexter. How would you like it if I called your mother a bean poled pea brained bigot? You wouldn't like it very much, would you?" Daisy looked at her aunt. "So, I punched her. It felt like the right answer."

"Not always the right answer, but it's an answer that we'll take today young lady." Poppi looked at her. "You aren't supposed to be fighting what will your mother think?"

"Can't we tell Grandma and Aunty instead?" She looked up at her aunt with hope. Poppi rolled her eyes.

"Sir I suggest you and your wife figure out who you want your children to be, if you want them to be hateful bigots when they grow up, remember that my kids will grow up too, and every time when they're met with adversity, they are going to fight it. And physical violence isn't the only thing we know." She clasped her hands in front of her.

"You wait till I talk to your mother!" He scoffed. "I'm sorry ma'am to all of you. "

"No worries." Daisy folded her arms. "They'll never get the chance to both Thea and Sawyer again. They're too good to go to a school filled with losers anyway." Daisy handed Thea her monkey and looped her arm into hers.

"Have the day you deserve." Zander turned Oli away and Sawyer followed. Poppi walked beside him. "I'm scared of you right now." He smiled. "I kind of like it."

She laughed. "Shut up Zander."

20

Hero

"Daisy you can't be fighting like this missy what will Grandma Paulette think?!" Brantley asked putting an ice pack on her hand.

"Man, what a clean right hook." Zander chuckled.

"You are not helping." Brantley shot him a look holding his laughter. "Young lady that gut punch could have hurt her."

"Aw come on Daddy Brantley she didn't even puke!"

"Uncle."

"Huh?"

"It's Uncle Brantley Daisy." Poppi looked at her sister. "Right?"

"You need to call Grandpa and tell him that Thea and Sawyer are coming to school with us." Daisy looked at Brantley.

"Honey, I don't think that's how that works."

"I told him about this it's fine!"

"Back to the subject at hand." Juniper folded her arms. "Why are my children throwing fists at a winter carnival."

Poppi looked at Zander who watched Sawyer and Oliver standing together. "Oli why were you fighting?"

"I'm tired of seeing girls get pushed. One day someone is gonna push them and really hurt them. Then what? What do I do Mom? Just wait?"

"Oli calm down." Daisy reached over the couch and rubbed his shoulder. "He was in the right Mom."

"And you stop defending him you're not out of hot water."

"This is our fault really, if we didn't come today, they wouldn't have been fighting."

Oliver wrapped his arm around Thea quickly. "Don't ever apologize for needing help, if you need me, I'm here that's what I'm for, that's what family does. We stick together."

"You're my hero Ollie." Thea laid her head on Oliver's shoulder.

POPPI walked Zander to his car after the children spent another hour together for dinner. She enjoyed being there with everyone, but her head was all over the place, what was going on between Juniper and her brother-in-law. Did anyone else know?

"I had fun today." Zander looked at her as they got to his car.

"I feel like I should be kissing you goodbye." Poppi half-joked. "It kinda feels like a date."

"That's rather improper Ms. Nichols." He chuckled. "I think I can be satisfied with a handshake if you'd like."

She wrapped her arms around him for a hug. "A happy medium." She let his arms hold her. Caress her back. She kissed his smooth cheek. His goatee tickling her. She could get used to this, being with him. Having moments like this.

"Take care of yourself." He hugged her tightly. "Please don't forget to call me any time." He kissed her forehead and walked to his car.

JUNIPER sat in the laundry room with Poppi folding laundry. Poppi was deeply focused on folding all Olivers clothes, fighting back her tears. She tried to keep their arguments on that trip private. She didn't want anyone, especially Paulette to realize they weren't on the best terms, and she couldn't protect the one person who needed it most. She needed to distract herself. "Why is Brantley here?"

"Is this because Daisy called him dad?"

"I'm so glad I'm the only one who is weirded out by that. Why is he spending so much time with them? What's going on?"

"Guilt Poppi. Okay. It's guilt because his wife fucked my husband and caused my divorce. He found out the same day I did, and he feels guilt for it, so he's trying to do his penance by stepping up because their dad decided to step out to another fucking country."

Poppi swallowed. "She must have a thing for things we have."

"She has a thing for mediocrity. She's getting below averaged dick from either of those parties and you can't tell me she's not. I married him right out of college I was still a virgin. But I know that it's not worth that. I got bored. And you're dying."

"Daisy wants to tell Lavender and Mama about what happened."

"Why so Mama can celebrate and beg to put her in sword fighting?" Juniper put her hands on her belly. "She practices her meditation every day so she can find her place of peace. She's been centered. You know how those old-world techniques are."

"Maybe it works." Poppi shrugged thinking about her stepmother. It had been years since she had seen them. She missed them incredibly, she wished she could reach out and say something that would make it okay for her father to come around again.

"I know you miss them Poppi, why don't you call them? Daddy would love to hear from you."

"I don't think he would Juniper. He hasn't spoken to me since his plea for my freedom at my wedding."

"You're his baby girl Poppi, he didn't want to see the girl he thought would light up the stage be dimmed by that man." Juniper folded a baby blanket. "None of us did."

Poppi looked at Juniper's round belly. She thought about the life that grew inside of her. Mitchell had already made such a dark impact on

Oliver's life. How could she prevent it from happening to them? How could she save them from the same fate?

21

Family

"Mother this is beautiful!" Rayden gushed over the beautiful handmade cookbook that Poppi made his mother. "Zander did you pay her for this?!"

"I didn't even know it existed." He chuckled. "It's very beautiful Mother, and it's an heirloom, you can pass it down to Thea, and so on and so forth."

"This is the sweetest thing that someone has ever done for me. Look," she flipped to the recipe 'Marry my chicken.' The page was decorated with wedding bells and two chickens getting married. "How cute is that!"

"She's quite the artist."

"You two should collaborate on the baby's room since you've been helping Juniper set it up."

"I've been painting again." Zander smiled. "In the baby's room. I've been going off the crib that Poppi painted. It's Fairy Tale, For every child. I hope she likes it. Juniper has been forcing her to stay out until it's done."

"Those two are so sweet. I love the picture she got of the kids making cookies together. I love it I think it's the sweetest."

"She's a sweet girl, I worry about her though."

"Did Crispin tell you about the black eye?" Rayden asked helping her bring things to the table.

"Black eye?" Zander looked up as he placed the napkin on the table "What black eye?"

"Poppi was staying at her sister's last week, she had a black eye, and was wearing pajamas at 4pm on a Tuesday."

"Maybe she had an accident." Zander tried to relax himself from the panic he felt.

"Maybe." Claudia looked at Zander. "Check on her for me, will you? I know that you what you're thinking, but I am just worried."

"No, I'll go check on her tomorrow before Carmen and I go to California."

"Is she coming tonight? Will she at least get to see what you've done to your place?" Crispin asked.

"I don't know." Zander shrugged.

"How much longer do you intend on keeping her around?" Crispin asked with his arms folded. "I can only be nice for so long."

Zander looked at him. "I intend on keeping her around for a while, she's my partner, not an employee."

"I'm glad you see *her* that way," Crispin muttered.

"What is that supposed to mean?"

"I'm here." Carmen strolled in and looked at Zander. "And starving!"

"I bet." Crispin rolled his eyes at her.

"WHAT brings you back into our lives Carmen?" Crispin asked sharply. "Zander's been here a month and we're just now seeing you."

"I'm sorry my presence has been missed, but I have a job that requires a lot of my attention I'm sure you, being the business owner you are, know that."

"Funny you should mention my business, Carmen." Crispin took a sip of wine. "We have had a lot of business in your world."

"You have?"

"We have." Rayden nodded. "In fact, we did the Jacaris family Christmas this year."

"I heard it was lovely."

"You heard?" Crispin looked at her. "You weren't there?"

"She had to do some reshoots in LA how is she going to be in New York celebrating Christmas?" Zander laughed cutting into the chicken. He chewed feeling the love cooked into each bite. He could imagine Poppi serving this for Sunday dinner. He smiled to himself. "Mother, this is delicious."

"Thank you honey, Carmen how do you like it?"

"I don't like tomatoes, but other than that it's delicious."

"Thank you." She smiled.

"Carmen, did you at least get to see your parents for the holidays?"

"Sadly no, they were busy when I was free and vice versa, you know how that goes."

"Really? Are you sure it's not because you were in New York with Keres Abraxas?"

"What the fuck Cris!?" Carmen gasped. "Why would you say something like that?"

"I'm sick of this! I'm sick of her coming in here every few months and pretending like she loves him and then shatters him to bits." Crispin took a sip of wine. "And if you think that I am going to continue to let some D-list knock-off wearing no personality having ass bitch keep hurting *my* brother-in-law because she doesn't know where she wants to be and has been bouncing between the Abraxas brothers for months."

The room was quiet. Zander knew that Crispin disliked Carmen, but he never knew anything about why. She wouldn't cheat on him, she knows that's how his first engagement ended, and he was broken by it, but was he any better for how he felt about Poppi? Maybe this was his sign to end things. "Is this true?"

Carmen burst into tears. "Of course, it isn't true! I love you Zander and for two years I have stood by your side I adore you. I came here tonight to announce that I'm moving to Maine because I get a vacation coming up soon and I want to spend it with you when I'm not filming in New York for the new sitcom I'm doing. Call that D-List bitch."

Crispin looked at her. "What do you want an academy award? He's fucking you he'll accept whatever you tell him, but your bullshit is about as clear as my mother-in-law's window and let me tell ya, babe. That's crystal fucking clear. You think you're untouchable, you think you're this brilliant being, but you're just a difficult, disrespectful, dysfunctional diva with delusions that you deserve a man like Zander when you deserve demise. How's that for D-list bitch?"

Zander knew that Crispin wouldn't have caused such a scene if he was lying. He would have been more careful about the information if there was time, but there was none. He wanted it out in front of her and their entire family. All eyes were watching the stare-down between Carmen and Crispin. He believed Crispin, even Sawyer said the part about him being a brat.

He stood "Thank you all for having us, but we've got to get home and start packing."

"Zander don't go because of me. I'll leave." He stood. Zander put his hand out.

"Cris, it's not because of you." He promised and Crispin sat back down. "I love you, all of you."

Claudia looked at him. "Please don't forget."

"I won't ma, I love you." He walked Carmen out of the door.

"Thanks for having my back." She hissed.

"I left my family dinner with you after my brother accused you of some very large things. I think that says what it needs to loudly enough." He helped her into the car and drove into the night. His head swimming with doubts.

22

Canvas

P oppi held hands with Daisy as they walked into the Paint palace. A cute paint activity shop that Daisy enjoyed coming to when Brantley took Oliver to Jujitsu or something else, they had planned. They walked in hand in hand as Daisy was talking about the statue, she wanted to paint to put in the baby's room.

"I'm going to make the princess look just like you, auntie and the prince look like Uncle Zander."

"Is that right?" Poppi chuckled. "Don't you think his actual princess will get upset?"

"Daisy!" Thea called waving as she ran up to them.

"Thea!" Daisy met her halfway hugging her tightly. "I am so happy to see you!"

"That makes two of us." Zander smiled standing in front of them. "Hi you."

"Hey yourself." She smiled. "How have you been? I thought you were going to California?"

"Tonight, I wanted to spend some extra time with the kiddos, so I took Sawyer to dinner and then Brantley came and got him for his lessons and now I'm taking my little miss here painting."

"My uncle Zander is a great painter!" They looked up at Poppi. "Are you good at painting?"

"I try, but I don't know if I'm well."

"C'mon Thea let's go pick out something to paint."

Poppi looked at Zander. "Is it bad I want to hug you?"

"I'd really like that." He wrapped her in his arms and squeezed her tightly. Her body sank into his allowing herself to for once feel wanted.

POPPI sat across from Zander. He was deep into his art. She watched him as he chose what he did and how. He looked at her from time to time as she watched him. She couldn't help herself. She loved his attention to detail. The way he held his brush to his lips when he thought about something he wanted to do instead. She wondered what he looked like when he painted at home.

"I don't know why, but I like it when you watch me." He looked at her from the corner of his canvas. "You make it seem like it's an event, instead of a bother for me to paint."

"When did you know that you enjoyed making art?" Poppi asked making another brush stroke on her canvas.

"My father's business partner Martin Hall was like a father to me, and he would keep me company sometimes when my father would have an extra phone call to make or something and he would ask me to draw him something from time to time, he'd frame them and put them on the wall. My dad used to tell me he showed them off to clients, so I always wanted to make them better."

"Did you ever think to go to school for it?"

"I got my doctorate in business and minored in Art then I went back and got my doctorate in art."

"Wow! That's brilliant." Poppi looked at him. "That must have taken a lot. I'm very proud of you. You took seven years of your life to do something that had nothing to do with your career. You did it because you love art. That's amazing."

"Poppi you're very sweet to tell me that." He smiled. "Did you minor in anything, or did you just know the law was it for you?"

"I got a two-year creative arts degree in a community college when I was with Lydia. I'd take the classes while she was there helping people study and prepare for exams. It was really great."

"I guess we could do something with those eventually." He looked at her. "We could skip town and do something crazy. Open an art studio."

Poppi laughed. "Wait til the world gets a load of us."

"Funny thought, isn't it?" Zander looked at her his lips turning into a sweet somber smile.

"What?" She asked putting the final changes to her painting.

"Us."

"Here, something to remember me by while I'm gone for a week." He handed her his canvas.

"Zander this is beautiful." She looked at the masculine hand reaching out from the darkness of the night to hold the feminine hand of the day. Her heart felt a yearning she'd never expected or experienced. She wanted to tell him not to go. She wanted to make him stay with them.

"I read some of the stories from creationism. It's kind of hard-to-find books on."

"It's handed down from generation to generation, not many people write it down, my stepmother has some books on it, but most of the time there is a very small amount of people who care."

"I read the story about Oryn and Keahi the light-bringer. I think it's absolutely heartbreaking. To see the man you love killed, and be banished to the underworld. Only to find out the one you love has been crowned the lord of the underworld with absolutely no memory of you. That's a punishment I couldn't endure. But to know he'd left a piece of him in this world in hopes she'd return breaks my heart even more. "

"You have been reading." She blinked shocked that he had worked so hard to understand her family's ideas.

"I relate to him you know, if something was happening to the woman I loved and I was captured I'd reach through every dimension I could to get her back to me."

Their eyes connected and a surge ran through Poppi's spine. She felt the buzz between them she'd been trying to avoid. She'd been trying to hide. She was falling in love with Zander Octavious Bell.

23
California

Z ander walked into Carmen's living room with two glasses of champagne. It had been two days since they'd gotten there, and he'd been having a good time spending moments with Carmen he wouldn't have gotten the opportunity to if he had spent the time in the office.

"Thank you, baby." She smiled kissing him. "You have been a different person this week." She grinned. "You've been in such a good mood lately."

Zander knew it was because he spent his last moments in Maine with Poppi. He knew there was something between them from the cold chills he felt the last time they looked at each other. The way they hugged goodbye, though they had to bribe the girls to leave apart instead of together as usually intended. "You're welcome." He smiled.

"You're making this such a nice trip I'm almost sad it's going to be over."

"In a few days, we still have plenty of time together." His phone buzzed. He pulled it out. "How cute is that? Poppi taught Thea how to make ties and she made me one. Now I'm going to have a seamstress in the family." He showed Carmen the tie, it was made of Spiderman fabric, his favorite superhero.

"That's cute honey, but do you think you should be so involved?" Carmen asked putting her things away.

"She is my niece Carmen of course I'm involved." He chuckled.

"I meant with Poppi. You and she share these children as if they are your own and they aren't. They are your siblings."

"I know that!" Zander scoffed. "My aunts and uncles helped out with me and my brother all the time. My brother runs his own business, does his own baking, and his own bookings. He works all the time and when he'd not working, he's with the kids. Sometimes he needs a break Carmen that's hard on anyone."

"And her sister? Does she need your help too?" Carmen folded her arms. "She's single and pregnant. She's been trying to get Mitchell's brother for years and he's stayed loyal to his wife, but you're not married so she might not even see me as a threat. She might just come after you. And if not her, then her sister. Mitchell told me she's got this weird thing with you, and I don't like it, Zander."

Zander looked at her. "To start, Juniper has been doing this fucking badass mom thing she does for a decade without my help. So, no she doesn't need my help. I offered it because I enjoy her company. She's a lovely person, and you'd know that if you came to anything I invite you to. You would also see that that brother you're talking about is head over heels for that woman and I would never respect another friend of mine."

"You are not friends with Mitchell's brother!" Carmen scoffed. "You're being used by these fucking banshees!"

"Carmen please, you have to understand I would never do anything to disrespect you so why are you coming at me this way? I have done nothing but try here and you're giving me grief because I helped a friend."

"You helped your employee's in-laws!" Carmen corrected harshly. "That's all they are to you and as far as their little brats go-"

"So, you did call Sawyer and Daisy brats!" Zander looked at her. "I can't fucking believe this Carmen. I don't appreciate you calling the children I love anything other than their names. If anyone is acting like a brat right now, it's you! I could understand if it were a serious issue but- "

"You took time off to spend with them! Yes, this is a serious issue!"

"I went to her house to help her paint a mural for her baby! Yes, I did do that, you were out of town!" He defended himself hotly. "And if you would have asked me, I would have told you that!"

"I came to surprise you and I had to have lunch with Mitchell because you can't be there for me the same way you can be there for that bitch and her family! She has a husband, Zander. And you're making him uncomfortable."

"Why can't *he* tell me that?" Zander looked at her. "Why are you pillow-talking with Mitchell over lunch like you can't pick up a fucking phone?" He held up a finger before she opened her mouth. "And don't say you did because I would have heard it!"

Carmen eyed him. "Why are you defending her so hard?! Are you fucking her?"

"Be serious Carmen. Be so fucking serious!" Zander stood. "I'm going to go."

"Go?! Go where?!"

"I don't know Carmen to get some air, obviously this isn't how you wanted this to go and now I'm just livid. I could understand if I've given you any fight or pushback. If I've given you an indication that I was cheating, but I've been nothing but transparent to you! I've given you nothing but my all and I thought I was doing a good job at it but obviously, I was wrong." Zander walked out with her calling his name in the background.

24

Freedom

P oppi and Lorna walked into the chambers of her favorite judge. Judge Albert Hops. He was a sweet older man with silver hair and youthful gray eyes. His smile was sweet and warm. He understood Poppi's hardship and wanted to help her the best he could. He pulled a lot of favors to get her conservatorship in his hands.

Paulette came in with her lawyers and sat beside her granddaughter-in-law. Mitchell used her lawyers without her knowledge to get the ball rolling on this matter, and her mother pulled the extra strings. She was told her mother would be here for this. She became nervous.

"Ms. Nichols," Judge Albert looked at her. "Are ya alright?"

She nodded. "I am not exactly excited, if my mother says the wrong thing–"

"There will be none of that. We can get started can't we Albert?" Paulette asked looking at him.

"Yes, we can, I believe all parties are here." He looked at the papers. He looked at Poppi. "Do you know the widow Baxter has given us enough evidence to grant you everything you've asked for, but there's some paperwork that's gonna take up to 120 days to be settled."

"What about the divorce?" Paulette asked her voice hopeful.

"We have to wait the 120 days, or until the paperwork is cleared, I'm sorry I wish I could do more."

"Tell me I'm free judge." Poppi held Paulette's hand tightly.

"On behalf of the state of Maine and everything I touch Ms. Nichols you're no longer under a conservatorship." He signed the papers to give her freedom back.

Poppi felt the tears pouring down her face. For once she felt something more than despair. She felt Paulette grip her hand.

"As soon as we get the opportunity, you'll be divorced quicker than you can say I quit." She promised. "I've got enough evidence to make this nice and easy." She promised. "Just like we said it would."

Poppi smiled. She was so close to being done. To being set free. To never looking back ever again.

25

Passions

Carmen and Zander sat in the VIP of her favorite nightclub. She was talking with her friends and making him the butt of whatever joke she could. She noticed her friends would laugh, but they would eye him as they did it.

"Can you take me to get a drink?" Gia, Carmen's softer friend, asked Zander.

"Sure, of course." He nodded and helped her down so they could walk to the bar.

Gia was beautiful, with long silky black hair, perfect almond skin, and beautiful silver eyes. She looked like a jellical cat. Mesmerizing and innocent when she looked up at him. "I thought you two broke up."

"She told you that?"

"She was with some guy last weekend. Michael? Mick? What the hell was his name?" Rami tapped her acrylic two-inch nail on the bar. "Damn, I can't remember. Anyway, they were all over each other and I thought she'd finally ended it with you until I saw you here tonight."

"Sorry to darken your party." He mumbled as he watched her order. He didn't want to be here with her either. He wanted to be at home painting or talking to Poppi. He wondered how she was. If she was thinking about him.

"No, you don't darken anything." Gia laughed. "I like you, but let's face the facts, Zander, Carmen doesn't deserve you. And you don't even wanna be with her anymore. You smell different and everything."

Zander laughed. "I smell different?"

"Yeah, when you two first got together you had your own smell, it was like a dark smokey passionate kinda smell, but now it's different.

Sweeter, floral. Powerful. And that's not from Carmen. Carmen is a bitter sharp pungent smell."

"What are you?" He asked paying for her drink. "Some kind of perfumer for humans?"

"No silly, I'm a hybrid between a Succubus and my father is the chairman of the league. I didn't know you were a creationist!" She swatted him. "Something else you and I have in common."

"I'm afraid I'm not, some friends of mine are." Zander looked at her. "I want to learn so I'm not ignorant."

"If it isn't my favorite little chipmunk!" A young woman stood in front of them. Her hair was in a sleek ponytail. Her body was coke bottle-shaped and decorated in leather. Her eyes were covered by large designer shades. "Who is this? Your next victim?"

"Actually, he's protected." Gia looked at him.

"By whom?" The woman looked at him. "I've never seen him before."

"A flower in your garden." Rami grinned mischievously. Zander didn't like the smile she held for her new and mysterious friend. Everyone was in on something that he wasn't.

"Bullshit! Neither of them is actively practicing." She looked at him. "Who are you here with? How do you know her?"

"He's Carmen's boyfriend Lavender lighten up. He doesn't know about it." She scoffed. "C'mon have a drink with us and stop being weird." She looked at the large man who looked like he moonlighted as a football player when he wasn't playing bodyguard to the angry lady in purple hair. "C'mon Alfie we're having' drinks."

"WHAT the fuck are you doing here?" Carmen spat at Lavender.

"Relax Carmen, I invited her." Gia waved her off. "I haven't seen her since the Halloween party, and I miss her."

"I miss you too hot stuff, but I'm really here on business. So, I can't stay."

"You can stay for a drink." She looked at her.

"Don't pull out those pitiful doe eyes on me you sweet little mere." Lavender winked at her.

"If you're gonna be all over each other go some fucking where else."

"What's wrong Carmen are you mad you aren't the center of attention for two seconds?" Lavender turned fully to face her. "You know I was actually hoping to find you here tonight."

"Oh really?"

"Yes, I was I was hoping that you and I could have a little chat. Since you went missing at the New Year's Eve party in New York and I haven't seen you in a while. My boss is climbing the walls, he'll be so thrilled to know that I found you."

"I don't know what you're talking about." Carmen rolled her eyes. "He and I have nothing to talk about."

"There are twenty-five thousand things he would love to talk to you about." Lavender looked at Zander. "This tall drink of water here being one." Lavender had an accent Zander heard before, it was slightly different, but the dialect and mannerisms were the same. He was curious about her. "Tell me darlin' where are you from?"

"Maine. Cole Harbor."

"Shut up! I know that place!" Rami, another one of Carmen's friends spoke up. She was beautiful with deep almond skin and bright hazel eyes. She was wearing a tight black dress and had her hair up in a bun with dangling earrings that danced in the light. "My sister moved there a few years ago, you might know her."

"What's her name?"

"Kantrella, but she goes by Kandi she used to work as a dancer, but she just got the okay to open up her bookstore."

"Does she have a boyfriend?"

"Derrick? She's head over heels for him, they've been together for a month, and they are insane about each other! I love him! They just left from seeing me, and I think they took my parents to the Aspen this week."

"Wow, good to know that he was serious." Zander chuckled. "He's never been in a committed relationship before."

"He is so good to her; I love them together."

"So, you know Roxanna?" Lavender eyed him curiously. "How long have you known them?"

"Not long, I just moved here from Texas."

"Carmen you used to live in Texas, didn't you?" Lavender looked at her. "Were you living with this man?"

"Yes." Zander put his hand on her knee. "We've been together for two years."

"What was going on for the past six months?" Lavender leaned in. "Were you moving the entire time?"

"No, I just moved the last week in November, then life became a blur with the holidays. You know how that can go."

"I'm sure." Lavender's eyes never left Carmen's. "Carmen wasn't with you?"

"No, I wish she was." He took her hand. "She could have been there for my Christmas miracle."

"What miracle?" Rami leaned in deeply interested. Her bangs haloed around her as her eyes intensified their stare on him as if she were going to watch the story play directly from his eyes.

"My brother called me on Christmas and informed me that I was on dessert duty for my family dinner, but I don't bake and no bakery including his was opened. I went to that small little grocery store on Main."

"Alberts?" Lavender looked at him.

"Yeah, that's the one." He nodded. "Anyway, I went and there was this hideous reindeer cake being all sad because I miss my girlfriend, my cake is hideous, and I am one reason away from seeing if it really is a wonderful life."

Rami laughed at his bad Christmas pun. "So, then what happened?"

"This angel in this blue dress comes up to me, well really, I crash into her with a loud bang, and she's apologizing and everything. She sees my cake and tells me she can't in good consciousness let me serve this to my mother and the next thing I know she's giving me a bag full of cakes and cookies."

Rami let out a deep sigh. "That's a Hallmark movie if I've ever seen one. I mean I can almost smell the love. Can't you?" Rami asked looking at Lavender.

"Wait a second." Gia looked at Carmen "I thought you said– "

"I was called in." Carmen cut her off. "What a sweet story. I hope you told the bitch thank you and kept it moving."

Rami looked at Lavender who was putting things together in her own mind. "Now do you smell what's cooking?"

"Oh, I smell it alright." Lavender looked at Zander. "I just can't fucking believe it."

26
Unpleasant

Poppi watched Mitchell eat his Pot roast as he sat across from her. "How's dinner dear?"

Mitchell looked at her. "It's fine, not the Ritz, but I do love your pot roast."

"I'm always glad to hear you like it." She looked at him. "I'm glad that you are home tonight I've missed you."

"What is that supposed to mean?" Mitchell looked at her.

"You've been working very hard Mitchell, that's all I meant was that you're working hard with Zander galivanting all over the coast with Carmen. Clubbing at night sunbathing in the day. Sounds kind of fun, maybe you and I could do it one day."

"What you go clubbing with your two left feet?" Mitchell chuckled. "Or embarrass you and me trying to run on the beach?"

"If you ever took me out you know I'd love to dance." She pushed a potato around her plate. "And I think that I'd look lovely running on the beach, I'm sure there are other people who would like to see me too."

Mitchell rolled his eyes. "Who the hell would want to see a whale in a bikini?" He scoffed. "Carmen is drop–dead gorgeous. She's beautiful, funny, and smart. We've had lunch together a few times when Zander is too busy, she's very wonderful, and people love her. They'd want to see her, but you. They'd pay you to put your clothes back on." He laughed.

Poppi didn't dare mention the thousands of dollars she made during her time at Lucky's. She was tucking it all away as the time melted slowly to her divorcing and being free of Mitchell forever. "Is that why you haven't slept with me? You're paying someone to take their clothes off?" She asked casually.

"What the fuck did you just say to me?"

She put her fork down and looked at him. "It's painfully obvious that you and I aren't happy. You hate everything about my appearance and personality. Why are you even here? To make yourself miserable?" She looked at him. "My conservatorship is almost over; you've gotten your money's worth out of me. Why don't you just divorce me and call it even?"

"Are you asking me for a divorce?" Mitchell stood quickly lunging at her. His hand wrapped around her throat. They both fell to the floor, and she hit the ground with a thud.

"Let go of me!" She screamed clawing at his face. She shoved him from her and scrambled to get up and away from him.

Mitchell grabbed her by her hair and punched her in the eye. "Where do you think you're going?!"

"Away from you!" She cried. She threw her elbow into his ribs, and she ran to the door. She knew it wouldn't be forever, but she could at least run for this moment. At this moment she could get away from him.

POPPI walked into the nursery with Juniper. "He's been so busy in here." She walked inside the empty room. All the furniture was being repainted to match. Zander had made each wall a different fairy tale scene from the series Happily Ever After: Fairy Tales for every child. She loved the amount of detail that he put into each wall.

Her favorite was Beauty and the Beast sitting together in the garden. The bright vivid colors and the deep brown skin of Belle made her want to jump right into the photo. She looked at Juniper. "This must have taken ages!"

"He comes over on his lunch a lot. When you take the girls, he'll have the boys help him. He even brought a projector so that he could get what he called true reference. I don't think I've ever had two men put more work into a room than Brantley and Zander. I mean look at this. Daisy has already said Zander is doing her room next." Juniper shook her head.

Poppi began to cry. She wished she could tell her sister that she was falling in love with him. She wished she could tell her sister more than anything in the world, but instead, she'd keep it private. No one needed to know, she'd just hurt herself.

"Poppi are you alright honey?"

"I'm leaving Mitchell in 117 days, and I really don't know if I can make it that long."

27

Conversations

Zander got up from the sleeping Carmen. She barely moved when he got up. He supposed that was a good thing. He hated not working, it was a Thursday and there was nothing for him. No working, no networking, not even his girlfriends' associates were amusing to him anymore.

He'd been vacationed out. Carmen worked, but he didn't want to bother her there. He was always told that he got on her nerves when he came to the set, so he just stayed in the background. Perhaps, he thought as he took a long hot shower, today he'd go to the country club his father listed him at since he'd been in town.

He pulled out his phone and called Poppi. It had been days since he heard from her and he missed her voice, her laugh, her smile. He missed the way she looked at him. He missed her being in his arms, no matter how short her time was in them.

"Zander?"

"Poppi?" Zander scratched the back of his head. "Is this a bad time? Did I wake you?"

"It's six am where you are. Why are you awake? What's wrong?"

"What's your favorite color?"

"What?"

"What's your favorite color? I don't think I ever asked you that before."

"Burgundy." She replied. "What's yours?"

"Green, dark forest green. If you could be any animal, what would it be?"

"I'd be a bear. I think they are beautiful, protective, majestic."

"Really?"

"Yes. I love bears, cows, and my all–time favorite animal which is a dog. Pitbull to be exact. What's your favorite movie?"

"The Wiz." He watched the skyline twinkle in front of him. "I love that movie. What about you?"

"God, to narrow it down? I guess Purple Rain."

"You're kidding."

"No, it's an epic tale of love and loss. Kid totally needed therapy and motorcycle lessons, but you have to admit that he worked hard when he was dedicated."

"I've never seen it."

"I'm sorry what?!" She exclaimed laughing. "How in the hell have you never seen Purple Rain?!"

"When given the chance of movies with the ladies of Vanity Six I go with the Last Dragon."

"I can't argue that it's a classic." She laughed. "Well, now we have to have a movie night."

"Don't get my hopes up." Zander tried not to sound excited.

"Are you going to tell me why you called at six o'clock in the morning?"

"Technically it's nine." He corrected.

"Not for you it isn't. So, what's wrong?"

"Mitchell thinks our relationship is inappropriate."

"I know that I told you New Year's Eve."

"He told Carmen that."

"When?" She asked. Zander looked back at Carmen who had shuffled but not rolled over.

"Over lunch."

"So, they're having lunch together, but he can't tell you that it's inappropriate for you and me to take our nieces and nephews to rehearsal and practice?"

"What do you think Poppi?" He sighed rubbing his shoulder.

"About what?"

"About you and I?"

"What is it you're trying to ask me, Zander? Do I find our relationship inappropriate?"

"Yes."

"Do you?" She asked after a long moment of thinking. Zander wanted her to say something that gave him an inch to take.

"Poppi, I called you because I was homesick, I missed you. I wanted to hear your voice, but I don't think it's inappropriate to want that from you."

More silence. Zander's skin was on edge when he thought about her just hanging up and never speaking to him again. She was all he wanted. He was thrilled with the idea of them being together in his apartment. Alone. If that's what he had to look forward to he was tempted to pack and catch the first flight out, no matter the seating.

"Will you bring me back a seashell? I've always wanted to see what they look like from California. Maybe it'll be a souvenir of the last time we miss each other."

"Yeah, I can do that." He took a breath of relief. "Sure."

"The Harkson case against your father starts today, wish us luck."

"You don't need it. You're my little lightning bolt. You'll knock'em dead."

"Thank you for the vote of confidence." Poppi chuckled. "I have to go, bye Zander." She hung up with an emptiness of a click. He would have stayed on the phone with her for hours if he could., but he was sure that duty called. At least he finally had something to do for the day though, finding the prettiest damn sea shell he could for her.

ZANDER searched for all the best shells for the best part of four hours on the chilled beach. He found as many as he could, and then he went to an exhibit and dug pearls from oysters so that she could have her own pearls.

Since Zander had hours before his jewelry order would be done, he went to the country club. It wasn't far from the jeweler he had chosen to do the work he wanted. Zander decided he'd have a nice lunch and wait the extra two hours to call his father to see how court went.

He couldn't believe Kyle Harkson was suing his father for a bad investment that they told him not to make. He even swore they wouldn't be liable for the matter, but due to some odd negotiations in the contract his father was being held suit. His finger drummed nervously as he thought about the situation.

He knew Poppi could handle it. He saw her win more with less. He'd even stepped into the courtroom a few times since they took the firm on as their own lawyers. She sounded different in a courtroom. Her body took up space unlike when she was with Mitchell, and she faded into the background. Her voice had that sweet southern warmth that drew people in but commanded attention and devotion to her version of events.

"Why if it isn't Mr. Zander." The voice from the club cut through his thoughts. "Where is your little lady this afternoon?"

"She's doing her job I assume." He replied. Part of him was talking about Carmen, but he mostly referred to Poppi when someone asked where his person was. He knew that was wrong, he was slowly starting not to care.

Lavender looked at him. "You know you aren't being forced to stay here; you can go home."

"What are you talking about?"

"My sister Poppi Nichols." She sat down across from him in a white skirt suit. Her lavender hair was flowy and her soft honey-brown skin was glowing as she crossed her legs. "That's the girl you're sitting over here looking like a lost puppy over, isn't it?"

He looked at her as she took a sip of coffee settling in. "Just who the hell are you?"

"I just told you. I'm her sister." She took her white designers off. Her bright lavender eyes stared back at him, without her glasses, she looked almost identical to Poppi, there were differences in eye color, her cheekbones were higher, and her nose was slender and pointed.

"How can I help you?" He asked putting down his book.

"You won't be helping her. You'll be helping me." An older gentleman with mahogany skin and deep green eyes that almost shimmered towered over the table. He wore a black shirt with marble green buttons and dress pants that matched. His tie had a clip on it with a lion wearing a crown of branches behind a sword and shield. "Our Lavender tells me you're an investment broker."

"I am."

"And you're good at your job."

"Hall and Bell happens to be one of the best firms in the United States, can't complain too much about that. We're top 10."

"I like the way he talks Lavender." He nodded. "You know who I am, I'm sure."

"Sol Abraxas, CEO of Nectar of the Gods brewery. We're four hours away from your only one on the East Coast."

"Lovely. I need a man I can trust, and something tells me that is you. Besides Lavender here vouched for you."

"She did?" He looked at her somewhat confused about why she would mention him of all people. Had Poppi mentioned him to her? It gave him a sense of hope maybe she did see something between himself and her.

"Let's just say I want you to owe me one," Lavender smirked.

"I'm coming to Maine for an event, and I would like to talk to you about this. Are you going to be there next week?"

"Yes, sir I will be."

"Wonderful." He shook his hand. "We will talk then. Lavender also tells me that you're involved with Carmen Grace is that correct?"

He looked at Sol, he was a strong-looking man. His face had a classic rugged handsomeness to it. He looked like he had never known a failure. And he was looking at Zander as though he might be his first. "Is that going to be an issue?"

"I'm sure you know Carmen's history with my sons?" He looked at him. "I don't want it to be uncomfortable for you since my business is very family heavy and their history is complicated."

Zander shook his head. "I have absolutely no problem with that sir, this is business, and I don't know your sons well enough to have personal opinions on them, but I can assure you this won't be an issue."

He nodded and looked at Lavender "Say your goodbyes my dear, the last time I got you back late my son wouldn't talk to me for a week." He looked at Zander. "Until we meet again Mr. Bell."

"I look forward to it Mr. Abraxas." He shook his hand. He watched him stand and walk out of earshot. "Do I say thank you or-"

"Don't mention it, and don't tell my sister." She stood. "I'll see you sooner than you think." She winked and followed him.

ZANDER went back to Carmen's place and fixed a steak and alfredo dinner thanks to his cooking class that he'd been taking with or without the guys there. He'd been proud of some of the work he'd been doing for himself. Preparing himself for the best things in his life to come.

He brought her a pair of lovely emerald earrings that he knew she would enjoy since he got a pair handmade for Poppi, but in his rush, the jeweler said something about replacing the earrings with something of lesser or equal value because there had been an issue with Carmen's. He didn't care, he was more excited about Poppi's going with the rest of the gift.

He set the box on the plate on the table and brought the food out. He even brought her roses. "Are you surprised?" He asked.

"Thank you for going all out." She smiled. "I feel so special." She looked at the black box. "Can I open it?"

"Yes of course." He dropped a napkin and went on his knee to pick it up.

"Oh my god Zander!" She looked up at him. "Are you fucking kidding me?!" She cried. "Babe! This is perfect!"

Zander looked at her placing a ring on her finger. "What?"

"Yes! Yes, I'll marry you!"

"What?!" He stammered. "You'll do what?"

"I'll marry you! I can't believe you would do something this fucking sweet! It's about time! I don't even wanna eat! C'mon, you! Let's go celebrate our engagement!" She took his hand dragging him from his stunned position and rushing him up the stairs.

28
Garden

Zander returned Carmen's deep kiss. He wanted to tell her that he couldn't marry her, but he would let her have tonight. He would hate to break her heart on their last night in California. He would just feel worse when he flew back alone. He also didn't want to tell her it was a mistake, because then he'd have to explain why.

Maybe Poppi was a silly little crush but crushes never made him feel the way he felt when it came to her. When it came to them. Even as he buried his face between Carmen's freshly waxed legs and began licking the sweet stickiness between her legs he felt the bubble of guilt that made him stop this act several times this week. He knew Carmen was getting suspicious.

Now she would just assume that this was why. He was nervously planning their engagement. He'd become a liar. He hated what he'd become. He hated that this was who he was. He never wanted to become this person. To become dishonest to the woman that he loved. He'd given her his heart; she wouldn't hurt him. Why should he put her in the same position?

"Oh, Mitch." She moaned "Right there, baby." She tightened her grip on him.

Zander froze mid-tongue stroke. That wasn't right. Was she thinking of someone else while he was in the act of pleasuring her? His own internal battle wouldn't allow him to feel her being at fault. He was hurt though, he'd never call Poppi's name out during sex, he felt terrible about even having feelings for her.

Zander slid on his condom and pushed himself inside of her. She gasped and opened her eyes. She looked up at him. He couldn't look at her. He closed his eyes. He tried to think of anything that would allow this to work for him. He took five deep breaths exhaling each one slowly as he thrust.

His mind became fuzzy and warm. He could hear birds chirping in the middle of the night. His body melted from his mind. He was left to wander. He walked to a door; the light was pouring underneath it. Handprints decorated it.

He turned the knob and let the sunlight pour onto him. He felt warm soft grass under his feet and when he looked back the door was gone. He looked at the scenery. The beautiful lake with ducks floating lazily along the sparkling water. The grass was deep and green.

He walked to the red blanket with the basket on it. She sat there curled in a ball. Her white dress had soft yellow flowers on it. The dress was worn and faded. He reached out a hand to her. "Poppi it's me."

She jumped and stood. "What the hell are you doing here?"

He looked at her. "What do you mean what am I doing here? You're in my head."

"What are you doing right now?" She looked confused.

Zander looked at her. "You won't like that answer Poppi." He sighed. "How did I get here?"

"If I knew I'd ask you to leave." She looked away. In all of their shock, Zander hadn't realized she was crying.

"What's wrong?" Zander reached out for her.

"Why are you here Zander?"

"Where is here exactly?" He looked around.

"My plane. My dream scape. I come here to meditate when I have had a hard day."

"You had a hard day?" He touched her. Her skin felt real under his fingertips. "Come here."
Poppi melted into his embrace. She exhaled clenching his bare back. She sighed. "Maybe this is why you're here. We needed this." She pulled away from him.
Zander looked into her perfect brown eyes. He leaned down and kissed her. Deeply passionately. His kisses went down to her neck down to her breasts pushing up her dress as quickly as she was tugging at him.
Their lips tangled together. Bodies pressed together in a breathy embrace. His pace was slow, steady, and passionate. "You feel so good mon éclair."

ZANDER heard cries of passion that weren't Poppi's. He looked down and Carmen was crying. She was flushed and her cheeks were wet. Zander quickly pulled away from her. "I'm so sorry did I hurt you?"

She shook her head. "No."

"What's wrong?" He asked cradling her in his arms.

"No one has ever made love to me that way before. I was just shocked. For a second it seemed like you weren't even here, and then you just were so good to me it made me cry."

"I'm sorry." Zander held her. "I guess that was just the excitement of everything."

"Yeah. I can't wait to see the wedding night." She kissed him. "I love you so much, Zander."

Zander tried not to think about her calling him someone else. He was thinking of someone else when he gave her the best love-making experience to date. Though he never had a fantasy where the person was asking him to leave.

29

Eros Night

Z ander sat in his VIP section. He didn't expect this kind of treatment from Lucky's, but tonight it had been transformed into a glitzy upscale bar with a masquerade ball of lingerie-embellished bodies. He waved at Kandi behind the bar, and she waved back happily. He was glad to see her, it'd been a while since they all had gotten together. He'd have to call Derick and change that.

Zander watched as the dancers came and went from the stage doing small floor shows or entertaining men in 500.00 haircuts and even sharper suits. Everyone here was dressed like they belonged somewhere very important. Zander even recognized them as his father's high-end clients.

He wasn't surprised since the getting-in process was just as extensive. He had to present his invitation and tell them who gave it. After running it under a black light they called Roxanna down to verify that it was him and guide him in. He had to hand his ticket to another woman after he was led in. She was dressed in a beautiful tight black evening gown and beautiful curly hair. She stamped his hand and pointed him to the VIP section.

Sitting there he couldn't help but wonder if he should call Poppi and let her know that he was home. He wanted to see her but now wasn't the time. He was really just here to network; he'd stay for an hour and then leave. If it wasn't too late, he'd call her.

A group walked into his section. The four men who looked like they should be playing the starting defensive line for the NFL dressed in matching black suits stood in front of him. He straightened looking up at them. He watched as they separated. Lavender walked between them wearing a green and black checkered dress with a heart cut out of the cleavage. Her lavender hair was in two heart pigtails and she wore Y2K flame rimless glasses with platform Mary Janes.

A man walked beside her, his mahogany skin deep and coated in the cool blue lighting. His eyes were dark green with bright flecks of gold in them that dazzled when they were caught in the light. He wore a black suit with a green tie. His clip matched Sol Abraxas's. His nose also matched Sol's. "Is this him little viper?" He slid his long finger from Lavender's throat to her chin.

"Yes sir, this is him." She sat on one side of him. Making herself comfortable. "Roxi girl gave him his ticket personally. Said this was supposed to be a real special night for him."

"Oh really?" He looked at Zander taking a seat beside him. "We'd hate to ruin that for you."

"I don't even know you, so I doubt I can help." He replied honestly.

"I do believe you can. I'm Keres Abraxas and I'd like to talk to you about Carmen Grace, and what she's done with my 25,000.00"

ZANDER'S brows were knit with confusion. Was this why she was so quick to accept an unwanted proposal because she owed someone money? He looked down at his glass and then back up at the man and his goons behind him. Lavender was lounging with her legs crossed on the couch looking down at the dancers.

He wanted to be surprised that Carmen was into something shady. He wanted to be angry and maybe even cause a little havoc, but all he wanted was out. He wanted to enjoy the act Roxanna had spoken so much about. She was so excited about it, and now he'd miss it because of something silly Carmen's done. He straightened his tie. "I don't know anything about that."

"If you don't know about it why did you take my father's deal?" He inquired looking at Lavender. "If not to cover for Carmen."

"I didn't know your father until Lavender introduced us. I have no reason to cover up for Carmen. As a matter of fact. Let's not have her ruin a perfectly fine evening." He held out his checkbook and wrote a check for 30 thousand dollars. "Consider that even, with interest. Let's leave it alone."

"Mr. Bell..." He looked at the check and back at him before folding it and handing it to Lavender who examined it. "You always throw his kind of money at an inconvenience?" He asked him."

"I don't like to brag, but yes, I've made a life for myself. I like civility as well, and if I'm working with your father, I want no issues with you or any other members of your family Mr. Abraxas."

Keres nodded and looked at Lavender. "I guess we will have to tell Carmen you've done this good deed."

"Don't." Zander shook his head. "I'd prefer her never know that I've done this. I prefer her never feel in debt to me, I'd like everything to be clean between us."

"Sounds like a lot of final talk for a man who just ask her to marry him, but thanks to you, now my little viper can take that leave she needed for her sister." He looked at her with a proud grin. "Isn't that right?"

"Yes, thank you, Zander." She stood. "I'm going to go check with the dancers, see if everyone is prepared in the rooms, you know my actual job."

"I'll keep Mr. Bell here company, I like him." Keres smiled softly at her kissing her hand.

"You just be on your best behavior, apparently he's very well-liked around here." Lavender snapped her fingers and two guards stood behind her.

"Oh, you don't have to tell me." He watched her go and then looked at Zander as if they shared an unspoken secret.

"DO you know why I love Eros night?" Keres asked sitting on Zander's left side for a better view of the state.

"Are you a Greek Mythology enthusiast?"

Keres laughed. "You can say that. I'm a creationist, they all go together. You know the creator was fond of them all. The Greek depictions, the Egyptian ones, and even the ones that have been long forgotten, much like the creator, but it's said that we celebrate Eros because he's the one who will restore magic to the world."

"Is that right?"

Keres nodded slowly. "Eros is the creator of love. Most of the world's magic is ruled by love. It could change the very trajectory of our very lives. I know I know it sounds sentimental, but it's true. Eros was born from the goddess Aphrodite, but neither of them would exist without the fire of Keahi. Eros forged her sword for the rebellion against the god Zephyr and his son Kenye. That sword was forged with the love of her and Oryn the god she was accused of killing. The god who left a piece of his soul up here to walk the earth until he found her. His true love. His light bringer. "

"That's quite the story Keres." Zander took a drink.

"The first sign that there Oryn is coming back to reunite with his lover, the bringer of fire, is a fertility witch igniting magic with her soulmate." Keres traced a circle in his pants. "That's what the Arrow shot is for, they're ten grand a pop and only given out during certain celebrations in hopes that she will come to some lucky SOB who is worthy of her." He looked at Zander. "Do you think you're worthy?"

Zander thought about what he was asking. He wasn't worthy of Poppi, not after messing up so badly with Carmen. If he knew she wanted this, if she was willing to run with him, he'd do everything he could to be worthy of her love, of her time, of her devotion. "I'm not a creationist Keres," He looked into his cup. "I don't think this applies to me."

"Who said the love of her life had to share her religion? It's ideal sure, but if you love someone you should just accept you love someone." The lights went down in the club. "Ah, show time."

ZANDER watched as the stage went silent. The entire club was pitch black and all he heard was the clicking of heels echoing from all over. 'Burn' by Lina J, one of his favorite R&B artists played The slow sultry piano keys played as a soft spotlight hit the center of the stage. There was a hoop there. A woman dressed in all gold walked up to the hoop in complete sync with the music. She sat in the middle of the hoop for a few moments. When the first verse started.

"My heart's been cold for so long.
I know you hear the same song
over and over again
I can't seem to when
but when you touch me
baby,
I can feel the Burn."

When the beat dropped into a beautiful bass line the hoop lifted with her twirling upside down with her legs spread. She moved her leg inside the hoop and swung back to the pole as Lina J summoned her lover from the shadows in her song. Begging him to touch her the way she dreamed he would. The woman in black, who appeared to be Roxi, latched on to her arms and they did aerial ballet to the music break. When the words started Roxi's leg looped on the pole and she twirled down into a split.

Their performance was breathtaking and didn't even have to be performed in a strip club for it to be taken that way. Their bodies told the story the song belted out visually. Their bodies moved to hypnotize the audience as money flowed down on them. Zander was infatuated with the woman in gold. She danced like she had so much to break free from. He was curious about her. Why did she feel like she was calling him? Like she was looking for him in the crowd.

"They are something else, aren't they?" Keres asked breaking the trance. "What a way to get the lucky golden ticket winners to open their minds, an entire dance about the history." He stood and emptied a suitcase full of money that rained on the two dancers.

"Zander!" Kandi stood holding a silver tray with a red card and a white translucent shot.

"What is this?"

"It's your Arrow shot. When you take it just relax your mind. Allow yourself to be in the moment. You signed all the paperwork, right?"

"Yes, though that's a lot of paperwork for a private dance." Zander took the key.

"Zander it's not a dance," Kandi smirked. "It's an experience. And don't forget if you panic your safe word is grape."

"Grape?"

"Grape." She nodded as he took the shot. It tasted like cherries. Sweet and crisp. "Enjoy your time in room five." She waved to Keres who gave her a nod.

Zander looked at him. "Here goes nothing."

He shook his hand. "My friend, don't let a very fixable mistake stop you from changing the world."

30
Trouble

P oppi changed into her outfit that matched everyone else's. A black lingerie set and a black plain mask. She even had to wear a black wig. Nothing about her could stick out. Thanks to her makeup skills her tattoos had been well covered.

"I still can't believe you're doing this! This is so incredibly dangerous!" Lavender hissed. "What if someone who isn't supposed to smell, or sense her is here and they do just that."

"I'm sure it will be fine." Roxanna hushed her. "Besides this is just a hunch of yours and Kandi's sister who hangs out with Carmen how credible can she be? No offense Kandi."

"I did worse when I was younger." She shrugged. "At least she's hanging out with the rich and famous."

"What if our hunch is true? I mean he's talking about her in LA. And he smells *just* like her."

Poppi looked at Lavender. "I'm not practicing, I haven't since Lydia died. So my scent, my magic, is dormant. I don't have anything. You know that. And if you don't, ask my stepmother. She'll tell you. She's a fucking elder."

"You can not practice and still have a smell, Poppi." Kandi corrected her. "The smell of your love pheromone in your soul doesn't change just because you don't practice, and Zander doesn't even know what you are exactly. What I can say is the whiskey warm smokey fire smell he had the first night I met him now has floral and strawberry undertones you know kinda like the same way you smell like a warm fire in a field of wildflowers."

"Maybe she shouldn't go." Lavender bit her lip. "What if the hunch is right? Fertility witches are supposed to be put to death so they don't accidentally ignite the end of the world. It's one of the big things Chairman Sepehr has made pretty clear. So what if she is one, and she does ignite the 'great awakening' and starts the end of the world."

"Then she had fun getting us there. Hell, the world is gonna end anyway bitch might as well fucking enjoy it."

"Says the succubus." Lavender scoffed.

"Your sister has been miserable for the past five years. Your family has abandoned her, she's been verbally, physically, and emotionally abused. She has been held prisoner in her marriage. Yes. I think she should go out and have some fucking fun. This world hasn't exactly given her a fair hand Lavender. Yourself included. You could have had that fucking asshole erased the day after her fucking accident, but you didn't! Don't come in here now and try to preach what's right and what's wrong. Let her have some fucking enjoyment knowing there is a man out there who is crazy about her."

All of them looked at the stare-down between Roxanna and Lavender. Poppi never felt as seen as she did when Roxanna said it. She was relieved to know her friends loved her more than anything in the world.

"You're right." Lavender handed her the shot. "Just remember if anything bad happens. If you need out. Call us. I'm literally bound to you. I'll know."

Poppi took the shot; it tasted like sweet cherries. "Wish me luck."

Poppi walked to the door. She knew that her appearance would change the moment he laid eyes on her, she was nervous to see what was going to happen when he looked at her. Would he see Carmen? Would he see someone else? She took a deep breath and opened the door.

31

Unreal

Zander's back was turned when the door opened. He was looking at his bar. Curious how they got his entire living room into a private room. He was glad not to be in a stuffy suit somewhere unfamiliar, but this was even more odd. It all felt real.

"Zander." Poppi called from behind him.

"There she is!" He smiled. "My bride-to-be."

"Your what?!" She looked shocked. She stood there in her normal outfit when they were settling in for the night. His old basketball shirt and knee-high socks. Hopefully she wasn't wearing anything underneath.

"You heard me." He smirked. "Or do you just want me to say it again?"

"Can't it be both?" She smiled. "Can't I be in shock to hear it and want to hear it again?" She walked up to him putting her hands around his neck.

"The fake you wouldn't have been surprised." Zander didn't pull her away, he just held her. "Where are you?"

"What do you mean?" She looked at him quizzically. "I'm right here."

"Where are you really?" He looked at her. "I'm at Lucky's and I know you're not there." He looked at her. "Where are you and how do you keep meeting me in here?"

"I wish I had the answers Zander, but I don't."

"Are you the fertility witch I've heard about?"

"No!" She exclaimed. There was uncertainty in her voice that displayed over her face. "I wouldn't know really."

"I don't want to waste time." He looked at her. "I'm sure we will see each other in person, and we have a lot to talk about." He looked at her *hand. A large half-moon vintage ring sat on her ring finger. "I'd like to enjoy tonight."*

He kissed her; it felt different. He felt her kiss him back. He felt her hands on him, and it didn't feel artificial. She cradled the back of his head as he kissed her neck. "I miss you." He moaned in her ear. "I miss you so much."

She giggled "I miss you too." She kissed him. Rolling him on his back. She sat on top of him. His hands traced her stomach. He loved her curves. The small rolls of skin made her look realistic to him. Every imperfection to someone else was a beauty mark to him. His hands went up and caressed her full breast. Her breath escaped her.

"Is this, okay?" He looked at her. "I don't want to push you if you aren't ready."

She looked down at him. "Kiss me." She leaned down. He gladly followed her instructions. Her body began to direct his hands in just the right way. His body began to react to her.

Zander felt his true self melting to the surface. She bit his lip and he growled at her tossing her on her back. Biting her thigh so hard she cried out. He could feel her flesh under his teeth. Taste the warm delicate skin, smell her perfume. He kissed the tender area. "I'm so sorry."

"Tell me this is what you want Zander." She reached out and touched his face. "Tell me I belong to you."

He looked at her, her brown eyes were glowing with energy. Tears brimmed his eyes. He could feel her pain, her angst for him. Being in this situation was hard for both of them. "You're all I've ever wanted since I first laid eyes on you Poppi Celeste Nichols. All I've ever wanted was you."

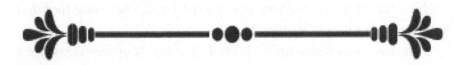

BRIGHT lights separated him from the dancer. Before she could run out of the door, he grabbed her hand, and she looked back. The wig fell off of her head and her frantic eyes locked with him. It was her! "Poppi!"

She ran out. Zander tried to get to the door. The guards stopped him. "No, you don't understand I have to catch her."

"No, you don't. You need to sit down."

"Fellas please!" He looked at them. "She's... She's the love of my life."

The guard laughed. "How many times have we heard that before?"

Zander sat down with his head in his hands. Caught between that didn't happen and it was the best night of his life.

32

Valentine

P oppi walked into her office. Her leg still tingled from the bruise. She couldn't believe last night actually happened. She was walking on air. She felt untouchable. Her body felt recharged and renewed. She was so happy she could scream, but she decided to keep it to herself. She took a deep breath.

"Miss P!" Her secretary a light-skinned young woman named Teressa with hair that changed every other day. Today she wore a red wig with a heart part on the side and a red suit to match it. Her lipstick even kept on the theme. She was one hell of a beauty vlogger when she wasn't trying to be a lawyer.

"Good morning, Teressa." She beamed. "How are you on this lovely day of...Well, love?"

"Not as good as you! Did DeMarco give you an extra shot of espresso?" She asked looking at her "You're glowing."

"I am? Must have been a good weekend." She shrugged. "What can I help you with?" She opened the door and her walk on cloud nine ended quickly and shot her back down to earth. "Mitchell, mother." She swallowed. "Hello."

"Hello dear!" Mitchell walked over to her kissing her on the cheek. "Your mother has decided to spend some time in town with us for a while and I wanted to surprise you with some lunch since I have to go out of town. Tonight. I'd hate to leave you alone."

"Honey, it's fine."

Mitchell looked at Teressa who stood at the door. "Could you get us some coffee or something? Whatever it is you're supposed to do here."

"Sure, I'll get security." Teressa walked out of the office and down the hall. Teressa hated Mitchell ever since she walked in on him yelling at her about not being able to miss work for some event he sprang on her last second.

"You haven't been home in a week it's time for you to come back and I brought your mother to make sure you did just that."

"Mitchell, I don't need a chaperone!" She broke away from him.

"Nonsense. It's clear you need to be with your mother for a while, and I'll be back on Thursday, so it isn't that big of a deal." He kissed her on her head. "Maybe now you'll think about questioning me." He whispered in her ear and left.

Poppi looked at her mother across the table. Her black hair slicked back into a formal bun with small gemstones gilding it. She was a petite older woman who was vain about her looks. Her lips were full, but they never looked like they enjoyed a smile, her eyes were fierce and firm. She pushed through her salad.

"You've lost weight." Her mother complimented her. "It's about time, I thought you were going to be fat forever."

"I like my appearance, Mother," Poppi replied shortly poking at her steamed salmon. "Not that that matters to you."

"Mitchell says that you've gotten a smart-ass mouth lately." She snapped at her. "What is going on?"

"I hate my marriage and soon I'll be leaving him." She took a sip of water. "And there is nothing you, or him, can do to stop it or change my mind."

"You belong to me! I'll never allow you to divorce him! He's the best thing that ever happened to you, just because your sisters are ignorant of good men and ruin relationships and marriages left and right doesn't mean you will."

"Callum was cheating on Juniper, and Lavender knows her worth! Neither of them ruined anything that wasn't already fucked up. But I guess to a woman who sold her daughter to an abusive piece of shit for money his grandmother just sneezes at that you wouldn't consider that an issue."

Her mother reached across the table and smacked her across the face. "I suggest you watch your tone!"

She stood and looked at her "Thanks for lunch." She threw her money on the table. "Find your own way to the damn house." She strolled out of the restaurant her head held high. Reminding herself sooner than later she'd never have to see them again.

POPPI sobbed in her office. She couldn't take the despair that came with being Mrs. Mitchell Baxter any longer. Now she was forced to go to a place she hated with a woman she couldn't stand. She wanted to call Lavender, maybe with the both of them in a room together she could escape, but where would she go?

Her door creaked open. "Poppi." She heard his voice fill her ears. It wasn't dreamy or full of whimsy like last night, but deep and present in this moment. "Teressa said you weren't taking visitors, but suggested I come in anyway. And by suggested, I mean forced."

Poppi laughed through her tears. She wiped her tears and looked at him. He stood in a nice Navy-blue suit and black shirt wearing the tie that Thea made him. He held a vase of red roses, LA hybrid lilies, and Soraya sunflowers. In his other hand, there was a black box.

She got up and took the flowers. "Oh, Zander these are lovely." Poppi was trying to hold back tears she opened the box a set of pearl earrings of two different colors looked at her. One pearl was a powder rose and the other was lavender. She looked up at him. "Where did you find something like this?"

"I did it myself in California. There were mostly bored kids at this science exhibit at this museum, but I was excited, I took them to a jeweler and had them make earrings." He looked at her. "Happy Valentine's Day."

She wrapped her arms around him. "This is absolutely the best worst day I've ever had. Thank you." She laid her head on his chest. Wishing that this was where her day could end, and not at home with her awful mother.

33

Paulette

"Zander this is a dear friend Paulette Baxter."

"Hello." Zander looked at the woman in her purple suit with her silver hair blown out, and she wore a diamond necklace. She had a clutch that matched the suit, and her smile and her golden-brown skin was ageless.

"Mr. Hall only calls me a dear friend because his investments from my grocery stores and other businesses alone can single handedly fund his retirement." Paulette chuckled holding out her hand for Zander. "It's a pleasure to meet you, young man."

"Pleasure is mine." He shook her hand. "How can I help you both?"

"It's no secret that I'll be retiring from being soon, and I want you to take over my accounts. Paulette here insisted that she should meet the man I feel so strongly about, and I was in agreement."

"Of course, Ms. Baxter let me answer any questions you may have. We'll keep everything the same, I'm sure you're satisfied?"

"You're correct I am. If I have issues?"

"You can call me any time." He looked at her. "Feel free to interview me if you'd like."

"Joesph why don't you leave us." She looked at him and then took a seat. "I would like to have a Q&A."

"Of course. Don't be too hard on him."

"Nonsense I'm nice as nice can be til you cross me." She shooed him. Zander sat at his desk and looked at her as she scanned the things in his office. "I hear that you're seeing a famous movie star."

"Carmen and I aren't exactly something I discuss at work." He replied honestly.

"Good for you keeping a balance." She nodded. "My granddaughter's husband doesn't have much of a balance. I'm sure you know him. Mitchell Baxter?"

"I work with him; I'm surprised you didn't ask him to take over your account."

"God no! He'd kill me to get his alleged inheritance." She laughed. "No, I'm fine where I am thank you." She looked at her watch. "You know I've got to meet my daughter and granddaughter for lunch, why don't you join me?"

"Really?"

"Of course, I always like to introduce my newest edition. My daughter likes to get a feel for them." She stood. "C'mon. Let's go."

"HI, dad." Zander stood watching his father and Poppi stroll toward their table. She looked lovely in her white pantsuit. Her hourglass figure is visible and commanding. "Poppi. What a pleasure to see you."

"You two know each other?" Sabrina asked hugging Frederick.

"Our lives have intertwined quite a bit over the past few months. We've been helping our siblings with their kids." Poppi kissed Paulette's cheek and then Sabrina's before Zander pulled out her chair for her.

"What lovely earrings Poppi where did you get them?"

"I got them for Valentine's Day." Poppi blushed as she answered Sabrina. "They were a gift from a very special friend."

"I'm so glad we're all here together. With so much to celebrate." Frederick looked at them. "Your granddaughter is quite the lawyer. She won our case today. It was a very smooth and quick battle."

"He's joking, it was grueling, and I barely won anything, but I'm glad I could help."

"She's being modest," Frederick ordered an expensive bottle of champagne. "Is she always like that?"

"Always." Sabrina smiled. "She forgets how proud we are." She kissed her head.

"Ma!" She laughed. "You're embarrassing me."

"Not as embarrassed as you're about to be," Paulette muttered. Poppi looked up as she cleared her throat. "Mitchell! Hello!" She waved him over.

Mitchell froze and turned around with Carmen in tow. "Grandmother. Mother." He sneered his nose when he saw her. "Poppi?"

"What are you doing here with my fiancé?" She looked at Poppi.

"Fiancé?" Sabrina choked on her water. "Frederick did she say fiance?!"

Poppi's eyes widened looking at Zander. "When did this happen?"

Zander was visibly embarrassed. This wasn't how he wanted her to find out if she had to find out before he fixed it at all. He wanted to tell her it was a bigger mistake, but he didn't want to do this at all.

"Last week not that it's any of your business." Carmen showed off the emerald ring that took up most of her ring finger. "What are you doing here?"

"Celebrating. What are you doing here?" Paulette glared. "I suppose business?"

"Looking for him." Mitchell nodded to Zander. "His fiancé came in looking for him and his secretary told us you would be here, so we came here."

Poppi quickly jumped up from the table after looking at her phone for most of the exchange. "I'm so sorry I have to go."

"What's wrong?" Zander asked noticing her color had gone from her body.

"My sister is in labor."

34

Baby

P oppi rushed out of the restaurant as quickly as she could, but her focus was all over the place. Why was Mitchell there with Carmen? What was going on with them? Where did she park? Did she even drive? Was Mitchell going to follow her to the hospital, she knew her sister and Roxanna would lose their minds if they had to deal with him when emotions were running this high.

Her mouth went dry, and her hands began to sweat as she took a deep breath, she had to think but nothing was making sense. She felt a hand take hers. "C'mon." Zander looked at her. "We've got to get the bags from her house and get to the hospital."

"YOU'RE doing great Juniper," Claudia reassured her rubbing her back as she bounced on the ball. She turned around to see Poppi walking through the door.

"Thank God you're here! The baby stopped."

"What do you mean the baby stopped?" Poppi chuckled kissing her cheek and rubbing her belly.

"I mean they said they weren't coming out."

Poppi laughed. "Don't be silly. I doubt that. Maybe they don't like the vibes. We'll start on getting it real cozy in a second." The sounds of *Murder, She Wrote* filled the room. "Now we've got some good television."

"Who did that?"

"That would be me." Zander stood raising his hand behind her. "Hi. Brantley texted me and told me he was two hours out and told me what to do."

"Of course, he did. I'm so glad you two have become such good friends." She sighed. "But what if he's not here? God, what if the baby doesn't want to come out and I don't get to give birth in water like I'm supposed to." She started to cry. "What if nothing goes right?!"

"Hey... Hey." Zander took her hands. "We're here, and this little being is going to come out just the way we all want happy and healthy right?"

Juniper nodded. "Right."

"We will do whatever you need to make you happy, and I'm sure Brant won't miss this. He promised he'd be here." He reassured her calmly. "We're going to be here with you until you tell us otherwise. Why don't we go for a walk, let Poppi change into something more comfortable, and get this place set up the way you wanted and see if that helps."

They looked at Claudia who was staring at her son in awe. She had a look of pride and sadness on her face as she nodded. "Yeah, that sounds perfect." She nodded. Zander helped Juniper up and they walked out of the door

. Claudia watched them walk out of the door Juniper looked like a weight had been lifted off of her shoulder. Claudia had a look of satisfaction and pride on her face. She started to busy herself while Poppi changed into yoga pants and a shirt that said 'Baby's favorite Auntie.' "I've never seen Zander so attentive to a pregnant woman." She lifted her head up. "As a matter of fact, I don't think I've ever seen him be attentive to anyone the way he is to you and your sister. Makes me proud though."

"I think that baby has everyone wrapped around its finger." She smiled. Changing the blankets to the ones Juniper washed and vacuum sealed herself. "I'm glad to see that she has such amazing support this time around. Her ex-husband left halfway through Daisy's birth because it was taking too long."

"I am too, the twins were six weeks old before we met them. So I've never really been in a situation where I already feel such a unique bond with the baby before, but I guess with Carmen as my future daughter-in-law, I doubt I will again."

She thought back to the lunch where she and Mitchell came storming in and ruining a perfectly good moment. "Did they tell you?" She asked, "Mr. Bell seemed shocked."

"He called me before you got here, I'd be surprised if Juniper isn't giving him an earful since she overheard it." Claudia looked at her. "Has he told you how it happened?"

"No," she replied and took a deep breath exhaling as she sat on the couch. "If I'm honest Mrs. Bell, I don't want to know. I don't even wanna believe it."

Claudia nodded. "You and my Son-in-law are one and the same when it comes to that."

"Crispin has reason not to be her biggest fan. I on the other hand do not."

"I see why Sabrina loves you the way she does." She sat across from her prepping the area for the birthing pool. "You remind me so much of her, noble, honest, and a heart of gold tied to someone who is everything opposite of those things. Sabrina and I were very close, but I also knew Mitchell's father, and if he's anything like him I can only hope you have an escape plan."

Poppi looked at her. Her warm eyes were deep with maternal knowing. She felt the urge to cry knowing what she'd been going home to for the past few days. All the mean hurtful things that her mother said to her. Telling her she'd never have a family like Juniper if she kept acting like a stupid bitch and realizing what Mitchell was to her. She couldn't let Claudia know what she was dealing with. "I'm fine Claudia, really. According to your grandson, I'm built 'Tonka tough.'"

Claudia chuckled. "I know you are." She took her hand a dark look waved in her eyes. "Just... Don't be too tough you can't ask for help. I've lost some I felt like I knew forever to that. Vivianite Abaraxas, Sabrina, and I were all close, I got luckier than both of them in the love department, but Vivi got the worst of the luck. She's been gone for 12 years because she wouldn't stop being strong and ask for help." She brushed a hair from Poppi's face. "And I just don't want the same thing happening to the closest thing I have to a...." She thought about her next words. She looked up at her and let a warm smile cover her face. "Let's just say... Zander wouldn't be the only one who would be lost"

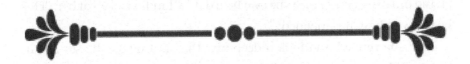

"SAY who you are and what you think the baby is." Roxanna held the camera up to Zander and Poppi. "Ready. Go."

"Hi, I'm you Uncle Zander, and I think you're going to be a girl."

"Hi, I'm your Aunt Poppi and I think you're going to be a boy."

"Seriously?" Zander looked at her. "I thought you'd be team girl for sure."

"Oliver needs to have a friend to grow up with that isn't Sawyer. Every boy deserves a brother."

"Every girl deserves a sister," Zander argued playfully.

"Speak for yourself." Poppi laughed. "You don't have any."

Roxanna rolled her eyes and looked up from the camera. "You two are disgusting." She closed the camera as they laughed at her. Roxanna's attire was the same as Poppi's only her shirt said 'Baby's Rich Bestie.' Which was her tagline for the children. "Like I thought that Kandi and lover boy were bad but you two are just despicable with cuteness. I'm going to smoke." She grabbed her bag and handed her the camera. "If Brantley gets here before I get back, get his reaction."

Poppi watched as Roxanna bounced down the hallway. Being this close to Zander after everything was starting to wear on her. She wanted to scream and shout at him. Cry about everything that Carmen had said to her at lunch.

"Are you going to talk to me about it?" Zander asked her finally as they stood there waiting for Brantley to show up.

"I-"

"I'm here!" Brantley rushed with a duffle bag over his shoulder with flowers in hand. He had a shirt on that said 'Future Dad Bod."

"Great!" Poppi turned back on the camera. "Who are you and what do you think the baby is going to be?"

"Hello, baby!" He waved nervously to the camera. "I-I'm your dad, and I think, no I know you're going to be my little princess! I can't wait to meet you!"

"It looks like you're just in time," Claudia stepped into the hallway. "Her water just broke."

35
Willow

Poppi stared in awe at Brantley and Juniper working together to bring the beautiful pale child into the world. Her skin was a deep tan and she had beautiful long black locks as she lay on her mother's chest as Brantley cried kissing Juniper's face and thanking her for everything she'd endured for him. Poppi wanted to be angry with both of them for hiding something so extreme from her, but were they hiding it really? He'd been hovering around her the entire time, Oliver was more open to him than his own father, and the time that Daisy called him dad. Poppi shouldn't have been so oblivious, maybe she was just happy to see her sister happy for once.

"Poppi." Juniper looked at her breaking her stare with the little loaf on her chest. "I want you to do the honors and cut the cord."

"Are you sure Brant doesn't want to do it? It's his first baby."

Brantley looked up at her. "I have this baby because of you. If you hadn't come into my life and introduced me to the woman of my dreams I wouldn't have had this moment. You deserve to cut the cord Pops. We love you."

Poppi looked down at the cord and snipped it where Claudia told her to. Claudia scooped her up and nodded to her to follow her to the baby bed. "How is she?" Poppi asked.

"She is 7lbs and 21 inches. All ten fingers all ten toes." Claudia admired the baby as she went over all of her stats. Poppi peered over at her. She had the perfect little round face and button nose. Her eyes were closed, but she had long curly eyelashes. Her eyebrows were barely there, but her face was expressive with her full little pouted lips. She was precious and the perfect blend of both her mother and her father. "She did good didn't she Pop?" She asked wrapping her in a rainbow blanket.

Poppi looked as Claudia handed her the baby. "She did perfectly." She looked at her. "Willow is absolutely perfect."

POPPI laid back on the recliner with her niece as Brantley helped Juniper shower and get comfortable. She was glad to have some alone time with the little person. Roxanna went to call Alton and get dinner for everyone. She wasn't leaving until it was absolutely necessary. Since Lavender's flight was late and she felt she had to have her sisters here. Poppi rubbed Willow's back thinking of everything that Claudia had said to her. She was right, there were a lot of people who needed her around. Especially the little being who was curled up on her chest. She planted a kiss on her forehead. She would make her proud. She would make sure she would never have to witness the mean and nastiness of Mr. Baxter. She'd see her Aunt Poppi as someone strong, she'd make all of them proud.

"I'm here to take my little princess." He smiled scooping her into his arms. "Auntie has done enough for us today, hasn't she? She needs to go hang out with Uncle Zander doesn't she?" He cooed as he stroked her small little hand. Kissing it. He looked over at Poppi. "He's smoking I think if you were curious."

"Yeah?" She stood grabbing her bag. "I think I'll get some air, maybe I'll catch him." She walked to the door and turned around. Juniper had the baby in her arms and Brantley thanked whoever was up there for their beautiful blessing. Fatherhood looked good on Brantley, and being loved looked better on Juniper. She was glowing brighter and smiling wider than she had after any other delivery. With Oliver, she cried herself to sleep. This time Poppi didn't feel guilt leaving the room. She felt peace.

She loved seeing her sister like this, she hoped one day they would get to see her and feel the same way.

36
Conflict

The February chill was more bitter than January's bite. Teasing spring in the day, but when the moon hung over their sleepy city the cold of everything hit her. He would be with her when he went home. Talking color swatches and cake tasting. Why was he the one her heart called to, the one who was unattainable? Her eyes focused on his silhouette carved out by low lighting. She thought about Eros's night, his hands on her. The way he made her feel...

"I can feel you. You know?" He looked over at her. "When you look at me, and your mind goes somewhere, but your eyes don't. I feel them looking at me."

She looked away bringing herself closer to him. "I'm sorry." She replied fiddling with her coat.

"I didn't say it was a bad thing. I just said I could feel it." He looked at her. "I like to feel it. I like to know you're with me."

"Oh." She tried to hide the smile that threatened to fester from his kind words. She returned his gaze. "Did you want to talk to me about something?" She tried to not think about the engagement while they were being a team for her sister. She tried not to think about the man she was in love with running off and getting married to the bitch she was constantly compared to.

He took a deep breath. "Depends are you going to tell me the truth?"

"I have no reason to lie to you."

"Okay." He exhaled smoke. "It was you on Eros night, wasn't it?"

Poppi looked away. "I didn't know you were engaged! I never would have done that if I knew."

"Poppi..." He sighed looking upward and rubbing the back of his neck. "My engagement is an accident. I bent down to pick up a napkin and I got up to being engaged. I never wanted that."

"So why didn't you correct her?" Poppi folded her arms.

"Shock," Zander replied honestly. "I never thought she wanted something like that, and I never thought you would be giving me whatever that was at Lucky's."

Poppi's face burned with remembrance. "I didn't think it would be like that."

"You know why it's like that Poppi? " He slid his hand around her waist. "It's because you're meant for me, and we should stop pretending that isn't the case. You deserve someone who values you, Poppi. I'd do anything for you to see that."

She felt his hand cup her face. The warmth of it made her feel beautiful inside. She couldn't believe this was happening. She couldn't believe she finally heard what she'd been longing for since he first caught her in the alleyway. She watched him lean in and felt their lips meet for the first time in the physical plane. She savored his tongue's gentle touch against hers. How he kissed her tenderly, but full of ambition.

"I can't do this Zander. I'm married, and you're engaged." Her eyes burned with angry tears. She was angry she couldn't bring herself to be how Mitchell was to her. He didn't care about his commitment to her at all. He cheated numerous times, but she couldn't bring herself to even with the man she was in love with. "You've made a commitment to her, and I don't owe her much, but the respect of her engagement."

"You're right." He held her close to him. "I should respect both of those things. And for now, I will, but I don't intend to be engaged to her for long. I'm not going to lose you Poppi. You are a piece of me. And there won't be a day or a moment where I won't think of you. Or be so far out of reach you can't find me. Give me some time and I'll fix this Poppi. I'll fix everything if it means I can come home to you." He kissed her once more. This time she could taste the salt from tears, she knew this wasn't just hurting her. He pulled away "Call me if you need me." His voice was graveled as he walked away from her.

Poppi watched him go. The knife twisted in her heart as every fiber of her wanted to run to him. Run away from all of this and one day she would, but for now, she was just exhausted and wanted to go to bed.

POPPI walked up the stairs to her home. She decided that it would be best to let the little family have their space and she wanted to sleep in an actual bed. Zander said his goodbyes after their discussion. They both needed time to think. She thought about her gift to him being shipped to his office and whether would she need to return it. Frederick had let it slip that Zander would be taking over as the Senior Vice President in a few weeks and she ordered him a custom watch, part of her thought now it was inappropriate, but she decided against canceling the order. She figured if anything it could be her goodbye gift.

Poppi's mind was all over the place as she opened the door to her bedroom. She looked at the two figures deeply entangled in a unique sexual position. She was on top of him facing the door. She stared at Carmen Grace on top of her husband. "Oh, you have got to be fucking kidding me!" She shouted.

"Poppi, you need to leave right now." Mitchell looked at her shoving Carmen off his erect penis. "This isn't what it looks like."

"It looks like you were fucking your boss's fiancé!" She swung at him connecting with his jaw. "You son of a bastard! I can't fucking believe this!" She cried as she kept swinging and landing blows at him. "I **hate** you!" She shoved him into the floor and turned her attention to Carmen.

"Don't." She looked back at her. "What will Zander say if he sees me? You can't tell him."

Poppi smacked her with an open palm and pulled her by her hair out of her bedroom. "Why the fuck would I care what Zander thinks about how you look? You ***dirty bitch!***" She began throwing punch after punch. Every blow for what happened before she got here. She could have enjoyed a night with the people she loved, but instead, she decided to do the right thing.

She felt a sharp pain in the back of her head, and she staggered back watching Carmen scramble from under her and flee down the stairs. "You would defend your fucking mistress over your fucking **wife** you **stupid Motherfucker!**" She threw another punch. She was tired of being the one who was being flung and thrown. She wanted her vengeance.

"Your mother is on her way back!" He tried to hold her down. "You need to calm down or you're going to St. Helens!"

"***Fuck you!***" She shoved him back. "I want out of this fucking marriage. I'm leaving." She threw her wedding band, something she'd tried wearing again for effort, back at him. "You'll never see me again! You can marry my fucking mother if you want someone who is going to stand for your stupidity!" She walked toward the stairs and as she turned, she felt a full-force shove topple her down the stairs.

37

Gone Girl

It had been five days since Willow's birth and Zander walked away from Poppi instead of staying there and fighting for what he wanted. He could have just as easily ended the relationship by bringing Poppi home and telling Carmen that it was over he'd made his choice and she wasn't it. Poppi hadn't called or texted him since. He sent her a text asking her if she wanted to join him in taking the kids and giving Willow a break but she didn't respond, he figured she'd had enough of him yo-yo-ing between what he wanted and what he needed. He knocked on the door and it swung open.

"Aunt Poppi!" Oliver's face was filled with hope and quickly dashed when he saw Zander. "Oh, hey Uncle Z." He glumly greeted.

"Everything okay kiddo?"

Oliver sighed. "I was hoping she would come by today."

"Your aunt hasn't been by?" Zander walked into the house. That was odd for Poppi even before Willow's birth she practically lived with Juniper and the kids. He walked into the living room and Keres Abraxas sat on the couch holding Lavender and Juniper was staring into space. Her expression was dazed and the beautiful glow that she carried was now dimmed with worry. Something wasn't right.

"Zander!" Lavender jumped up at the sound of his voice. She hugged him tightly. "Thank god! I was going to call you, but I really didn't want to chance Carmen being there. Have you heard from Poppi?!"

"I sent her a few texts." He admitted. "But I think she and Crispin are giving me the cold shoulder because of the engagement." He searched Lavender's bloodshot eyes. Her nose was red and she rubbed her temples. "What's going on?"

"My sister is missing," Lavender replied quietly. "We don't know where she is and I mean no one can find her."

"I've even called in help from the Jacaris family, and I got nothing."

"Jacaris as in–"

"Yeah, the famous ones. Nothing's out of reach for my little viper and her den." He stood and kissed her head. "I'm going to call Cas, I'll have him check once more. And if I can't find her–"

"My mother is in town and it's hard to know who she's called a favor in from for that motherfucker!" Juniper finally exploded with angry tears. "My baby sister is missing! And no one is doing anything about it."

"Have you called the police?" Zander asked the obvious.

"Not that I enjoy dealing with law enforcement because they are worthless most of the time when it comes to her," Lavender sighed "but yes I have. And they told us if her husband doesn't make the report, she can't be considered missing, and he won't make the report. He says she is fine, but we've all tried calling or texting and nothing."

"Have you tried other means?" Zander asked looking at them. "'Power that be' means?"

"No, we can't do that." Juniper shook her head. "She is picky about who she lets in, and we've never been it."

"I've seen her," Daisy spoke behind them. Her eyes were tired like she hadn't slept in days. The house that was usually so filled with love and laughter was so dim and dull. Zander looked at her and Oliver, they both looked tired.

"You have?"

"We both have." Oliver nodded. "But it's only in our dreams."

"More like nightmares." Daisy yawned. "But yes we see her, it's one of the reasons why we're worried."

"Well, she's their godmother." Juniper sniffed. "When she and Lydia were practicing together, she meditated and bonded with Oli so many people thought they were his parents. And then Daisy would barely go to anyone else other than she and I when she was born. So it makes sense."

Lavender nodded. "Tell us about the dream guys." She sat them beside their mother and sat across from them on the table. Zander sat behind them. Hoping that there would be something that would come out of them having the nightmares.

"It starts off in a room. It's dark and dreary. Like the Haunted Mansion." Daisy looked over at Zander. "Like you just know a ghost is going to jump out at you and scare you." She looked at Oliver. "And it's always raining like really heavy. Sometimes you can even hear thunder that makes you jump. Right?"

Oliver nodded. "Then she's just kinda laying there." Oliver's lip quivered. "Like she's dead."

"Have you two tried to call out to her? Or reach out to her or anything?"

Daisy shook her head. "Anytime we get close to her, it feels like a buzz from the game Operation and we're awake."

"A buzz?" Zander looked at him. "Like electricity?"

"Yeah, just like that." Oliver nodded. "Y'know like I touched the sides."

"Maybe I can reach her." Zander looked at them. "As you both said, they are her godchildren, most days they are all she has. Maybe she's blocking them from seeing what's really wrong because she can't bare for him to see something he shouldn't."

"Maybe he's right." Lavender looked at Juniper. "Maybe you should try."

"I don't exactly know how." Zander looked at them. "I'll try tonight after I take the kids out. Get their minds off of this and let them enjoy it. Then we'll figure this out."

"That means you're gonna have to make the elixir." Lavender looked at her. "You're the only alchemist we know."

Juniper nodded as Zander gave her a deep-tissue hug. "I'm scared Zander, I'm really fucking scared." She whispered to him.

"Don't worry." He hugged her tightly. "We are going to find our girl."

38

Bitter

"*A unt Poppi! Wake up!*" She heard Dasiy call for the seventh time. She groaned feeling the hardness of an unfamiliar bed. Her head banging and her body hurting more than it had when she got to where she was. "W-where am I?" She asked into the bright fluorescent lighting. "Where is Daisy?"

"I don't know who Daisy is. But you're at the hospital dear, how are you feeling."

The voice was fuzzy in the wake-up as she blinked into the sterile whiteness around her. Her body was cold. The room was cold. Was she in the morgue? Had Mitchell finally killed her? "I'm confused and I have a headache. How long have I been asleep?"

"72 Hours." The nurse replied matter-of-factly. "You must have been exhausted.

"I've been asleep for three days?! Where is my phone?!"

"Now Mrs. Baxter, you know you can't have your phone, those are the rules." The nurse rolled her eyes. "You've been here enough haven't you."

The voice became quickly recognizable. All of her fears of ending up here were realized when she yanked her arm and felt the restraint clink to the bed. "No, no I can't be back here!"

"Mr. Baxter said you had an extremely violent episode and tried to harm him and his coworker's girlfriend."

"I wasn't trying to harm them! I tried to leave! Let me out." She demanded, "I've slept my hold time."

"Oh no, you're here for three weeks this time." The nurse cooed pleasantly tightening the restraints. "Mrs. Booth and Mr. Baxter have both put that in strict order. You can't come out until you have shown *real* change this time. no more of that fake funny business."

"Neither of them has that right anymore!" She wiggled. The restraints only hurt her already broken body more. "Let me go now! I wanna see my attorney! "

"I'm sorry Mrs. Baxter I can't do that; you have to at least speak to a therapist first."

"My therapist's name is Rita Sheffield, and I don't think she would approve of this hold."

"Dr. Sheffield isn't our list-approved therapist." She grinned smugly. She was enjoying this a little too much for her liking. When she got out of here she was going to ask Lavender if one of her friends could burn down this hell hole. "One of them will be back to check you in a few days."

"Can I at least pee?" She asked looking at the nurse with snow-white skin, deep black hair, and a wicked smile. She looked like the wicked stepmother Poppi would read about, the ones her mother warned her that her father would marry a woman just like that. But she was thankful her father had sense.

"Of course. Then we can call your husband."

"He isn't my husband. He is just the man I'm married to." She muttered and followed her to the bathroom. She couldn't even cry about being captive in peace. Once they got to the room the nurse put the receiver to her ear so she could hear her slimeball husband's voice.

"Hello darling how are you feeling?"

"Let me out of this fucking place Mitchell and don't play games with me."

"I can't do that; you still sound angry."

"I woke up in a hospital tied to the fucking bed!" She let out an agitated chuckle. "Yeah, I'm *a bit* miffed!"

"We can't have you being miffed honey. We need happy Poppi. Can you be happy Poppi before I come and get you? Don't you want to see the baby? Lavender's here don't you want to see her? " He patronized. "You can do all of that if you come home and forget about this silly divorce and what you saw."

She took a deep breath and tried to sound cheery. "Please quit talking to me like a goddamn child and let me out of this hell hole please."

"I'm sorry honey, I can't do that. Not until you promise me, you're going to be on your best behavior."

She had images of what she was going to do when she got out of there. She had an idea of watching Lavender cut him limb from limb. Or her catching him outside of the office and beating him to death with a baseball bat. She sighed it would still be too good for him. She would do what she'd been wanting to do since the night she got here. She'd kiss Zander this time. She'd be with him the way she'd dreamed of seven thousand times. "Fine, if that's what you want.Goodbye, Mitchell."

"I love you, honey. I'll talk to you later. Your mother said she was coming to visit."

"Mitchell no!" She heard the click. "Hello?! Mitchell!? **Motherfucker!**"

"Good thing anger management classes are next for you, young lady. You're very angry."

She wanted to tell Sonya to choke on the orderly's cock she was sucking in the supply closet during rounds last night, but she thought against it. "Guess so." She spat.

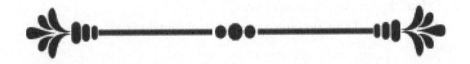

"I KILLED him because my daughter was in trouble. I killed him because if I just left then someone else's daughter would be in trouble and I couldn't do that to another fucking woman! I killed him because every day I spend in here my daughter doesn't have to look over her shoulder for a release date. That man is good and dead never to haunt her again."

"Do you feel any remorse for it, Sheryl?"

"Killing a pedophile? Absolutely not. I haven't been angry since. I released all my anger with his brains on the wall." Sheryl was a small black woman with a 70's afro and a gap between her front teeth and full red lips. She smiled. "My daughter gave me this yesterday." She held up a picture of a newborn. "She named her Infinity Sherie. After me, she said I gave infinite days of peace, I got two years left and I'm gonna make the best outta being the best goddamn grandmother I can. And if someone hurts her, well my name will be engraved in this place."

The therapist looked at Poppi. "What makes you angry?"

"Seeing my soon-to-be ex-husband fuck his boss's girlfriend." She said numbly. "On the day my niece was born. Seeing her laugh at me as he beat me unconscious. And then stick me in here and make sure no one knows where to look for me."

Sheryl looked at the therapist and then back to her. "You didn't kill they asses? I find it weird you're in a criminal ward if there was no crime?"

"No ma'am I didn't. I was trying to leave before I made a mistake. Turns out my mistake was even being there."

"Why didn't you try to express your anger calmly?" The therapist asked, "Why didn't you tell them how it made you feel?"

"What the fuck was that going to do doc?" Sheryl asked a thinly plucked eyebrow raised. "Please stop fucking. You're hurting my feelings. What would you have done? Would you have been rational if your wife was banging administrator Langston? No! You would have been pissed off. This girl is numb. Look at her face! It goes with her story doc, she's black and fucking blue yet, she's in here! I don't want to cut off your sharing, but what the fuck kinda question is how does that make you feel?!"

"It made me feel angry. I can't breathe." Poppi admitted aloud. "I hurt, and I slept for three days. No one checked on me, and he told my mother I'm here. Which means he wants me to be emotionally berated. Guess you guys don't ask the imprisoned what they would prefer when it comes to visiting."

"You're under a conservatorship."

"No. No, I am not. You can call any court and they will tell you any document that says otherwise is falsified. So, this is false imprisonment."

"I mean the girl's a lawyer so she's not wrong." Sheryl looked at her. "And I'll vouch for her if you ever say you never heard it."

An orderly walked into their group. "Baxter you have a visitor."

"Thank you for coming to the group today. So glad you could make friends." The doctor refrained from rolling his eyes, but Poppi could feel them on her back as the orderly lead her to the visiting room.

POPPI'S mother sat at the table. She was an older identical version of her. It made Poppi hate herself, but she was glad inside she was a garden and not a pipeline of patriarchy like her mother. She sat in front of her. "Hello, Merigold."

"I'm your mother you should address me as such."

"What do I owe the pleasure."

"Well, Poppi I'm here to see what happened."

"My husband cheated on me with his boss's movie star girlfriend who, in my opinion, really downgraded." She replied flatly. "I walked in, and I beat her ass, then his ass, and then he beat my ass and put me in here. Now I'm in a mental hospital for catching my husband cheating and I can't get out unless one of you agrees to it, and since he called you, I doubt that will happen."

"He is a good man Poppi," Merigold spoke through tight teeth. "Why do you keep doing this to him!?"

"Doing what Mother? Existing? Being his wife. Breathing? Which is the one that made him fuck Carmen? Or Patricia? What exactly did I do for him to tell you I attempted suicide and you needed to put a conservatorship on me because you fuck a judge who just grants whatever motion gets you wet? And all for 50 fucking grand. You sold me for fifty thousand fucking dollars Meri. You didn't even know what you were selling me too! Just that you didn't want a bisexual daughter."

"I was doing what was best for you!"

"Look around bitch! Does this look like what the fuck is best for me?! I'm in a goddamn institution because he cheated on me, and I can't get out! My father won't speak to me because I had barely any choice in the matter and when I tried to leave, he almost killed me. **You said stay!** You don't give a damn about me! You need to leave."

"Poppi Celeste Baxter! You do NOT talk to me that way."

"No she doesn't, but Poppi Celest Nichols does, and she's telling you, that you need to get the fuck out of my face before I tell everyone what you two did to me."

Her mother stood a silver lock falling into her face. "I did this for your own good. You'll see what a good man he is when it is too late! I know about that Zander boy! Do you think he is good? He will drop you the second you give him what he's after, and then what?"

"Then I will have had mind-blowing sex with someone who showed me real love and how to love myself, and I'll go on with my life, and I'll never have to be with Mitchell again." She smirked. "If you ask me after years of two-pumps and snoring I'll call that a win."

"You'll regret this, Poppi. I promise you." Merigold watched her stand "You don't ever walk away from your mother and not regret it."

She put her hands on the table and got as close to her as the table would allow. She looked at the woman who applauded and added to her torture. "The only thing I have ever regretted is having you for a mother."

39

7 Whole Days

After the visit with her mother, the doctors upped her meds and it made her sleep mostly. She didn't mind. She would sleep as long as she could in the dreams she wanted. Most of the time they were black. Just her sitting in nothingness until her next dose. She could hear people calling to her from the darkness but every time she tried to reach them she would be jolted awake for more treatment. She was starting to wonder what kind of place wanted to keep a patient so doped up. She was sure it had to be unethical.

Other times she would dream of the lands before man. Where gods and goddesses would walk free without the need for prayers or temples. Only one would notice her. He was taller than an average tree with deep green skin and one eye the color of stone and the other of land. She would walk beside him and tell him the things she was suffering. He would listen, but his mouth would downturn with anger when she would mention her woes with Mitchell and being trapped in a place she couldn't escape from.

She thought he was someone imaginary her mind had made up, but she felt safer when she was around him. Stronger. Like she could endure this for as long as it took. He would tell her things like how serious it was for her to be free of these shackles and call forth the light-bringer. Whatever that meant. She enjoyed those.

Sometimes when the medicine was good to her she would go back to their place. The bubble they'd met in by pure accident. She'd relive their moments together and she would live in them until they'd make her take another dose or sit in another classroom, but she was with Sheryl most of those times and it made her feel like someone understood her at least.

Poppi lay back in her bed and curled into her ball. She missed Oli and Dasiy. She missed her sisters and Willow, she'd barely got to enjoy time with her. After vowing to make her proud she ends up in here. She yawned. Most of all she missed Zander. She wanted nothing more than to wake up in his arms the way she'd dreamed a million times before.

POPPI walked into a gray and cold condo. The warmth that once was there was replaced with a dreary rainy day and there was no Zander in site. She felt herself begin to panic. Mitchell couldn't take her dreams from her, could they? He couldn't take every good thing that she had from her.

"You're here!" Zander ran to hug her. "Thank God! I was afraid it wouldn't work!" He smothered her bruised and battered face with kisses. "How are you? Where are you?"

Poppi looked at him in shock. "You're in my mind." She looked at him. "This is what it looks like?"

"I think you're upset, and it's changed a lot, but yes. This is where we met on Eros night! I can't believe you kept this as a memory." He sighed. "I miss you so much Poppi. Promise me you'll never go this long without speaking to me again."

"This isn't my fault. I'm in a psych ward." She pulled away from him. "How long have I been gone?"

"You've been gone for a week! We've looked all over. Which one."

"Saint Helen's. It's in New York. I guess they thought you wouldn't have found me."

"Well, they're wrong. I found you didn't I." He kissed her. "I could do that about a million times, and it still wouldn't feel good enough. What happened to you?"

"Zander listen there are so many things we need to talk about, but I can't do it here. I need you to tell my sisters where I am."

"As if you had to ask. Hold on Mon Éclair I'm coming for you." He kissed her head softly.

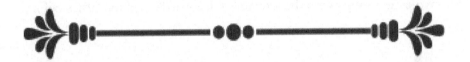

"HARVARD!" Sheryl shook her arm. "Harvard you need to wake up now."

"W–what's going on?" Poppi felt like she was wading through the mud as she sat up. "What's wrong?"

"You've got visitors, and they're trying to turn them away, but I see no reason in you not making an appearance." Sheryl pulled a groggy Poppi into a wheelchair and strolled her into the lobby where nurse Sonya was standing there telling her sisters she wasn't there. "Hey, did you say the ginger brown skin girl with a scar on her eyebrow?"

"Yeah." Lavender looked her up and down. "I did."

"Is this her?" Sheryl wheeled her in. Poppi looked up and thought she saw her sister. This dream was getting better and better. She was seeing everyone she'd missed.

Juniper fell to her knees looking at Poppi's drugged body in the wheelchair. "Oh my god, what did you do to her?!"

"I will have your job for this!" Paulette shouted. "I'm going to own this entire damned hospital! This is illegal Sonya, and you know it! Discharge her now!"

"Of course, Ms. Baxter." She looked like she swallowed a baby mouse. "I'm very sorry for this mix–up."

"I'm sure you fucking are." Lavender looked at her. "You're lucky there was someone with common fucking sense because I was about to start taking limbs." She looked at Sheryl. "Consider me in your debt Ms. Sheryl."

"Nah, you just take care of Havard, she's been here enough. I hope she's outta here for good this time. Take care, Harvard." She called to her as Juniper rolled her out of the dreadful hospital.

40
V.P.

"We are very sad and proud to see Joseph Hall retiring from his position in this company. He and I built this place from the ground up. He and I have seen the best of times and the worst of times, and now I will watch him take the plunge into a lovely life with his wife Rene, and their beautiful children and grandchildren. I hope this life is built around joy for you Joe."

"I love you, Freddie." He shook his hand. "Thank you for 35 years of success."

"And the other five we don't count." They laughed together.

"And it is my pleasure as Senior Vice President it's an honor to get to pass the title to Zander Bell, you are going to do great things with this company, I don't think that I could have picked better if there was." He shook Zander's hand "Congratulations, son. I am so proud of you."

"We would also like to congratulate Mitchell Baxter on his promotion to Vice president of Hall and Bell." Frederick ushered Mitchell up to the podium in front of the board of directors.

"Thank you all so much!" Mitchell shook their hands. "I am very excited to show you all how much this means to me. I'll make you proud. I promise."

Frederic nodded. "I have no doubt you will Baxter. You are an amazing addition to the team."

"Thank you, sir."

"Mitchell I'm having a dinner party for Carmen and myself Saturday, and I think that it would be great if we returned the favor of hospitality that your wife extended." Zander looked at him.

Mitchell's face had gotten tight, and his eyes squared on him. He cleared his throat "Poppi has been under the weather. But I'm sure she would love to get out of the house."

"Oh?" Frederick looked at him. "I'm sorry to hear that."

"Yes, she's been doing better though. She'll be happy to be there Saturday." Mitchell looked calm, but Zander could feel him squirming. "I think I'll call her and give her the good news."

"Sounds great." Frederick and Zander watched him leave. "Why do I get the feeling he is lying?"

"He is dad." Zander looked at him. "I just want to know why."

ZANDER walked into his office still going over everything that he had been through in the past twenty-four hours. He read about St. Helens after she told him where she was. He thought about the terrible things a place like that could do someone, he was sick to his stomach to think of her in there. Anyone with half a brain would know that Poppi was far from criminally insane. He didn't think that someone could be put in a place like that without reason, but the way Lavender talked of their mother she seemed like the kind of woman who would do such a thing. Poppi didn't deserve that, she didn't deserve to be tortured by someone who was supposed to love and protect her.

He walked to his desk. There was a simple black box in the center with a bright green bow. He smiled his mother must've wanted to surprise him with a gift since his father couldn't hold his excitement for the promotion. She was always doing these kinds of things for him in Texas and he couldn't imagine Carmen ordering him anything to celebrate. He told her about it and she rolled her eyes saying "Good for you babe." He couldn't imagine she would be so nonchalant and then go all out.

He opened the box and there was a wooden box with his initials burned into it. He ran his fingers over them. He opened the box and three watches sat in front of him. On the left there was a vintage black diver watch with unique dash marks for the numbers. It was on a matching thick band. He admired the dark brown open-face antique-styled chronograph watch on the right.

He picked up the one in the center, its intricate skeletal design was made completely of oak and onyx. The face of the watch was the most beautiful one that he'd ever seen. He turned the watch over. *'Lightning only shines to the call of thunder. -P'* While he sat admiring what Poppi had done for him, tears burning the back of his eyes his phone rang. "Hello?"

"We found her." Lavender spoke softly. "She's home, but I'm going to ask you not to see her. I don't want you to see what that son of a bitch did to her. I'll call you if there's an update." She hung up.

41

Tour

"How are you feeling sweetheart?" Mitchell asked as he walked her up the stairs. He stroked the side of her face. She tried not to wince and pull away. She wanted to scream and throw the bottle of wine she brought over his head.

"Like I want to go home." She took a deep breath to bottle the unbridled rage that bubbled in her torso. "I don't want to be out."

"C'mon, the doctor said it would be good for you to get some air." He wrapped his arm around her kissing her cheek. "All your friends are going to be here."

"I don't think he meant with the woman who kicked me in the face and the man who put me in a mental institution that drugged me so bad I've been sleeping for long periods and have no concept of passing time."

"Sweetheart can't we please have a good night?" Mitchell asked. "You got out of the house today, didn't you? You took that nice little trip to Cabot and got your gown for your niece's birth celebration tomorrow, didn't you?" He looked at her with warm deep eyes. "I trusted you, didn't I?"

"Right." She handed him a bottle of wine from the Abraxas winery that was down there. "Here. It's for your host, I thought it would be nice to have it since you'll be working on that account with him."

"You're still so perfect." He kissed her and bile rose to the back of her throat. "I know you're upset, but that fine-tuning at St. Helens was perfect."

"You threatened to send me back there if I didn't come home." She hissed hatefully. "And now you're parading me in front of her. I don't want to do this."

Before Mitchell could answer the door swung open. Carmen stood there looking beautiful and glowing. Her skin was radiant, and she was wearing a silky sapphire blue evening gown. She looked at Poppi. "Well hello, Mrs. Baxter so nice to see you!" She smiled.

"Hello, Carmen." She replied monotoned. "May I come in?"

"Please." She led them into the condo. Poppi looked around. It looked exactly like it had when she went there countless times during her stay at St. Helen's. She touched the black sofa with memories of him kissing her there. "Make yourself at home. Mitchell, is that for me?"

"Of course. It's the finest wine for the finest hostess." Mitchell smiled.

"You always know what to say to me!" She giggled. "Thank you. Why don't you help me chill it for dinner." She looped her arm in Mitchell's and walked him to the kitchen.

Poppi wondered if the reading nook was real if that was just something she imagined. Or if he had really carved her out a space in his in case, she ever needed it. She walked to the hidden corner with the hippie beads that acted as a door. She pulled the beads and there it was. Perfect.

The burgundy bubble chair and soft lighting welcomed her as she kicked her shoes off and hid inside. She curled into a ball swallowing her tears. She wasn't much for being the life of the party anymore. She didn't even want to enjoy it. She looked over and there was a vase of plastic flowers like the ones he brought her for Valentine's Day. She reached out and touched them.

She let the tears fall for a moment and wiped her eyes as quickly as she allowed them. She sat there for a moment, enjoying the quiet. Letting herself enjoy the freedom of being in her real happy place.

"I knew I would find you in here!" Roxanna spread the beads open. "I told Zander if he built it the way he wanted you'd come. I saw that aint shit dust rag of a husband and that F-list actress kiki-ing so I figured I'd come and find you." She laid on top of her for a hug."Don't you ever decide to go off the goddamn radar and go missing on me without letting me know woman! I was worried sick."

Poppi wrapped her arms around her best friend inhaling her scent deeply. She'd missed her more than she thought she did. "I didn't intentionally go missing Roxi it was more or less me being forced to disappear."

"By whom."

"I... I was in Saint Hell." She whispered.

"Why the fuck were you there?" Roxanna stood. "Who put you in there Poppi?"

"Good, you found her!" Kandi popped her head in. "Why does it look like you're going to murder?"

"'Cause I am!" Roxanna snapped looking back at Poppi who was deeply curled into the chair smelling the cologne that Zander sprayed on a gray fleece blanket that laid across the arm. She wanted to wrap up and fall asleep until the dinner was over.

"No murdering tonight we are celebrating!" Kandi held up her hand showing a 5-carat diamond ring on her engagement finger. "Girls! I'm getting married!"

"HE did it in front of my parents. He said 90 days is all he needed to know that I was the one he wanted to spend his life with. I told him I wanted a prenup, not because I was going to be famous or anything, and his parents love me, but I wanted him to know that it wasn't for the money. He made it favor me, but he still let me have my way."

"Good for you." Poppi looked at her as she led her into Zander's room. "Why are we going in here?"

" I need to fix your makeup. And you need to tell us why you look like a zombie." Kandi looked at her with concern.

"I can't. I would if I could, but I truly can't. Not tonight."

"Then when?"

"Not tonight, okay?" She was growing more agitated with the situation. Moreso now with Kandi fussing over her. "I just want to get tonight over with."

"You look like you need to get some rest." Roxanna looked at her. "And you need to tell me why Mitchell put you back in Saint Hellen's."

"That fucking hell hole Mitchell put you in when you threatened to leave him for good?" Kandi asked looking at Roxanna.

"Yeah, that place." She looked at her. "And there is no Alton and his miracle transfusions there that make me feel better after I have been beaten to a bloody pulp by my husband and his lover."

"Mitchell is cheating on you."

"Again?!" Kandi scoffed. "I fucking hate him. Who did it? I will fuck them up for you."

"I'm going to get Alton. Maybe he can fix you before dinner."

"I wanna go home! I don't even wanna do this." Poppi followed Kandi into the walk-in closet Zander turned half of it into a vanity. He listened to her. He turned his home into a love letter, and she hadn't even seen him. "Where is Zander?"

"He's working so hard to make sure everything is perfect. We've been here all day. I mean he's asked our opinion on everything you would like or want. It's why we know about all this." Roxanna sat her in front of the vanity. "I'm going to get Alt I'll be right back." She kissed her cheek.

"He's crazy about you Poppi, he's shown off his watches to Derrick and Alton, and it's so adorable the way he tells his stories about you two being there with Willow. You are holding her on your chest while he snuggled you both. It's one of the pictures on his family wall which has more pictures of you than Carmen. He's revealing a picture tonight I'm really excited."

"He painted a picture?"

"It's the centerpiece, he can't wait for you to see it. I'm melting." Kandi sighed. "I touched it, and the passion of that painting is enough to make someone like me salivate." She looked at her. "Now tell me what happened."

"Kandi, you really cannot tell anyone." She looked at her. "Seriously not even Roxanna, especially not Roxanna."

"Oryn's sake this is bad." She looked at her and nodded. "Okay, spill it."

42

Reveal

"This is delicious Zander." Alton gave his seal of approval. "The lamb is seasoned and seared to perfection. Those cooking classes have been paying off."

"I have to agree, I'll never be a good chef because I have a wife like Poppi, but Carmen is lucky to have someone who is going to care for her." Mitchell kissed Poppi's cheek. She barely twitched.

Zander looked at her as she stared down at her plate pushing food from side to side like no one would notice if she didn't take a bite. "How is it, Poppi?" He spoke to her softly.

She looked up at him. "It's lovely Zander thank you." Her face cracked a small smile. "It's very sweet of you to learn to cook for your future spouse."

Mitchell smiled. "That's my Poppi always knowing the right thing to say. I love her so much. I don't envy you, fellas. You had to wait so long to find your happily ever after. I've been living mine for five years and I am so glad we get to be a part of all of yours."

Carmen rolled her eyes. "Thank you for such a lovely speech, Mitchell." She looked at him. "She is such a sweetheart it's no wonder you're so happy and you've got to keep her hidden away all the time."

Zander looked at Carmen who took a drink of wine, but her eyes never left Mitchell's. He looked at Kandi who whispered something to Derrick and he nodded. He stood and walked to the kitchen.

"She's a busy woman, Carmen, I'm sure you understand that." Mitchell smiled. "After all, you're busy yourself."

"Yes, but I still make room for Zander, she never seems to make the time to attend any of the events you've been at. Is that because they occur when she's being a busy little worker bee or an adorable little sweetheart who takes care of the cookin' cleaning."

"I don't think that's any of your business bitch." Roxanna looked at her. She put down her fork and interlocked her fingers glaring at her. "And I don't like how you're coming at my friend."

"I've not said anything!" Carmen defended innocently. "I was just saying what a sweetheart your friend is. Zander thinks so too, I mean he practically jumped out of his skin when he found out this sweet little angel drove four and a half hours for a bottle of wine and a bottle of scotch."

Zander looked at her. "I don't think that's what I said. I said it was kind of them to do that." He looked at the couple. "Mainly since we're going to be spending a week checking out a beautiful winery with them in Italy. Thank God it's one of the languages I'm good at." He chuckled.

"That's terrific."

"It'll be a great birthday present for Poppi since we're leaving two days after her birthday." Mitchell looked at Zander blankly. Like he couldn't figure out the correlation.

"My birthday is May tenth honey." She whispered before going back to pretending to eat.

"Oh, that's right it is!" Mitchell's realization snapped him to reality. "Well, I guess it is."

Zander wanted to be visibly angry, he wanted to make everyone but her leave and take care of her the way he knew she needed. "I hear congratulations are in order!" He looked at Kandi and Derrick. "I'm very happy for you two."

"I know this isn't exactly the right time, but I'd like to ask you to be my best man."

"As if you had to ask! Of course!"

"Poppi, I want you to be my maid of honor." Kandi looked at her. "I wanted to do it some fancy-ass way, but I think this will work better than anything. Will you?"

"Of course." Poppi smiled.

"How sweet," Carmen muttered. "I wonder who my maid of honor will be?" She looked at Zander. "Maybe Taryn."

"When is the big day?" Derrick looked at him. "I didn't even know you finally asked."

Zander looked at Poppi who stared deep into the plate. "Well, I never really found the right time, and Carmen made it clear she never wanted to get married so I never thought this would happen. But it did."

Carmen wrapped her arm around Zander's arm. "Mitchell isn't the only one with a sweetheart." She kissed his cheek.

ZANDER walked them over to the wall of pictures he'd been placing like tile on the wall. There were pictures of all of the children. Some were at events, others were just candids he had gotten from their parents. He even had baby pictures of Daisy and Oliver. His favorite one was the one of Poppi in her Carebear pajamas reading a textbook while Oliver rested sweetly on her chest. She was so special to him. She'd graced his wall several times. He watched as Poppi, Kandi, and Roxi examined the wall.

"Oh my god Poppi! It's the Halloween we all dressed up as Disney Princesses! Look at Lyds as Prince Eric!" Roxanna laughed leaning her head on Poppi. Poppi's deadpan face showed more emotion than it had all night in the memories of his wall. "How did you get these?!"

"It was a group project really. I asked Alton, Juniper, and Kandi to find pictures of them and they included some they knew you guys would love." He looked at Poppi. "Do you like it?"

"Bit weird to have my wife and my family plastered all over your walls don't you think?" Mitchell asked him taking a sip of scotch.

"She's not plastered all over the wall. There are only four maybe five pictures, and in most of them, she's with the kids including his niece and nephew. But if you spent any time with them you'd know that." Roxanna answered for him and kept Poppi protectively away from him.

Zander looked at the three of them. Poppi had been placed between Kandi and Roxi, their partners were in formation behind them. Derek was watching Mitchell like a tiger waiting for the big kill. He was curious about what his friend knew that he didn't. Poppi looked like she wanted to be anywhere else the entire night and he was starting to settle into anxiety. He walked over to the centerpiece and stood in front of it. "Well, I guess now is a better time than any to reveal my painting to you all.

"The suspense is killing me. I can't wait to see it." Roxanna looked at him.

"I call this love and betrayal in the soul of Eden." Zander pulled off the white sheet that protected the painting. He heard the gasps from the crowd. It was a beautiful garden scene on the right and a dark smoky version of the same paradise on the left. A woman who looked like she was made of darkness with long red flames for hair reached out for a man who was emerald green with a golden crown around his locks who reached back to her trapped in the scorched paradise but couldn't reach her. The art was deep and detailed. He was proud of the work and time he put into it. It was a welcome distraction when Poppi was missing.

"Handsome, rich, and talented." Carmen schmoozed. "Back off ladies this one's mine." She giggled.

"Poppi?" Roxanna asked as Poppi walked up to the picture. She reached out and touched it.

Zander reached out for her and she stumbled into his arms. "Poppi are you okay?"

"I think it's time to go," Mitchell said taking her by the arm and pulling her away from him, but her hand clutched to him as he pulled her to him. "She looks like she's coming down with another headache. She's been getting them a lot."

"Oh, you poor dear it must be hard to be in so much excitement after where you've been."

"And where has she been Carmen?" Kandi asked folding her arms. Zander could feel the anger radiating off of her.

"In bed, ill, duh." She rolled her eyes. Then she touched Poppi's arm and gave her an odd smile. "You get her home, we wouldn't want her having another accident."

Mitchell shook his head. "No, we can't have that." Mitchell turned her away by the small of her back."Goodnight everyone. Poppi, tell them good night." He instructed her.

Poppi looked at everyone, her face still twisted in some thought even she couldn't express. Her face relaxed when she settled on Zander. "Good night, thank you for having me." She replied almost robotically.

Zander clenched his glass as he watched them walk out. Something about it didn't feel right. Carmen and Mitchell spoke in code and he could tell that Kandi had already deciphered it from her fist being balled up and a droplet of blood dropping on her shoe. She looked at Zander with bitter anger. *Zander.* He looked back at Poppi looking at him as Mitchell put her coat over her shoulders. *I need you... I need you to help me.* She turned and continued to be led out.

"Zander!" Carmen snapped at him. "Derrick asked you something."

"I'm sorry." Zander shook his head trying to resist the urge to run after Poppi. She needed him and he was trapped in the loop of small talk. "What was the question?"

"What made you paint something like this?" Derrick asked. "It's not your usual style."

"I saw someone who made me want to be different." He watched the door close before looking down into his glass of wine. "I saw something that made me want to try something new and I liked it, they made things that were black and white seem filled with color and I can't be more grateful to them."

"Aw, babe." Carmen kissed him deeply. "I love you right back."

43
Ceremony

The temple of Keahi was one to be marveled at. There weren't many temples of the light-bringer, since she was considered a cursed goddess, but being here made Poppi feel at ease. Like she had a sense of peace and protection knowing no one from her living nightmare would dare step foot in this place. She walked up to the stature carved in black stone of a woman holding a child and a torch. She was beautiful, she looked a lot like the woman Zander had painted as the centerpiece of his wall. She walked through the temple and there was another one of her holding a sword outward pointing to the hall of fellowship. Flowers were at the feet of this statue.

Women prayed to Keahi for strength. She held a bouquet of red roses and dropped to her knees thankful for the deep purple dress her sister picked out since they had petticoats and her knees were still sore from the fall and the beating after. She placed the flowers at the warrior goddess' feet. *'My goddess.'* She began *'Please hear my cries. Free me from the hell I have endured and bring me peace. Give me a sign that I can be free. Give me a sign Zander and I are meant to be together and I'm not just imagining what I feel.'*

"Poppi? Poppi baby is that you?" A deep voice spoke behind her. A voice that made her heart swell. It couldn't be real, she stood and turned to see him. He stood at a towering 6'6" in a tailored deep purple almost black suit with a brighter purple tie against his black shirt. His eyes, her eyes, crinkled into a tearful smile as he gripped the bouquet of flowers staring at her. "You're really here?!"

"Daddy!" She cried running into his arms. She felt him hold her. Everything crumbled away. She felt the safety a daughter felt from her father instantly. Something she had desperately missed. She felt him squeeze her as if she would run away again. Being banished from speaking to her father because he was a bad influence was awful. She was forced to have most phone calls monitored in the early years of her marriage and if she tried to call him the punishment was more than she wanted to endure. By the time Mitchell had stopped monitoring, she figured he'd never wanted to speak to her again for allowing someone to come between the close bond they shared.

"Oh let me look at you! Let me look at my star!" He pulled away studying everything about her. She looked at him. His hair had gotten more salt and peppered. His jaw was covered by a matching salt-and-pepper beard that was well-groomed. His bright brown eyes looked filled to the brim with happiness. "You look just like her. Your grandmother Agnita. She would have loved you so much." He wrapped her back in his arms for another hug. She savored the smell of his Old Spice cologne and Cool Water aftershave. "I've missed you so much my little Poptart."

"Daddy it's been so long. I have so much I wanna say." She pulled away from him holding his arm. "So much I want to explain. I need to apologize to you."

"No, Poptart, it's me who should be apologizing and explaining." He sighed "I should have been there for you when you needed me. I should have fought harder... I could have done something! Instead, I let them take you from me like a coward. I love you so much. I checked in every chance I got, but I got blocked or you never responded to my letters."

"Daddy I never got any letters." She looked at the gentle kind brown eyes that nurtured her for years in her life. His eyebrows knitted in confusion. "I thought you never wanted to speak to me again after the wedding." Poppi felt Zander's eyes watching the exchange from a safe distance, protecting her. She could feel him thinking of her. Feel the way his body was at attention waiting for her to say something to him. She turned and waved him over to them. "Zander I have someone I'd like you to meet."

Zander walked over to them. "Hello, sir."

"Zander this is my father, Ahern Nichols, Daddy this is my person, Zander."

"So, you're the one who has my star coming into her own." He held out his hand. "I am so pleased to meet you."

Zander looked at him. "The pleasure is all mine sir."

He looked at him for a long moment. Zander's tuxedo was black with a deep purple vest and tie that matched the knee-length corset dresses that Lavender and Poppi wore. He looked back at Poppi and then back to Zander. "I would tell you to take care of her or I'll kill you, but I feel like I'd be wasting my breath."

Zander nodded. "I'd give anything to protect her sir." He wrapped his arm around Poppi. "She means the world to me."

"'AS a child goes through a world of darkness, they must have a village of light.'" The priests lit the first candle handing it to Juniper. "Their mother is their first voice of the Gods, the first light that they are guided by, that they feel warmth and love from." She lit another white candle and gave it to Brantley. "Their father is the light of protection, the warmth of shelter, the giver of strength." She looked at them. "Who are their godparents?"

"Poppi Nichols and Zander Bell," Brantley answered.

"Me?" Zander looked at them stunned. "Really?"

Juniper nodded. "You have been such a wonderful friend to us in this time, I feel safe with my children in your care and if something ever happened to us, I think you and Poppi would be brilliant carriers of light for our baby girl."

"Do you accept?" The priestess asked looking at them.

"Yes!" Zander walked up with Poppi. They were given two candles and Poppi walked to join the side of Juniper and he stood beside Brantley. He looked over at her with the biggest smile. She returned it looking out into the crowd of people who loved her, loved her niece, she exhaled. She finally felt like Keahi was listening.

"What a beautiful village." She smiled looking at them. "I'm so pleased that she will have the best of the best in protection." She stood in front of the candle that was at the head of them. "Please recite the prayer with me."

"As we walk behind Willow in her path of life may we light her way with guidance, understanding, strength, dignity, and truth. We ask Keahi, the bringer of light and love, to protect and guide us as we lead this beautiful soul to her purpose in life. Blessed be the brightness of the world."

They lifted their candles above the sleeping Willow and recited the prayer. Thunder cracked as they finished. A gust of wind opened the closed sanctuary doors and all of the candles that were held above Willow's head went out, all but Poppi's which burned taller and brighter. A flash of lightning illuminated the dark sanctuary behind her. She looked down at her niece who was looking back up at her with a babbling smile.

"Well," The priestess spoke when the lights came back on. "I do believe we have been blessed." She took the candle from Poppi and placed it at the top of the altar where there was an empty space for a candle. "I think we should be thankful she graced us with her presence today."

44

Recital

"You're making more fuss than her actual father." Crispin rolled his eyes as he watched Zander set up the motion-activated camera he brought for Thea and Daisy's first recital. Zander was excited things were getting back to normal after a very eventful month. He was even more thankful that Carmen said she'd rather be gagged than be here. He wasn't going to complain about getting to enjoy some much-needed family time.

"Our parents are going to kill us if they can't see their granddaughter dance in expert quality since mom had a baby emergency tonight and dad was stuck on a flight."

"Hi, guys!" Juniper smiled walking in with Sabrina and Poppi. "So glad to see you tonight."

"Where is the baby?" Crispin asked excitedly. "Please don't tell me you left her at home with our sons and husbands."

"I did, I'm sorry, but I'm going there after, Poppi has prior engagements."

"Oh?" Zander attempted to look casual "What are you doing tonight?"

"The couples are going out on the town for Kandi's engagement. She said she didn't want to take away from you and Carmen, so she wanted to celebrate on her own."

"Do you need a plus one?" Zander asked trying not to be too eager to spend some time with her. "I am free, Carmen's busy."

"Sure! I'd love that." She smiled and sat beside Sabrina who eyed him. She whispered something to Poppi that made her giggle and tell her to behave.

Crispin sat beside Zander his eyes boring into him. "You like her."

"Cris please."

"No, tell me the truth you like her!" Crispin nudged him.

"She's two feet from you, this isn't high school, and in case you've forgotten, I've got a fiancé."

"You don't even wanna marry her. When's the big day going to be? Have you told Mama?"

"I will in my own time Cris please." Zander watched as the curtain opened for the girls. "Let's just enjoy the show."

THEY applauded after they were finished cheering as Thea walked up with her long black 4c braid. She made a beautiful Rapunzel and Daisy made a beautiful fairy. Daisy had been proud of Thea since she told them about it. She was Thea's biggest fan. Even at curtain call, Daisy was jumping up and down screaming Thea's praises. "Did I do good Auntie?" Thea asked Poppi taking a bouquet of flowers from her.

"Oh, honey you were perfect!" Poppi gave her a squeeze. "Absolutely perfect Thea, I am so proud of you, you did just like we practiced!"

"She was beautiful up there wasn't she." Crispin sniffed. He'd started crying when she danced her first solo and hadn't stopped until the curtain call. "I can't believe how good you are Thea."

"Thanks, Daddy." She laughed. "Daisy was so good; did you see her pointe and spin? Flawless."

"I did! Daisy, you were great." Poppi smiled as she took pictures of both of them. "Daisy I am so proud of you. Auntie is so glad Uncle Zander recorded it. Now Grammy Paulette can see it and we'll have you in Jacaris School of Dance before you know it my little star."

"You think so?"

"You're the best fairy I've ever seen." Zander handed her a bouquet of daisies and Thea one of the same multicolored flowers with ballet shoes on them. "You two are so spectacular. Not that you had any question of that."

"C'mon, girls" Crispin took Thea's hand and Daisy took Juniper's "Aunt Poppi and Uncle Zander have to go, but they did say we could take your brothers out for pizza, their treat."

"Thanks, guys!" Daisy hugged her once more. "You're coming back this time, right?"

"You better believe it angel, I'm never gonna leave you without a phone call again. I promise."

She hugged her. "I love you." Poppi stood beside Zander watching the four of them bustle out of the auditorium.

"I guess now is the time to tell you, the best dance you will get from me is the funky chicken." He smiled. Looping her arm into his.

"Better than me. All I can do is the hokey pokey." She grinned and walked in front of him out of the door.

45

Full Moon

"Oh shit, it's a real party now!" Derrick smiled taking another shot before hugging Zander and then Poppi. "My two favoritest humans in the whole world other than my wife!" He looked back at Kandi. "She's so damn beautiful." He walked back over to her kissing her cheek. "Hey, where's your beard?" He asked Zander.

"My beard?" He looked at him confused. "I've never had a beard D."

"You know that ain't shit bitch you parade around like you really like her, but in reality, you wanna be with that pretty lady right there." He pointed to Poppi before trying to take another shot when Kandi took it from him.

"Okay, honey." Kandi laughed handing the shot to Zander. "No more buttery nipples for you."

"Shhh honey don't tell them our bedroom business." Derrick kissed her cheek. 'Full Moon' by Brandy started to play and Derrick froze at the cool beat. "This is my shit!" He took his fiance's hand dancing to the beat. "C'mon, baby let's show them what we expect on the dance floor at our wedding."

"Okay, hot stuff." She smiled as he kissed her hand and lead her to the dance floor. Kandi and Derrick began to dance on beat and fluidly together. Like they rehearsed. They laughed and enjoyed each other's company.

"Here's to the luck son of a bitch who got to keep his love at first sight." He thought as he held the shot up to the two of them grinding on the dance floor and swallowing the sweet but harsh liquor.

Poppi watched him take the shot. "Do you always call your friends sons of bitches before toasting to them?"

"I didn't say anything." He looked at her. "I think you are in my head Starshine." He smirked as he took her hand leading her to the dance floor.

THE six of them danced together for hours. Switching partners and dancing like they were celebrating all the things they had wanted for so long. Poppi had enjoyed the feel of Zander's hands wrapped around her waist as she grinded on him to 'Can I Take U Home' by Jamie Fox. The slow grind of her waist was starting to make him hot. He didn't realize how full her ass was until it started to wine against his belt and his hands were in the right spot for her to do what she wanted. He wanted to live the lyrics. Get her all alone and do her how he wanted. Kissing and loving her until she couldn't handle it anymore. He could feel her thinking about what it would be like to be with him. Wondering if his hands would explore her or handle her the way that she was right now. "Why don't we get out of here and I show you."

Her body froze. She turned to him. His blue eyes were dark and serious. "You aren't supposed to be listening to me." She scolded.

"Neither were you, but you did." He looked at her.

She looked at him biting her lip. His hands were wrapped around her waist when the slow jam by Enzo Jacaris started, and he started swaying with her. Pulling her closer to him. Her hands rested at the base of his neck. "What are we going to do Zander, we can't keep this just being friends thing up forever. Not since we hear, feel, and according to my sister and Kandi, smell like each other now."

"I thought you said you didn't believe what they were saying about you." He looked down at her.

"I don't, but I can't deny it's happening and has been since–"

"California." Zander nodded and placed a hand on her face. "We don't have to talk about it right now, but I want you to know I've never believed in magic or the creators until now, and knowing you I wish that I would have learned things I didn't. I wish I could pretend it wasn't happening and ignore it until we were both ready, but I don't think that our souls are going to allow it."

She lay her head on his chest, and she held onto his shoulders. "I didn't mean to bring you into this, but I don't want to change it, just the part where I was married."

He lifted her chin to him. "I think we can arrange for that to be fixed, can't we?" He leaned in and watched her follow until she froze and turned her head to look at a very angry Carmen in a bright red dress with folded arms and her eyes were fiercely focused on the scene. He watched her pull away from him and all he wanted to do was pull her back and kiss her in front of him. He was tired of hiding how he felt.

"What the fuck is going on here Zander?!" Carmen screeched. Before he could answer she held up a hand and looked at Poppi. "Mitchell is looking for you, I guess he got done at the office. You should probably go make sure he doesn't get into another screaming match with Derrick since you're so good at that kind of thing." She shooed her.

They looked at each other. *"I can end this right now Poppi. I'll leave with you, and we won't look back."* He stared into her eyes. *"Say yes"*

They stared at each other for longer than Carmen liked. "I told you where your husband was bitch why don't you leave my fiance alone!" She hissed and Poppi snapped out of her trance. "Thank you for the dance." She whispered as she walked out of site.

46

Birthday

P oppi opened her eyes from the same dream she'd had since the ceremony. Her in the middle of Zander's painting trying to pull them together, but it was impossible. Until Zander arrived and together they pulled the hands together and rain poured down dousing the fires that he'd painted. The garden began to grow again and she felt at peace. She lay in bed staring at the ceiling of the guest room. She'd slept there since she'd returned home. She hadn't spoken to Zander in a week, since the club. She missed him, but running from him was far easier than facing whatever fate for her.

She'd been in constant contact with her father and stepmother Vanessa, who was the alchemist witch for the Jacaris family immortals. She would prepare magical serums to allow them to live like most mortals. She called Poppi last night and told her that she'd done a birthday reading for her at midnight, and she received a very clear message of death, rebirth, and divine blessing. It made Vanessa worried and she wanted to call and see if there were any new developments, Poppi wanted to tell her everything, but she couldn't even decode it herself.

Poppi got up and showered taking the time to enjoy the heat of the shower. Her birthday present would come after Italy. She and Paulette finally got the final okay for her divorce. Paulette planned for her to come home a day early and then when Mitchell got to the airport he would be served with divorce papers. She'd already gotten most of her important stuff out and in storage. Mitchell barely cared about her enough to notice. He was so sure she'd become back to her docile self. She was buying her time, and with or without Zander by her side, she would be happy, and most of all she would be free.

Poppi walked downstairs and was surprised by the black designer luggage with balloons tied to them. Long–stem red roses and balloons holding various amounts of money lined the hallway. Mitchell stood at the end of the hallway holding a cupcake with a candle on it. "Happy birthday beautiful." He smiled. "I love you so much!" He kissed her. "Make a wish."

She blew out the candle. Wishing he'd cut the bullshit like he hadn't forgotten her birthday for the past two years. Like he hadn't smacked her so hard she had a nosebleed when they got home from the club. "What is all this?"

"I have been thinking about how terrible things between us have been and I'm sorry about that. I miss being your husband, your friend." He touched her face. "You're all I've ever wanted, I've done so much to get us here I can't lose you. I want Italy to be the start of the rest of our lives together Poppi. I love you."

She looked at him flabbergasted at his words. She wanted to burst into laughter. After lying, cheating, and beating her for years he finally wanted to do better. Had someone hinted at her leaving? She smiled. She knew she had to play along, but she was suspicious. "Thank you, honey." She kissed him. "This is the best birthday ever!"

"HE gon kill yo ass on that damn trip." Teressa shook her head walking with her through the hall to her office. "He's gonna offer to take you on some damn hike or boat or some white people shit and he's gonna kill your ass."

Poppi laughed, but she knew Teressa was serious. Poppi didn't want to admit it but she agreed with her line of thinking, making everything special and sweet to tell people things were fine between them and then bam, he kill her because she knows too much.

"Poppi your grandmother is here to see you," Lorna popped her head in. "She said that she was taking you out for your birthday."

"Great! Now you can tell granny big bucks that her actual grandchild is planning on murdering you!"

Lorna looked at them. "What?"

"Mitchell went all out for my birthday and–"

"Have you updated your in case I go missing file?" Lorna looked at her. "I'm going to need that when you go on vacation, and I expect Roxanna has one as well?"

"You two are making a lot out of this." Poppi sighed.

"He put you in an asylum that could have gotten you disbarred if he wanted. You need to be thinking safely."

"We're going with people, but fine." Poppi walked into her office and behind her were her two closest friends in the office. She unlocked her cabinet and handed it to Lorna. "I updated it Monday, I knew you'd be asking for it."

"Good. Enjoy your time with your grandmother." They walked out with the file and smiled at Paulette.

"HAPPY birthday darling." Paulette took her hand across the table as they sat for lunch. "I'm glad we could get some alone time, though I won't pretend like I don't miss the kids. I can't believe Brantley took them to Jamaica."

"He said as soon as the kids could take their exams early they were going, I can't believe they convinced Ray and Cris to go. I am so glad they did though, they deserve the break."

Paulette smiled. "Brantley took to fatherhood like a fish to water, he and Juniper were supposed to be together, I think that's why you were brought to us, Brantley never would have met her any other way with that damned Patricia around." Paulette patted her hand and You've done your job for our family; I think it's my turn."

Poppi looked at her. "What are you talking about? You do so much for me Paulette, I really can't thank you enough."

"You know, I'm always going to be your grandmother, I will never leave you. You mean so much to me. You, Brantley, and Sara are my prized possessions. I know, you're people, but you all are my crown gems. When I show people my wealth you three, you three are who I show. I cannot for the life of me bare your mother, but I will always be grateful to her for you."

Poppi smiled holding back tears. "Was this your idea of a birthday? To make me cry?"

"I want to tell you this because I can't show you your birthday present yet."

"You didn't have to get me anything," Poppi giggled as she put her cup to her lips. "But why do I have to wait?"

"It's a surprise, it's not ready." She looked at her. Her flawless face became serious. "What day were you planning on leaving without him?"

"The plan is Sunday to Sunday. So I was thinking maybe Saturday night?" Poppi traced the table. "But today he came in this morning and made this big gesture for my birthday."

Paulette nodded with an eye roll. "His father did the same thing to his mother begging her to come back, he died the next month after he beat her so bad she was in ICU for two weeks." She made a written note in her planner "I'll send the jet out Friday Night. Do you have the phone?"

"Yes." She nodded. "It's in my luggage."

"Good. Leave your old one in the garbage can outside the airport. I'm so excited for you honey." Paulette raised a glass of champagne. "Here's to your last birthday as Poppi Baxter."

47

Flight

Z ander had been kept busy with fake wedding plans for Carmen's grand wedding that was supposed to take place a month after Kandi and Derrick's New Year's Eve midnight wedding. Kandi said it was a good omen going into the New Year as husband and wife because it showed their fate for years to come. Carmen then insisted on having theirs on Valentine's Day. When she was around him they were practically inseparable. She barely let him out of her site. When she was in California it was a different story, Zander might as well have been a stranger.

He wanted to talk to Poppi, but she'd been avoiding him since their heated conversation at the club. He'd sent texts, but she didn't reply. He was worried about her. He stared at their picture from Willow's blessing. It was Poppi and Zander holding Willow with Brant and Juniper beside them. Everyone was smiling at the camera. Zander thought he looked happier in that picture than the one that was once there. It was a professionally done photo, and Poppi was in it. He could stare at her all day, but it would only send him into his continued brooding over missing Poppi's birthday, though he did send a box of cookies to her office. He still missed it. He hoped that on their flight in the private jet, she would at least say something to him. Paulette walked into his office. "Hello, Ms. Baxter what do I owe the pleasure?"

Paulette walked into his office. Her white hair was in a clean bouncy bob of silver. It didn't add age to her youthful face, it only enhanced the beauty of her high cheekbones and fierce piercing brown eyes. Her rose-petal lips were pursed as she strutted in her purple pantsuit to sit in the chair across from him. In her pearl pink manicured hands, she held a manilla folder. He was worried this wasn't good news. "Is everything alright Ms. Baxter?"

She waved her hand at his greeting. "I think we are past formalities, Zander, I need you to tell me right now if you're in love with my granddaughter Poppi." She looked at the shock on his face. She tried to relax her face. and took a deep exhale. "I'm sorry, I'm very forward. My grandson Brantley told me. You're my great-granddaughter's godfather, you were going to come up in conversation at some point and my grandson told me all about how you talk about Poppi, and how much you care for her and her family. Brantley gave you his seal of approval. And he's like her big brother."

Zander was honored that Brantley thought so highly of him, but he wished he'd clear a conversation like that before he decided to announce it to one of his biggest accounts. He would understand if she thought the worst of him. He was sure this wasn't ideal for her. Did she think that he would use Poppi to weasel his way into her pockets deeper? "Are you here to terminate your account with me because of this?"

"God no! Why would I do that? I've made more money than Scrooge McDuck." She laughed and then shook her head. "No Zander what I need is for you to do me a favor."

"Anything." Zander looked at her. He didn't want to show visible relief, but he felt it. He thought he was going to have to explain losing one of the biggest losses to his father. "What can I help you with?"

"Firstly, I need you to stay close to Poppi, she's coming home from Italy early and I need you to come back with her."

Zander looked at her curiously. Had she not spoken to Poppi? "I doubt that she will want me to come with her." He admitted. "She and I haven't exactly been speaking."

"I suggest you be insistent. Something tells me you two are going to need each other more than you think." When she looked back up to him from the envelope her face was filled with guilt. The worry that had just passed from him slowly started to creep back up. "The second part of the favor is your forgiveness." She looked at the envelope. "I am always, particularly about who I let handle my money, so I do checks, you'll understand I have my own PI company. So I used them to do a check on you when you took over for our dear retired friend Mr. Hall."

"Of course Ms. Baxter, as you said I've made you more money than Scrooge McDuck, that's a lot of temptation. I would advise everyone be as careful and thorough as you have been." He agreed. "Was there something in my background that was to your disliking?"

"If you mean your eagle scout one parking ticket since you were 16 years old, background no." She tried to make the mood light for herself, Zander could tell it was weighing on her. "No, this is something I must apologize for. But I can't say why." She handed it to him. "Just know that It's not always like this." She stood and walked to the door.

ZANDER sat in the jet staring at the envelope. He was curious as to what she could have possibly found that would require him to forgive her. He was anxiously waiting to see Poppi. He couldn't wait to be close to her again, but the worry of what was in the envelope made it hard to concentrate on the good that was ahead of them. He felt the angst of opening it, but when he looked at Carmen peering over at the envelope he decided he'd wait til he was in private.

"What's that?" Carmen asked him, looking at the envelope.

"Something Mr. Abraxas needs me to look at before we get there." He tucked it back into his laptop bag. "Nothing serious."

"I thought you said you weren't going to work, that this is a vacation." She folded her arms. Her face was painted with aggravation.

"It's a working vacation," Zander sighed rolling his eyes. "I've got three meetings while I'm here. I told you this."

"Hi everyone!" Poppi's voice filled his ears and his heart with relief.

"There she is!" Claudia jumped up and hugged her tightly. Dancing as she did it. "I have missed you, young lady! We are going to have a blast birthday girl! I told Pearl about it and she said she is planning something very nice."

"I can't wait." She returned his mother's hug. Zander had never seen his mother so excited to see Carmen or any other girl he'd brought around. She had his family's approval far before he'd decided she was the one.

"Carmen," Mitchell nodded and then looked at him with malice. " Zander."

"Mitchell." Zander shook his hand. "Poppi."

"Hello, Zander." She smiled. "So nice to see you again."

After the plane took off he watched as his mother and father curled together to watch their favorite show. Hart to Hart. Carmen was listening to something in her earphones and Mitchell was reading. He locked eyes with Poppi, the look she gave him sent chills down his spine, and heat to his groin. He wanted her then and there and from the look on her face. She could feel it.

THREE hours into the flight Zander got up and went to the back to watch television and finally look in the envelope. He looked over and Poppi was reading a book with her head slightly cocked. She was distracted. He walked to the television room and shut the curtain.

He opened the envelope. He pulled the paper out first. It was the information of a private investigator and all of their credentials. He felt the hairs on the back of his neck stand up. Paulette hired a private investigator, maybe she saw Zander and Poppi together, but they were careful. They were never inappropriate.

He was a deep thought not paying attention to the show he put on in the background. He pulled out the first picture of Carmen walking into a hotel. Zander wasn't worried, she was an actress she slept in a lot of hotels. He flipped it over to 'Oakman Hotel 12:45 pm Monday, January

7th' Now Zander was more confused. Oakman was 15 minutes away from his office. She came straight to his house why did she need a hotel?

"Do you mind if I join you?" Poppi asked breaking him out of his puzzle. She looked delicious in her leggings and cropped tye-dyed crop top. Her hair was in a curly ponytail at the top of her head and bounced when she walked into the area, closing the curtain behind her.

"Of course not!" He moved out the papers aside. He would have to know about whatever was going on later. "Please. Be my guest."

48

Mile High

They watched the screen until he felt Poppi's hand on his joggers. He felt her body cuddle into his. He looked at the closed velvet curtains. Praying that no one would ruin this. Her head was on his torso, she looked comfortable like she didn't care that her husband was just a few feet away. He felt her hand sliding under his shirt and a shiver went down his spine. "Poppi what are you doing?" He whispered. "M–my parents."

"Won't know if you're quiet." She whispered in his ear making his erection instant and harder than he'd ever felt it. She giggled deviously with her hand wrapped around it. "Someone agrees with me."

All of him agreed with her. He wanted this more than he could ever express. He missed her, he needed her. But some questions needed to be answered. "Paulette came by today; she said something about you leaving early. What's going on?"

"I don't want to talk about it, Zander." She kissed his neck. "We can go back to reality later, but for now," Her lips met his. She kissed him deeply, lifting her leg and straddling him. His hands were allowed to explore her torso this time. He could feel the warmth of her flesh under his fingertips, against his chest. She kissed his neck and nibbled his earlobe. Finding pressure points on him that other women hadn't even thought of. "I can't wait to have your cock in my mouth." She whispered kissing his neck.

Zander watched as she pulled his penis from his pants. She took a long lick from shaft to tip. Then she spat on it and began putting it ao the back of her throat. His entire penis disappeared in her mouth. He thought it would be difficult with the curve. Carmen gagged and said she couldn't. He never pushed her. Never liked when she did it anyway, but Poppi's tongue worked in ways he'd never felt. Finding places that he didn't even know did things for him.

Zander fell into deep enjoyment watching Poppi's full lips covering his cock. She'd take breaks and suck on his balls while stroking them in her hand. She went back to deep-throating him when she took his hand and put in her hair. "A-are you sure?"

"Yes sir," She looked at him.

He pulled her head back and kissed her deeply "I'm gonna face fuck you now, my precious slut."

She smiled her eyes hazy from their interaction. "Yes sir."

"Now get up here." He commanded. "That's right just like that." He slid his hand in her panties feeling the soaking "Is all this for me? What a good little flower you are."

Her moans were muffled by her bobbing made the vibrations go down his shaft and he bit his lip to not express how amazing this felt. He couldn't wait to do this over and over again, repay her by making her body convulse in pleasure until she was unable to move. She was going to be rewarded for this. For making him feel like the only person on this plane.

He wanted to praise her, he wanted to tell her how good she was at this, how his toes were curling with the way she made the figure eight on the crease between the tip and shaft. He loved how she noticed his body's movements and acted accordingly, he would pump his hips for more pressure, and she would suction onto him so tight his mouth went immediately dry. Her tongue was amazing he felt himself slipping.

"I'm gonna cum princess." He whispered. "You should move."

She kept going, her body grinding against his fingers. Her soft moans drove him insane. He kept pumping his hips into her mouth. He loved the way he fit inside her mouth. He wondered what it felt like everywhere. Would it be just as perfect? His body began to buzz with pleasure, he put the fingers he once had inside of her into his mouth to stop himself from calling her name as loudly as he could He felt the plane quake as he pumped his hips, but he was sure it was his imagination.

His seed burst down her throat and still she kept sucking. Making him whimper and arch. She came up when was completely soft, wiping the side of her mouth. "I like the way you taste."

He kissed her deeply. "I like the way you do everything. Why don't you lie down and I return the favor." Her smile widened, before she could say anything the speaker began to crackle with life.

"Attention passengers." The pilot crackled over the speaker. "We're experiencing turbulence, please return to your seat and buckle your seat belts. Thank you."

49

Abraxas

When Poppi stepped into the villa her breath was taken away by the foyer. There were two black staircases leading to the left or the right and a two-step stair platform where they met. The railing was a deep green intricately looped design framed in gold. A chandelier hung above them on a beautifully painted scene that had two angels holding the light fixtures. There was a green velvet settee under *'In Italian'* by Jean-Michel Basquiat. Another green velvet chair with gold trim sat by the dark marble staircase. The entire room was an oak color with plants growing from the large archways, a black orchid grew in the middle of the archway. Even the rugs were earthy. She wondered if the entire villa was like this.

"It's beautiful isn't it honey?" Mitchell asked her as he wrapped his hand around her waist. She wanted to shove him off of her and tell him to knock it off with the lovey-dovey shit. He had five years to treat her like this, and he didn't. He just made her feel less than human and made sure she was reminded of how he felt about their marriage daily.

"It is." She replied with a simple nod. She watched as Carmen clung to Zander talking about all of the things they were going to do while they were here. Zander looked like he wanted to be anywhere else but close to her. She was happy she wasn't in this alone, but she was curious about why it was happening. She wondered if they were trying to butter them up to hide the fact that they would be trying to sneak off together. Poppi could care less if she was honest with herself, she'd welcome it.

"Welcome Baxter and Bell family to our home." A breathtaking brown-skinned woman stood at the top of the steps. She wore bright blue billowy pants and a silk white quarter-sleeved blouse. Her black hair was in a bun at the top of her head, and when she turned to either side there was a perfectly placed gray stripe. She had an angled face with a perfect button nose and hooded almond eyes. She looked as if she should be staring at technicolor musicals that she and Vanessa used to watch on rainy Sunday afternoons. She clicked down the stairs in her open-toe shoes.

"Pearl it has been too long." Claudia hugged her tightly. "You don't look a day older than when I delivered Silas. What is your secret?!"

Pearl laughed. "Never let your sons or your husband worry you. She looked at Zander. "And since this is your son I doubt you're going to need that advice." She watched Poppi and Zander admiring the painting while Carmen and Mitchell stood close enough to hear them breathe.

"Lovely isn't it?! It was such an honor to get a piece of his work. You must be Zander, and this must be Mrs. Bell." A taller man in a white silk button-down with a blue tie and dark blue pants. He wore a blue hat and sunglasses. "You look so familiar." His eyes were deep and vibrant hazel. He studied Poppi's face trying to place her. "Where have I seen you before?"

Poppi basked in the idea for a moment waiting for Zander to correct her. Instead, he smiled and answered for her. "I think her sister works for your family, Lavender?"

"You're Lavender's sister?! Why didn't you say that!" Pearl's face beamed in delight. She looked at him. "You're practically family! But Sol, she said her husband's name was Mitchell."

"It is." Mitchell stepped up. "I'm Mitchell Baxter ma'am. I'll be working with Zander on the project."

Pearl looked between them. Her eyes squinted. "I think I started vacationing too early." She chuckled. "I could have sworn-"

"It's okay Mrs. Abraxas." Poppi shook her hand. "It's a pleasure to meet you either way." Poppi looked at Pearl's face and she looked totally different. Her skin was glowing and her eyes were completely green. Her hair was down to her back and there were flowers all through it. What was she?

Pearl softly pulled her hand away and shook it like it was hot. Her husband looked at her like something was wrong. "I think Poppi is warming up to me." She chuckled. Her appearance was back to normal. She was smiling at Poppi until her eyes focused on Carmen. Her mouth went down turned and her arms folded. Her body language went from excited and joyful to defensive in a matter of moments. "Oh, if it isn't the whore who ruined my son's relationship with his brother. I forgot you would be darkening my doorstep."

"Is there a problem?" Frederick looked from Carmen to Pearl. He put his suitcase down as four men in black suits started to bring in luggage. Poppi watched each of them. They all looked like the human version of bears. Big and burly with expressionless faces and sunglasses.

"What's she talking about Carmen?" Claudia looked at her. Her wheels visibly turned with concern for her son.

"That isn't how it happened!" Carmen defended. Tightening her grip on her Zander. She looked from him to his mother her face shocked by the accusation.

Pearl looked at her, the smile she once wore returned with a bitter strike. "I'm sure it isn't the way you explained it to my friend and her son, but I know for a fact that my sons haven't spoken to each other since December because of you, and I'm not exactly pleased with you being here mainly since Keres and Lavender will be arriving in a few hours. So I suggest you be on your best behavior or you will be on the next flight out of here." She looked at Poppi. "I have a room I'd like to show you, since your sister is coming I'm sure you girls will want to spend some quality time together and Mitchell is gonna need his rest if he's gonna try to keep up with the Abraxas men in the board room."

"Thank god," Mitchell muttered. "Last thing I need is for you two to keep me awake with your cackling."

"If I were you, sir, I'd keep that kinda talk to a minimum when my son arrives, he's very protective of her. And I have a feeling it's already going to be uncomfortable for the six of you in a room, anyway," She narrowed her eyes. "Won't it?"

"I don't know what you mean by that, I'm perfectly capable of handling myself accordingly ma'am." Mitchell glared at her.

"You'll have to forgive my wife, she can be a bit eccentric when it comes to her boys." He chuckled and looked at Poppi. "Or in this case her girl. She loves Lav like a daughter so she's going to be a bit protective of her baby sister while she isn't here. Isn't that right honey?"

She stared at Mitchell for a long second. "Right." She looked up at him. "Sol darling show everyone else to their rooms, will you?" She looped her arm into Poppi's. She smiled and her Kanines were longer and sharper than they were when she'd first showed them her award-winning smile. "I'd like to talk to Poppi."

"Of course, dear." He bent to kiss her cheek. He looked at the rest of the group ."

"We'll all gather for dinner around six, does that sound alright?"

"Perfect." Claudia hugged her and then Poppi. "Holla if you need me."

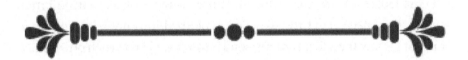

PEARL walked Poppi up the opposite staircase, and down a discreet hallway. "Lavender called me and told me something about your grandmother needing you to have a separate room, she's asked me to keep you away from Mitchell as much as I can until she gets here. I don't know what's going on but when she asks me I usually try to do my best to help. She opened a black door with the number 1 painted in gold. There were windows that started at the floor and rounded at the top inches away from the ceiling. The room was bigger than two of hers. There was a glass door that lead to the balcony, and there was a thick oak door that lead to a private bathroom.

The oak canopy bed looked like it came right from a fairy tale and behind it was a window that let her look down at the crystal blue water that danced with the wind in the pool lined with luxury pool chairs that alternated between black and white. plants grew up on the deep blue wall and a circle armchair sat in front of the window across the bed. There were dark brown tables with long stem lamps on either side of the bed. She wanted to crawl in it and fall asleep.

She walked over to the walk-in closet, she'd enjoy putting her clothes in it. She watched Pearl as she opened the bathroom door and she followed her into the bathroom. There was a white and gold garden tub in the most perfect natural lighting. She could imagine riding Zander as they were surrounded by the bubbles. The tub was within arm's reach of a counter with vases of beautiful flowers, a stack of towels, and a wall-to-wall half mirror. She looked at the counter across from the luxury toilet with a heated seat. It had a deep bowl sink and she slid her finger across the countertop. "Pearl this is the most beautiful room I've ever been in."

"It's all yours, fit for a queen!" She put her hands on her hips.

"I'm no queen." Poppi laughed.

Pearl folded her arms. "I wish I could believe that, but only a fertility witch can make someone in the immortal bloodline show their true form." Pearl leaned against the door handle. "I haven't felt that form in 70 years, and here you and that sham of a husband come. You and Zander can hide all you want, but I know what you two are. And since you're able to expose my true form I'm going to take a wild guess and say your bloodline was the one who gave birth to Oryn's immortal, my mother, and that was so long ago I doubt we can even trace it. But to have *you* in my home. That's about as close to royalty as we are going to get. Mainly since the last fertility witch from the Abraxas line did rule the realm of the Fae."

"Is this why we're here? You want us to join the Legion?"

"No, Zander got this job all on his own. And I want you to be as far away from Legion as you can possibly be. If anyone who isn't us smells what you are, they might not be so kind to you. Keres wanted me to check you out before they got here." She walked with her to the couch back in the room and sat beside her. "Have you had any new powers?"

"I levitate when I'm doing meditations, but my stepmother said that was normal when a witch was coming into her own, and then there is the whole dream realm thing where Zander and I can meet, but it hasn't happened for weeks."

"She's a priestess of magic, not a fertility witch, but I'm sure for her levitation is normal and comes with the territory. You haven't been able to physically go into the realm have you?"

Poppi looked at her. "I haven't, and I'm not sure I want to. I don't want too many lines in my life blurred for something I wasn't allowed to practice until I was of age and even then, I was bad at it. My powers aren't anything of value."

"What are they?"

"Honestly, I thought I was just a regular old witch who was good in the kitchen, I'm great at gardening, and I love music and dancing. None of that is going to bring back the light-bringer or whatever I'm supposed to do."

"Maybe you're putting too much on yourself. Fertility witches are powerful in their own way." She rubbed her arm. "When the time comes for you to bring us whatever it is we need I'm sure that you will. Immortals have had no signs; their powers are still dormant. Weird things like flashes of my past lives have come to me, but nothing that should make you worry."

"So why does everyone think that it has to do with me?"

Pearl looked at her. "Your sister. She woke up screaming for you, she was holding a Guardian witch wand, you don't get one of those because you're born one. They come to the protector of the fertility witch. Which since you two are sisters, would make sense."

"I don't know Mrs. Abraxas I'm not sure if I have something of value shouldn't I go to the LOEMC and document myself."

"The Legion of Extraordinary and magical creatures won't understand. And the chairman, Sepher will have you assassinated. Maybe that's why Mitchell is here, he's probably one of his agents, it would also explain Carmen's involvement." Pearl thought aloud. "No, you should just enjoy your life; you don't even know what's happening to you. Why bother them with a what-if?"

"Why do I have a feeling that you are keeping something from me." She folded her arms.

"It's for your safety Poppi. Nothing else." She hugged her. "I should let you get settled. I'm so excited for our shopping trip tomorrow. Lavender says you have quite the eye for fashion, I'll see you for dinner." She closed the door behind her. Leaving Poppi with so much to think about.

50
Inquiring Minds

Z ander sat in the bedroom Sol had offered to him and Carmen. It had a four-post king-sized bed with a fireplace across from it. He was in the hidden corner where a thick oak desk sat in front of a window that showed the beauty of Italy's countryside. He stared out of the window wondering what Pearl would have to talk to Poppi about. He wondered where she'd taken her since she hadn't been seen around Mitchell since they'd gotten into their rooms. He'd just gotten dressed for dinner. He decided on a black suit with a paisley green button-down under it. He wore the watch that Poppi had gifted him religiously and tonight was no different.

He thought about how Sol thought she was his wife. He wondered what it would be like if she was his wife. If they spent the rest of their life together what would it be like? What would it feel like without the thrill of being forbidden? He traced his lip with his finger. It would be replaced with the thrill of having her in his bed every night. Or the toe-curling eye-rolling pleasure she could administer with her mouth. Guilt festered behind his daydreams of Poppi's lips wrapped around his cock. Carmen was still his fiance and she deserved respect even if he didn't want to be with her. Though it was clear Poppi didn't feel the same. She was done respecting a man who didn't give a damn about her, she made that much clear on the plane.

Zander looked at the unopened envelope. He pulled out a note first. It was addressed to him.

'Zander,

It was never my intention to hurt you. I consider you and your family to be my friends, and if I was in this position I'd want to know, but it's what you do with the information that makes the difference.'

Zander re-read the cryptic message from Paulette. He looked back out of the window even more curious now. He shook the contents face down on the desk. He pulled up a clear picture of Carmen and Mitchell lip-locking in front of a hotel. The same hotel she booked down the street from his office. There was another of them holding hands in an upscale restaurant in LA. There was one of her and him in the alley behind the club on the night they came in and ruined his moment with Poppi. Her legs were wrapped around him. Her mouth gaped open as he fucked her. His jaw clenched as he went through the compromising photos and receipts of expensive gifts he brought for her on the company dime.

How could he be so blind? How could he have not believed Crispin who wanted nothing but the best for him and all he did was walk Carmen out instead of hearing him out? He thought about all the time he wasted that he could have spent dedicated to Poppi giving her his all and loving her so she didn't have to be with that human scum. He thought about when she disappeared. Carmen knew something about that. The way she spoke during their dinner party, he should have pressed her until she broke.

Zander was trapped in his loop of thought he didn't hear the door open. "Well if it isn't my niece's favorite godfather! And my future brother-in-law!" Lavender peeked her head around the privacy wall. She looked at the scattered papers on the desk and she looked back at his soured face. "What's wrong? Poppi not gonna let you do the Lady and the Tramp thing?"

"Carmen and Mitchell have been having an affair for months." He handed her a picture for proof. Her smile turned into a grimace. She wasn't shocked, but the look on her face was more so confused than anything.

"Wow..." Lavender turned her head to understand the compromising position they were in. "When did you get these? Who gave them to you?" She turned her head to the other side.

"Literally when you were walking in, they were fucking at the hotel down the street from my job!" He quietly shouted. tossing the envelope down. "They had a goddamn standing fucking reservation! Why didn't she just end it?"

"If she ended it, why would she have to stick around? It would have been weird. Poppi would have caught on if she hasn't already." Lavender sat down on the desk going through the rest of the pictures. She looked up at him. "Are you going to tell her?"

"He's been acting like such the fucking perfect husband to her she'll just think I'm being some jealous brute with a crush right?" He shook his head. "How could he do this to her?! After everything she's gone through in their marriage, he'd stoop this fucking low."

"Wait a minute." She held up a picture and her face looked like a light bulb went off. "Wait a fucking minute." She jumped up from the desk. "She knows!"

"What?" Zander looked at her. "How?"

"Poppi, I think she knows about the affair." Lavender slammed a picture of Mitchell and Carmen holding each other while Poppi was being dragged away by an all-white medical bus. She pointed to the time stamp. "This was the same day Willow was born. She said she was going home to grab some stuff after you two were doing whatever it was you were outside."

Zander looked up at her. "Why didn't she tell me if she knew."

"A stay in Saint Hellens could have her disbarred. It's for criminals, and they could consider her incompetent. If Carmen knew this information she could ruin Poppi's life if she told you. Not to mention as you said, how did she know you wouldn't have thought of her as the crazy girl with an obsessive crush? And you know Carmen would have twisted it that way."

"She has to know I wouldn't have thought of her like that right?" Zander sighed. "I'm going to kill that bastard with my bare fucking hands!"

"Keres is here, he might cause bloodshed if he puts two and two together. Speaking of," Lavender twirled around in a green cocktail dress.
"Dinner is ready."

Zander hid the envelope in his suitcase. "What do I say to her? How
do I even look at her?"

"Who Poppi? Sadly she's used to it. When they got engaged, Mitch was
banging his sister-in-law. A year ago it was that sweetheart in your
accounting department. Susie?"

"Cindi?"

"That's it. He put her in a nice little place for about a month, they had
her on such high medications she wasn't lucid more than two hours a
day." Lavender sighed. "As for Carmen, that's your own shit babe."

"I wanna be mad at her, hate her, but I guess I'm glad it's over. I guess
it's been over for months and I'm too dumb to realize."

"Don't say that, she's an actress. She acted like she loved you and for
once she was good at her job." Lavender looped her arm in his as they
walked to the door." Fuck her, go after what you really want. Stop being
so damn scared. Find your happiness."

"You're right." Zander sighed. "I think I'm going to like hanging
around you."

"You're just now figuring that out and I've been around you five times
now." She scoffed. "Thanks. C'mon Ms. P went all out for you guys."

"Lavender, one request."

"Of course."

"Don't tell Poppi, I want to tell her in my own time."

"If that's really what you want." Lavender looked at him. "Doesn't
mean I have to be nice to the fucking bitch who got her put back in that
fucking hell house."

"No I would say be easy on her, but I think Pearl solidified she wasn't
welcome when she called her a whore five minutes after seeing her."

"She didn't slap her?"

"God no!"

"Damm." Lavender sucked her teeth. "I lost the bet."

51

Uncomfortable

P oppi was one of the first ones to the dinner table to check the seating arrangements at Pearl's request as the cook staff brought out trays with silver lids. Sol was at the head of the table. Pearl was to his left and Fredrick was to his right. Claudia of course was seated across from her husband. She put Keres across from Lavender and beside Poppi. Mitchell sat between Carmen and Keres. Zander sat on her right side and there was an empty place setting for her son Silas who said he may stop in. She was excited to be sitting between her sister and Zander, it would be like her own bubble of protection. She looked up at the two guards who stood by the back door. She was curious if Pearl thought they'd need extra security for Keres and Mitchell.

The staff begin lifting the lids and the smells became fragrant in the large dining rooms with skylights that let the twinkling twilight rest above them. The table was large enough to hold six meals. Spaghetti bolognese, Gnudi, Fuslli with lamb ragu, steak with salad, Salmon alfredo, Lobster ravioli, and bruschetta. Poppi's mouth watered looking at the display, she thought about the meal Zander had cooked for their friends, it was the last time she'd seen delicious food she didn't have to cook herself. She was excited to enjoy a meal with so many people she cared about.

She watched Zander walk into the dining room and the smile she had faded when she saw the tense anger storming in his face as he walked to the patio. He looked back at her and she quickly followed. She saw Carmen lounging at the pool most of the afternoon, did she say something to upset him? She walked into the warm evening air. "Are you alright?"

"Did you know?" He asked shortly.

"Did I know what?" She asked praying it wasn't what she thought he was talking about. She hoped Mitchell wouldn't do anything so foolish in the proximity of his boss and his wife.

"Yes or no Poppi. Did you know?!" He repeated hotly. "Be honest with me."

She sighed. "Zander, honey now isn't the time–"

"So you did know!" He sat down on one of the chairs his hands smoothing down his face. "Is that why you were gone!? What did they do to you!?"

Poppi's eyes welled up with tears. She didn't care about Carmen or Mitchell, but the idea of seeing Zander upset or hurt would break her heart. She walked over to him and got on her knees pulling his face to hers. "We don't really have the time to talk about this now, the others are starting to make their way to the dining room."

He looked up at her his eyes were wet with tears. "Why didn't you tell me Pop? Why did you keep this from me?"

"What if I told you what would it solve? What would you gain?!" She shook her head. "Listen, Pearl gave me my own room. You and I can talk about it tonight."

"If he hurt you–"

"None of that." She touched his face. "You're my date tonight. We're sitting together at least."

"At least." He stood taking her hand and kissing it before looping it into his arm. "I'll be with the most beautiful woman in the world tonight." They walked in as everyone else was taking their seats. "Good evening everyone." He smiled at them.

"I saw you two outside." Lavender sat as Keres pulled her seat out "Is everything okay."

"Everything is fine," Poppi reassured as he pulled her seat out. "Just fine." She smiled as he took his seat beside her.

DINNER was quiet at first. Pearl and Sol chatted with Claudia and Frederick about things, and occasionally they would pull one of them in for input. Silas, the Abraxas' other son, joined them, he sat down and introduced himself to the group. He scoped out everyone but remained focused on his plate like something was going to jump out of it. Poppi nervously tucked a hair behind her ear as Lavender was telling her favorite story about her and Poppi skipping school and driving down to the beach for the entire weekend. "It was where I first met Keres."

Keres looked at her and beamed with a bright smile. "I have to say I think it will go down in history as one of the best days of my life, but I can't believe that was you Poppi!" He laughed. "Your hair was what... Green?"

"Oh god!" Poppi laughed out loud. "I forgot all about that."

"You would. You shaved your head that summer." Lavender sipped her wine and gave her a nudge.

"Please tell me there are pictures of this!" Zander looked at Lavender as he slid his hand onto her thigh rubbing it with his thumb. Poppi tried to hide the grin on her face and the physical melt that her body did under his touch.

"I have the perfect one you can put on your wall." Lavender winked at Zander. Who went back to his meal with a small smile. It was the most emotion he'd shown at the dinner table. Poppi was becoming worried about where his head was. She would never take a peak without permission, but she could feel the anger still coming from him. She looked up at Silas was studying her again she gave him a small smile. He returned and went back to his meal.

"I'm so glad you two came, if you didn't, I think we'd be bored out of our minds." Keres laughed taking a sip of wine. "I'm almost sad that I'm going to miss the shopping trip tomorrow."

"If we finish early enough, I don't see why we can't join them." Sol looked at his wife. "If that's alright with you."

"We should have lunch by the pool, if you all get done in time, we can make it a whole event!" Pearl looked at them excitedly. "Silas, are you game darling?" She over to him. "You've been complaining of a headache all evening."

"I'm so sorry if I'm dampening the mood, Mother." He smiled, Silas had a warm smile. He was handsome, she could understand why Carmen wanted to bounce between them. He was the taller of the brothers and according to Pearl, he'd just retired from playing pro football with the Commanders to run the beauty branch of their business. His shoulders were broad and he looked like he could wrestle a tiger barefoot. "I don't know where this headache came from, but I assure you I won't miss your lunch tomorrow, though I may skip the shopping."

"Speaking of dampening moods." Keres looked at Zander. "You alright man? You seem a little... Irritated."

"Me?" Zander removed his hand from her thigh and wiped his mouth with his napkin. "I'm fine."

"My presence here isn't making you uncomfortable, is it?" Silas asked "I mean no disrespect. They are my parents."

"Why would your presence here bother him?" Claudia asked taking a sip of wine.

"Hopefully it doesn't." Keres looked at him. "I was hoping we could all become friends. You know since we're all working together right Si?"

He nodded. "Right."

"I have no ill feelings towards you. Either of you..." Zander pushed a piece of ravioli around on his plate. "It's just been a very long day."

"The flight can be a pain in the ass." Carmen smiled. She reached out for his hand. "After dinner, we can take a hot bubble bath and go to bed."

"I'm going for a swim." Zander looked at her hand like it was poisonous. "I think the night air will do me some good."

Keres eyed him, and then his eyes went back to Silas who was rubbing his temples. His eyes traveled back to Poppi and settled on her. "What did she do to you?"

"Keres! Not at the dinner table darling." Pearl pleaded putting her fork down in aggravation.

"It was you she did something to. Wasn't it?" Keres pointed his marina-drenched fork at Poppi. "What did she do to you?"

"Jesus! Can you not think the worst of her? You don't even know her." Mitchell spat. "Can't you all lay off of her? It's been like this since she got here! Accusing her of stealing 25k, treating her like some masterminded villain when neither is the case."

Poppi closed her eyes and pretended she could be anywhere else when the table became silent after his outburst. She opened her eyes and everyone was looking at Mitchell with a look of confusion. He never had that kind of energy when it came to anything about her or their marriage. If he did maybe it would've worked out for the two of them. She looked at Carmen who was beaming with satisfaction.

"You would defend her," Silas replied coldly. Poppi's eyes snapped to him and he was staring at Mitchell with annoyance.

"I would be doing the same if he accused Poppi of something." Mitchell waved his hand at Zander "I'm surprised Zander isn't angry."

"It's because he knows I'm not lying, don't you?" Keres looked over at Zander who gripped Poppi's thigh under the table. She could feel the heat of his anger in his hands. Coming off like waves. She took her hand and placed it on top of his.

"What is he talking about Zander?!" Carmen looked at him. "What isn't he lying about? What I'd do to her?"

Zander looked at Mitchell and then back at Carmen. His face was blank. "I don't know Carmen, what'd you do to her?" He asked raising his brow.

"Okay, maybe this isn't something we should discuss at the dinner table." Poppi rubbed Zander's shoulder. "It's probably best done in private."

"The perfect Poppi trying to save the day again!" Carmen laughed bitterly. "Why would he listen to you? You're crazy. Just ask her where she spent those two weeks."

"Where was she?" Lavender asked picking up her steak knife and slicing flawlessly through her meat. She looked up at her. "Since you seem to have the boldness to call my sister crazy while I'm sitting right the fuck here."

The air was tensing around Poppi. She could feel the anger bubbling inside of her. She wished Carmen and Mitchell would fade into the background and let her get back to living a semi-normal life. She wished Carmen could go one night without embarrassing her. They were going to be in Italy for a week the least she could do is act fucking civil! Her jaw clenched with every angry thought she had. She knew that the act they were putting on when they got there was just that. Some bullshit facade to make her look even more crazy than she is already on paper thanks to Mitchel. She wanted this dinner over. She wanted to be as far away from the two people as she couldn't stand the sight of as her bedroom would allow.

Silas' fork clattered to his plate and he grabbed his temple. She looked over at him and his skin was the color of emeralds. His eyes were the same radiant eyes from her dreams in St. Helens. He quickly stood. "I'm sorry, I hate to leave like this but my head has become unmanageable. Please forgive me for my rudeness, but I'm going to get back to my apartment."

"Honey, why don't you stay here? It'd be safer wouldn't it?" Pearl asked looking at her son with worry. She put her napkin on top of her plate and stood. Sol followed behind her.

"No Mother," Silas looked at Poppi once more like he was trying to figure out something even she couldn't explain. "I'm afraid staying here may make it worse. It was a pleasure meeting all of you." He shook Zander's hand. He looked at him. "I do hope we can be friends. My brother told me a lot about you. I look forward to working with you in the next few days."

"So do I." Zander smiled.

"Poppi, right? I look forward to speaking with you again as well." He squinted his eyes at her when he smiled. He looked at his brother. "Call me." He told him as he hugged Lavender goodbye. "Goodnight everyone." Everyone replied with a mutual goodnight. They watched Pearl and Sol follow after their son.

"Well, children I do believe we will also bid you a goodnight." Frederick pulled out Claudia's seat and hugged his son, and then Poppi. "Thank you for always looking out for him." He gave her a gentle squeeze and then wrapped his arm around his wife. "C'mon honey, we've got dessert in the room." He grinned.

They watched them walk up the stairs. "Babe promise me we are that fucking adorable when I'm older." Lavender sighed leaning against Keres. Poppi smiled shaking her head, she turned back to Zander, but he was already walking to his room. Carmen quickly followed behind him.

52
Nightcap

P oppi crept out of her room, the entire villa was pitch black as she tiptoed down the stairs she jumped when she saw two armed guards playing cards in the sitting room by the door. They looked up at her and smiled. She held up her hand to them and walked out of the back door closing it softly. She wondered what the Abraxas family did in their spare time that they needed armed guards 24-7. She wouldn't let that bother her, now was her time to unplug. Her time to enjoy the quiet after a more than eventful dinner.

Pearl told her about the jacuzzi in the greenhouse when she was showing her around her bedroom. She told her it was absolutely beautiful at night, and she was right. Where she'd placed it gave her a perfect view of the countryside with the full moon strung above the hills like a pearl. The stars twinkled in the deep black sky above her. Everything was perfect, she looked beside her and thought of Zander who probably was upstairs listening to Carmen beg and plea for forgiveness. She wondered if he would accept.

"Do you want company?"

She looked up at Zander's half-naked frame. His brown skin was deep blue in the moonlight, the water droplets that traveled down his pectorals down to his muscular abdomen looked like diamonds. His thighs were thick and there was a bludge between them. Her mouth watered looking at the statue of perfection in front of her. "I would love some company." She exhaled the smoke she forgot she was holding. "Is everyone asleep?"

"Well, it is two in the morning." He slid in beside her and she passed him the blunt. He inhaled and looked at her exhaling. "So, I'm going to say yes."

She watched him look at the flowers and vines that thrived in the heat and moisture of the hot tub. "I thought you'd be in there listening to Carmen explain everything. Since you know, I'm crazy," She laughed trying to cut the idea of yanking his trunks off.

He cut his eyes at her and tilted his head back as he huffed. "I'm done with her Poppi, I know it's crazy, but there is this woman I'm in love with and I think it would kinda stupid to keep letting her get away." He handed her back the blunt. "So I'm not."

She looked at him. "L–love?" She asked. "You love me?"

"Poppi I'm over the moon about you. I'd shout it from the rooftops if you would let me." He smiled facing her. "You're all I think about. All I dream about. If you weren't here I'd be miserable. I intend on making every moment we have here together special, and I'm flying back with you when you go. Paulette's already arranged it."

She sighed relief washed over her. She didn't want to make that trip alone and now she'd be making it with the man who loved her. "Zander, you've already made this trip special for me. You don't have to do anything else."

"I guess it's a good thing I'm not done yet." He kissed her neck and pulled her close to him. His hands traced the tattoo on her ribcage. He let his kisses trail up to her ear. "You don't know how badly I want to be inside you, starshine." His husky breath smelled like smoky spearmint. He pulled her on top of him. Her lips danced with his. He let his hands trace up her ribs to her full breast teasing her wet nipples. She let a soft moan out of her lips.

"We shouldn't do this here." She whispered. "I don't want to be disrespectful." She pressed herself against him feeling him hard was making it hard for her to be the perfect house guest.

"You tell me where." He spoke against her lips. His lips trailed down to her breast sucking on her nipple and flicking it with his tongue. Her hand her arm braced his head there. He put his hands against her grinding her clit against his shaft. His body was ready for her. She could feel him aching for her. He could feel her throbbing against him.

Poppi felt the urge to be in nature. Their first time should be memorable. It should be shown to the gods and goddesses to show them she survived the worst and came out of it smarter. Better. Happier. She was ready for her rebirth, her freedom. She wanted to feel the earth the moment she gave herself to him. "There." She pointed to an empty patch of land. She got off of him and held her hand out to him. "I want you there."

He smiled. "With pleasure." He stood and the length of him stretched his swim trunks noticeably. He grabbed her sliding his hand between her legs and rubbing her clit as they walked pressing her ass against him and kissing her neck. He laid her down on the ground and took off her bottoms. He opened her thighs and licked her budding clit. He took long strokes between her folds. Teasing her entrance. Her legs tightened around him as she wiggled back, but he grabbed her thighs and kept stroking her slowly.

Poppi's body quaked at the way he focused his tongue and fingers on her most sensitive places. His thumb would rub her clit as he nibbled on the inside of her thigh to tease her. His two fingers would press against her G-spot as he sucked on her clit using his tongue to lap up his reward. She never had so much attention to her body after Lydia she just thought her sex life would be Mitchell centered and she would never enjoy indulgent pleasure like she was now.

Her legs looked amazing on his broad shoulders. She liked the way his head looked devouring him the way he was. His hands bracing her thighs his fingers making indents into her glowing skin. Poppi laid her head back, the visual of him was starting to get her off. He started to hit the spots that made her back arch. He started to get rough with the right amount of pressure on her G-spot and her hands clutched the dirt. Her hands sank into the earth as she moaned.

"Yes Starshine," He coached her. "Work that pretty pussy on my face." He instructed as he started to stroke her with his flattened tongue that covered every inch of what it needed to. She worked her hips against his face. Her body felt like she was floating. Her cries were loud and rattled her chest. Her toes curled and her back arched so deep her head was off of the ground.

"What a good girl." He coaxed pulling her onto his lap. He wrapped her legs around him and slid her on top of his extremely hard cock. He let out a hiss and clung to her. "I want you to ride me the way you were thinking about when you were in your room."

Poppi looked down at him, she was surprised her thoughts traveled so far. She was too focused on how he filled her. How the slight curve of his penis hit a spot in her that made her feel rabid and the pressure from his girth made electricity shoot through her spine. Her fingers clung to his shoulder and she started to work her hips like she would if she was in the bathtub. Letting her hips roll with the running water from the stream. He planted kisses down her chest, her breast, up her jawbone, and back to her lips.

"I can't wait to make love to you for the rest of my life." He whispered against her lips. "My soul belongs to you Poppi, you're my sun, my moon, my earth. I give you my everything. I will stand beside you in front of God and man and claim you as mine." His voice was strained with passion their bodies desperately feeding from each other.

"Oh, Zander." Her voice stretched with tears. "Your love is my magic. You have changed my life so much in such a short amount of time. I love you more than I thought I could ever love a man. You have my soul. You have all of me if you want it." Zander pulled her face down to him. Kissing her passionately. His body rocked against hers. Keahi wouldn't have put him in her path if she wasn't meant to feel this deep amount of belonging in a place where she once ached. She'd never dreamed of a love that felt like this. One that was so deep that she could feel it in the core of her. That it connected pieces of her that had been lost to the ether for so long she'd forgotten they existed.

Their eyes locked as their orgasm hit them. A flood of intensity hit her spine and flooded through her. She felt a rush of cold wash over her as she clutched to him. He pulled her back down to him and they kissed ferociously nipping each other's lips and clinging on to each other like they may disappear if they let go. Poppi broke the kiss and looked at him. "That was amazing."

"Poppi, we're floating."

"You feel that too?" She laid on his shoulder. She looked down and she saw her claw marks on the ground and her bikini thrown in two different directions with Zander's trunks. "Oh god! How did we-"

"I think the best thing to do is get down, go inside, and we can see how high I can get you on round two." He kissed her deeply and she felt them sink back into the earth.

53

Invitation

P oppi stretched her fingers across the empty bed. She was sure last
night was a dream. There was no way she was floating during sex
with Zander in reality. She didn't know what was in the weed her sister
gave her, but she'd be sure to smoke every night she was here if it gave
her dreams like that. She felt recharged and refreshed as she walked
into the bathroom and took a steamy shower. Poppi relived Zander's
touches and kisses along her new body. She washed in her favorite body
wash and felt there were no stretch marks that she hated. She looked
down at herself and she couldn't see the many scars and knicks that
happened along her marriage.

She stepped out of the shower and walked into her closet. She looked
at the full-body mirror and studied her reflection. Her scars from her
car accident were gone, the things that she hated most the things that
Mitchell hated about her, were gone. Her breast sat high. Her curves
framed her body to the perfect hourglass. Her ass was the perfect-sized
peach to round out the curves of her thick thighs and black-painted toes.
She looked at the small pouch over her waxed vagina. She saw the bite
mark on her chest, it was the only blemish other than her artful tattoos.
Last night was real. She was tangled in the sheets with Zander all night
and she still couldn't believe it was real.

She looked at her face. Her eyes were lighter brown they sparkled
like gemstones. Her lips were fuller and poutier. Her skin had a golden
glow to it like she had been dusted in highlighter. She was smiling at
herself in the mirror. The body from her marriage had died in the
field last night. She was free really free, even her body showed it. Even
her hair had gotten lighter. It was a rich honey bronze color that was

almost blonde. She twirled around. She was going to have fun and enjoy showing what Zander had done to her, she looked at her outfit for the day and grinned. "That's going to be perfect."

Poppi strutted down the hallway in a backless vintage navy blue sundress with white trim. She wore her hair up in a curly bun thanks to the new beautiful coil curls that her hair decided to turn into. She wore red open-toe pumps and white sunglasses on the top of her head. Her face was shimmering with moisturizer and her full lips were painted perfectly with red lip gloss. She looked like a bombshell and she couldn't wait to say good morning to the one who made it possible. She felt herself be pulled into another room and the door slam behind her. She felt a hard slap to the side of her flawless skin. Anger boiled in her. She turned around and punched him in the jaw. "What the hell is wrong with you?" She snapped. "You don't get to put your fucking hands on me anymore you fucking animal!"

"Where the hell were you last night and this morning? You missed breakfast! I had no idea where you were, Pearl asked me where you were and I had to lie."

She looked at herself in the mirror. She thought there would be a bruise or at least a red mark, but there was nothing. He couldn't even hurt her anymore. She fixed the lipstick smudge and looked at him in the mirror. "Well at least you're good at that, and I doubt you cared where I was Mitch, I'm sure you were fine with keeping Carmen company."

"Fuck you bitch! You're my wife did you forget that?! You're to be in the room tonight and I'm not arguing about it."

"Firstly," She turned to him. "I'm *not* your wife. I stopped being your wife when you started fucking your boss's girlfriend and you two jumped me and put me in a goddamn psych ward. Secondly, since I'm tired of you putting your hands on me and cheating on me, we're getting a divorce; I'm not asking anymore. I'm telling you. I'm done with you. I'm done being your punching bag, I'm done being whatever you think your version of a wife is supposed to be. I am done being Mrs. Mitchell Baxter. It's over Mitchell, we're done."

"You can't do that! I'll have you back in Saint Helens so fast your head will spin! How dare you be so ungrateful!?"

Poppi heard herself laugh at him. "With what reasoning? Not with the lawsuit we have on them for unlawful imprisonment, they're holding people against their will, and I do mean sound mind and body will not mentally ill unstable against their will. Do you think that you're going to get that bullshit hack job of a conservatorship to hold up now? Absolutely not. My mother can't save you, babe. It's over."

"You won't get a dime!"

"I'm a lawyer at a high-value firm, my sister is a world-renowned psychologist and my other one works for one of the most famous families in the world. You don't think I can't be fine?" She laughed and folded her arms. "Mitchell my father is one of the most famous classical producers in the Jacaris records. He's been dying for this day, Mitchell. I'll be fine without your money. Not that I even needed it."

"My mother will disown you!" Mitchell shouted. "My grandmother will never allow you to get anything from us ever again! My brother-"

"Is my brother-in-law. And as weird as it sounds, I don't think I'm going to be too far from the Baxter-Holden family. I just won't ever have to speak to you again." She smirked. "Get a lawyer, Mitchell, I want this done quickly."

"You can't do this to me! You can't leave me! I own you."

"I'm sure you think that, but sadly, like always, you're wrong." Poppi felt him lunging for her, she swung open the door and Zander stood in front of her. "Good morning Mr. Bell."

"If it isn't my favorite little flower." He smiled at her. "You look beautiful this morning. Did you do something with your hair?"

"Thank you." She touched her hair. "I woke up and it was this color."

"You look well rested." Zander complimented. "Glowing even."

Poppi blushed. "Did you sleep well?"

"Like a rock." Their eyes stayed on each other 'I want to kiss you. Bad.' He fidgeted with the door panel.

'Me too.' She smiled even wider. Leaning forward a bit closer to him.

"If you're going to eye fuck my wife at least acknowledge me first." Mitchell pushed past her. Poppi tried to ignore the small smirk on Zander's face. "Are you ready for the meeting?"

"Yes, I was coming to let Poppi know they're looking for her at the greenhouse. Your sister just passed me. And we've been invited to go out tonight since my parents and the Abraxas had a prior engagement."

"Awesome! Knowing Lavender, she's picked a nice little dance spot."

"You do know your sister so well." He looked at her. "Enjoy you're shopping trip."

Mitchell watched Zander leave. "We aren't finished talking yet. You're not leaving me." She watched him storm off behind Zander's confident and relaxed stride. Zander looked back at her and kissed the air. She blushed and kissed back. Poppi tried to conceal the large grin she had as she walked to the garden.

54

Unique Findings

P oppi walked through the greenhouse to see if there was any evidence they had been there. She picked up the blunt that was tossed under a long vine. It was barely smoked. She tucked it into her pocket. She smiled thinking of him pulling her up on him and kissing her in the warm water. The breeze let the fragrance of new floral smells tickle her nose. She hadn't smelled anything like that while she was out there the first time. She saw Claudia, Pearl, and Lavender standing around the spot where she and Zander made love in. Heat rose to her cheeks, they weren't exactly careful, and the way he made her scream was far from quiet. She walked behind them joining the crowd.

"Pearl this is stunning." Claudia squeezed her shoulders. "You did a hell of a job."

"Thank you, but I can't take responsibility for this." Pearl tilted her head. "Even I could never perfect flowers this way in such a short amount of time. These were grown."

"What is going on here?!" Poppi asked clearing her throat. Claudia turned first and she saw a glimpse of color.

"There she is!" Pearl turned to her holding a bright and vividly red poppy in her hand. "I almost feel like I should curtsy." She pulled her up close to the empty nest of land where her claw marks used to be. Flowers and fruit trees coated the once-empty plot of land. She was shocked at the vivid colors of the three different roses, the poppies, bursts of lavender, and flowers she'd only seen in books growing between two trees connected in some of their branches.

"Oryn's ashes who are you and what did you do with my sister?" Lavender twirled her around. "Girl you look good as hell! What got into you?"

"Zander." Pearl giggled like a schoolgirl. Claudia visibly blushed. "Oh, I'm sorry darling! I forgot he was your son." She laughed aloud wrapping her arm around Claudia. "But you saw him this morning, his eyes were brighter, he had a pep in his step, and he swam for an hour before he ate breakfast with us. And he out ate everyone, including Freddie, and Freddie loves breakfast."

Poppi felt the heat burning in her ears. She looked down at the ground and prayed it would swallow her whole. She didn't want to tell Claudia that she and Zander were together until after the divorce, but thanks to whatever it was that they had together it was louder and more obvious than either of them intended. She could see that it had affected everyone. Pearl was giddy and filled with laughter. She wasn't anywhere near this peppy last night, even her eyes were more vivid. Showing light green flecks in them that glistened like the sands of time. Her fangs in her smile looked sharper, and so did her cheekbones. She wore a green sundress and it made her deep skin stand out. Her hair was in a high pony and she was smiling with black lipstick from ear to ear.

"Is this true?" Claudia asked. Her face was stern, and Poppi felt like she was caught with her hand inside of her purse. "Did you sleep with my son?"

Poppi didn't want to look Claudia in the eye. "I am so sorry Mrs. Bell." The embarrassment made her wish she could drop dead.

"Claudia don't be too hard on her, it takes two, and let's be honest here they have every right to do whatever they want they're adults with cheating partners. No one enjoys cheating, but Poppi's getting divorced, and Zander has never wanted to marry Carmen. You don't need powers to know that."

Claudia looked at Poppi. "Do you?"

"Do I what Mrs. Bell?"

"Love him? She said that this couldn't have come about unless something really powerful came about and according to her that something was love, and if you two were the ones who were out here... Then that means you love him. So do you?"

Poppi looked at them. Did she love him? She adored him. He was the only thing to get her out of bed other than the children on the days when she just wanted to die. Did she love the way he talked to her? Or the way he looked at her? What could be said about the feelings she had for him to his mother? Poppi took a deep breath. "Yes, Mrs. Bell. I love your son more than I think any other woman could love your son. I love him with all of me. And I am getting divorced, I'd never string him along, I will never hurt him with malice intent. He means the world to me."

Claudia hugged her tightly. She was expecting a different reaction but eased into the hug. "I am so thankful for this." She sighed. "You don't know how scared I was for Carmen to be my daughter-in-law when you were sitting right there."

"Ladies let's get a picture in front of it!" Lavender said finishing her picture-taking.

"I was just about to say that." Pearl wrapped her arms around Lavender and Claudia and Claudia wrapped hers around Poppi. "Everybody say Shopping!"

55

Elevator

Z ander stood in the front of the elevator trying to ignore that for the next eight floors he would have Mitchell staring at him from the back. He couldn't even enjoy the bliss of his evening with her in worry that he would come looking for her and they would cause an issue at his newest client's home. He couldn't stop thinking about how she felt sleeping against his chest. Or how she rolled over on fours and let him fuck her from behind before he took his shower this morning while they were both barely awake. He felt like Mitchell was trying to read his thoughts. He took a deep breath and cleared his thoughts.

"Poppi went missing last night," Mitchell spoke finally. "Do you know where she went?"

"Nope." He looked at his reflection in the glass mirror door. "Did you ask her?"

"She's gotten crazy in Italy. She thinks that she can disrespect me like I'm nobody." He muttered. "She's been acting weird ever since she met you. I knew I should have nipped it in the bud the second she introduced herself to you." He continued making Zander roll his eyes. He wanted her the first night he met her, nothing was going to get in his way of knowing her, other than respecting her boundaries.

"Maybe if you weren't fucking my fiance five minutes from our office she wouldn't have felt inclined to grow close to someone else." He shrugged nonchalantly.

"So, you were with her then?" Mitchell shook his head. "That fucking whore. She's going back to that hospital and I'm not going to let her out until she's fucking brain-dead."

"What did you just say?" He turned to him. His jaw clenched. They had three floors left and that was plenty of time for him to do some of the damage he'd inflicted on Poppi for all of their years together if he said the wrong thing.

"I think you heard me motherfucker. I'm going to put her ass away," He folded his arms and let a smug grin cover his face. "And after I do I'm going to fuck Carmen on our bed, we'll recreate what happened the first time she tried to pull this getting brave shit."

Zander nodded and swung as hard as he could. His fist connected with Mitchell's jaw and he staggered back. He stood up and walked up to Zander throwing a wild blow that didn't connect but left his ribs open. He took his left hand slammed his fist into his ribs and caught him again on the other side. He swung for every unexplained sadness spell he felt for the past five years and put the pieces together that he and Poppi had been calling to each other for ages, but he never realized it until last night.

Zander pulled him from the floor and looked at his scrunched face he covered his hands with. "Do you feel that? That fear that it's never going to end? That panic that he's going to kill me heart racing panic? Poppi felt that every time you walked in the fucking room, but lucky for her, and for you, after this elevator ride you'll understand to keep your fucking distance from my girl!" He punched him square in the nose and dropped him.

Mitchell spat blood from his lip. "I won't let you get away with this you son of a-" He flinched when Zander lifted his fist to him again. He glared up at Zander's amused laughter. "I'm telling Frederick. I'll get you fired for this!"

Zander straightened himself as he stood. "What are you going to tell our boss, one of the most family-oriented men I've ever met, that you were constantly calling your wife outside of her name and I, your superior, defended her honor? Or are you going to tell my father that you were fucking his future daughter-in-law and that's the reason there will no longer be a wedding?" He fixed his tie. "Shut up you sniveling worm."

The elevator dinged and Keres stepped into the elevator and the door closed behind him. His back was facing Mitchell and looked at Zander. "I take it you finally released that anger?"

Zander let the hot air flare through his nose. "I don't want you to think I just go around punching my coworkers in elevators." He shook his head. "I lost it and it won't happen again."

Keres pulled out a spare handkerchief, "Sure it will." He turned around and handed it to Mitchell. "Those Nichols women are women you feel the need to ride into battle for. And with what you and Poppi have..." He dabbed Mitchell's nose and hissed in grimace. "I'm surprised it took this long. The first woman to ever speak to my little viper out of turn, well they lost their tongue." He stood. "Be glad it was him you were dealing with and not me, if it were me you'd be going to this meeting without a few digits." He chuckled taking his place beside Zander.

56

Executive

F rederick and Sol were chatting in the conference room as Zander
and Keres walked in. Silas was going over some files beside his
father but wasn't much for the conversation. Sol looked up at Keres
whose eyes were filled with mischief. "Why do you look like the cat who
ate the canary?" He asked standing to shake his son's hand. Keres' lips
curled into a smile. He nudged Zander and shook his head playfully.

"It appears your son has found someone who has the same overprotective gene when it comes to the ladies of the Nichols family." Silas
looked up from the files he was studying, his heterochromatic eyes were
playful. "Am I right?" He grinned. "I mean you and my brother are just
oozing with prince-valiant testosterone."

"Oh fuck you Si." Keres rolled his eyes. "If you would let this celibacy
thing die with the stone ages you'd have some Prince-Vailiant testosterone too." Keres sat beside his brother who rolled his eyes and stood
to shake Zander's hand.

"Pleasure to see you again Mr. Bell. I hope you know I'm only joking.
I was told by my PR that I don't do it enough." He sat back down across
from him. "I suppose you don't have that problem."

"Well, I'm not the one who is the CEO of an international beauty
brand." Zander shrugged. "I suppose you have to be out there shaking
hands and kissing models." He pulled out his folders for the investments
he wanted to work in. He heard Keres laugh aloud at his last comment
and he looked at him. "Did I say something funny?"

"The idea of my antisocial brother kissing models and shaking hands
is a vision I'd die to see. I've asked this stick in the mud to come out
with us, we're in a foreign country and although I have one of the most

beautiful women in the world on my arm, I'm sure there is one out there that isn't a complete knock out with the matching personality, but my brother doesn't really enjoy the dating scene anymore. He's just waiting for love to fall out of the sky."

"If we could get off my love life and the reasons we're here." He looked at his father. "Are we waiting on anyone else?"

Frederick looked up from his paperwork. "Hey, yeah, where is Mitchell?" He asked looking at Zander. "I thought that you and he were riding together."

Zander shrugged. "We were dad, I don't know know maybe he had to use the bathroom." He looked up and Mitchell walked in. His face was hastily cleaned from their conversation in the elevator. He watched him as he walked to and sat in the seat beside him. Keres stifled a laugh as he tapped his pen on the folders. Keres was playful and Zander enjoyed it. He was sure he would get along with Brantley, and now he was having hopes of having a brother-in-law group chat where they took the kids out and watched football in a sports bar while the women did whatever they wanted.

"Well now that we have anyone." Sol eyed Mitchell suspiciously. "Are we okay to start?"

Mitchell looked up pushing his glasses up to his bridge with a wince. "Yes sir, we're ready."

Zander went through all of the investments that Sol and Silas wanted to him to look after. He expressed how he was a fan of the idea of Silas opening a few spas/hotels in tourist areas around the world. They agreed that Carmen Grace would be a good look since she just landed the part in a new Disney film. She could usher in the New Era of Bone and Berry. They also agreed on several other things, like the villa as an amazing investment and the way they'd decorated made it even more of a destination than before. Zander looked at his watch. "Sol, I do believe we have enough time to join the wives or hit the course."

"I'm taking it you and Keres are joining the ladies?"

"Like you had to ask." Keres stood. "You wanna come?" He looked at Silas "You know Ma always loves to fuss over you."

"I'd rather not, Dad, what do you and Fred say to a few rounds?"

Sol smiled. "Mitchell, how about you join us?"

"Gladly." He stood gathering his things and walking out behind Sol, and Frederick."

Silas looked at the two of them as he packed his suitcase. "Tell me, Zander," He looked up at him. "How does it feel to know that your life is about to change forever?"

"What do you mean?" He asked.

"You're officially going to be the investment broker for an international beauty firm. I can't expect that is going to be something that happens to you every day." He held out his hand. "Congratulations on everything."

"Thank you." He shook his hand and they watched him go. Keres clasped him on the shoulder.

"Forgive my brother. He's... High strung. Now, c'mon, we've got women to spoil."

57

Shopping

Poppi held up a deep green shirt with silver buttons and a black tie. "Do you think Zander will like this?" She asked Lavender who was debating herself for a dress shirt for Keres for the Oprea. "Or do you think I should go with this since I brought that dress in the same color?" She held up a deeper green shirt with a silver tie. She dreamed of doing this with her sisters. Gushing about their partners while surprising them with exquisite gifts. She could picture Zander in either of them, but she was leaning toward the one that matched her dress.

"You two have to look like a unit now, you know since you're practically royalty! You're literally gonna be the queen of the fae!" Lavender gushed. "My sister the queen!"

"Can you keep your voice down and tell me which one."

"Ugh fine." She pointed to the green and silver. "You know you're taking all of the fun out of this 'my sister is the ultimate magical baddie of the fae realm.' Like what am I supposed to brag about to all of my legion friends if you aren't going to let me?" She held up a black shirt with blue silk patterns and a blue shirt with a black tie.

"You know I have other accomplishments other than an alleged magical ability." She pointed. "The left combo looks better."

"You would say some shit like that while you're literally shimmering bitch." She rolled her eyes. "You'd better be lucky I've been told that you're level 1 access and no one can even breathe a word to Legion about your existence, but I literally saw Pearl materialize a bouquet of roses on the breakfast table this morning so it's going to be kind of hard to answer why immortals have powers again without a great fertility witch."

"I'm sure they will come up with some sort of good lie." Poppi ensured. "Maybe they don't even believe it so they will keep it secret." Poppi shrugged. "Who knows."

"Poppi, can I talk to you?" Carmen asked looking Lavender up and down. "Alone?"

"I've got to go look at cuff links anyway, but if you need me call me."

"I'm fine." She insisted and went back to looking at the shirts.

"Mitchell hates green." Carmen fiddled with a shirt. "He says it makes him look pale."

"So I've heard, I've only been married to him for five years." Poppi rolled her eyes and looked at her from her search for shirts. "What do you want?"

"Where was Zander last night? Did you tell him anything?"

"I didn't tell him anything." She looked at her. "Why would I? It's not my place, he'll just think I'm crazy. You saw to that didn't you?"

Carmen bit her lip. "I did what was best. I thought you needed some time you were acting insane!"

"My husband was screwing a woman I know in my bed while my niece was being born. Yeah, I was a little angry." She shook her head. "Not for my marriage I mean that thing is as dead as your performance on the soaps, no I was angry for Zander. He didn't deserve that."

"You don't know him, he's a workaholic who never cares about me. He didn't even check on me for the month I was away. I'm going to end it with him soon so I can be with Mitchell full-time."

"You don't know Mitchell either, so I'll give you a warning. You should go, you should leave well enough alone and finish whatever sad pathetic fling this is and go. I've seen what you can do to a woman, and you know what they say about Karma."

Carmen laughed "You know he told me the happiest day of his life was when he and I watched you go out on the stretcher together. He told them that you were some crazed ex and if it wasn't for me, he'd be dead. He told me he loved me; we spent every night together."

"I bet he called you his good luck charm, or something too, didn't he?" She handed her a blue shirt with a bright yellow tie. "Here, these are his favorite colors to wear. Enjoy your life with him, Carmen, at least it's your choice." Poppi took her things and walked to the counter.

Poppi brought the shirt and tie. She wanted to be angry at Carmen and cause a scene, but she knew that all Carmen wanted was to have a reason to prove Mitchell right about her, and she refused to give her that. She had a perfect thing with Zander, a man who cared about her deeply. She hoped that Carmen would never have to endure the things that she did. She hoped Mitchell really loved her, and they lived happily ever after. Poppi walked outside where Lavender stood with Keres, and Zander stood alone. "What are you two doing here?" She asked looking up at him.

"We're here to celebrate closing the deal, and having the most beautiful women in the world on our arms." Keres wrapped his arm around Lavender. "Right?"

Zander held his hand out for her she slid her fingers in with ease. "Absolutely."

58

Exposed

Z ander moaned loudly in their private walk-in shower. Poppi had pressed him up against the wall and started sucking his dick. swallowing all of him down. "Shouldn't I be the one thanking you?" He moaned under the shower. "Didn't you buy me a gift?" He held her wet hair in his hand. She always put his hand on the back of her head when she wanted his dick in her mouth, something he was becoming all too happy with. He watched her bob up and down on him and he couldn't take it anymore. "Stand up Poppi," He commanded. "I wanna fuck you."

She stood on his command and he bent her over the shower chair. He knelt down and gave her pussy a few good licks. Savoring the taste of her on his tongue. He was excited they were leaving together in just a few days. Soon they would be doing this all over his apartment, or wherever she felt safest. Her legs began to quiver and he pulled away. He lay a satisfying little swat to her bottom and she let out a frustrating moan. "What happened to you wanting to fuck me?" She looked back at him.

"You're right baby girl, how could I be so cruel in teasing you? We've had to wait all day for this." He slid inside her and she let out a moan that was mixed with relief and pleasure. He gripped her hips and long stroked her sweet wetness. Teasing the both of them until the strokes became deeper and harder. She griped around him and he let out a groan. "I didn't think you were spiteful, trying to me cum already." He teased her kissing the back of her neck.

He quickened his pace making the sound of their flesh and moans merge together in the echoes of their bathroom. "Fuck Poppi! Your pussy feels like heaven." He rubbed her clit desperate for another taste of her he licked her fingers. His strokes became faster, hungrier to fill her with his cum. His legs wobbled, but he couldn't stop. "You treat your dick so good Starshine, I am so honored that you chose me. I love you so much, Poppi Nichols."

Her body shuddered and he felt the warming sensation of her juices coating him. He could spend the rest of his life using everything in him to make her cum multiple times a day, the smell of it was enough to drive him insane "Thank you, Starshine, thank you for cumming on me." He clenched her breast. His orgasm wasn't far behind hers now. Her cumming always brought him to damn near full orgasm. He thrust deeper inside of her as she moved her hips with him. He knew he would have to leave her soon and wanted to have something to think about while they tried to keep their hands off of each other. "I want you to taste me cum. I want you to taste how we are together.

She happily dropped back down to her knees and started to suck again. The moans and slurps she was doing to him made his toes curl as he sank into the seat. "You suck my dick so good angel, I don't think I've ever had my dick sucked like this." He groaned as he used her hair to set the pace. She licked his tip and then suctioned herself down to his shaft. "Do you taste how spectacular you are? This is your dick Poppi, you treat it so good." He pumped his hips into her mouth some more before expelling his release down her throat. She sucked until he was completely flaccid and with a long chain of drool pulled away.

He dropped to his knees kissing her passionately. "God, I hate to leave you." He sighed.

"It's okay honey, I know we have to pretend tonight. We are so close to leaving and being free together that I can almost taste it." She grinned as he dried her off and slid a robe onto her body. He kissed her neck as he looked at them in the mirror. A grin pulled across her sex-drunk face. "If you don't leave now I'm going to make you bend me over the counter."

He kissed her behind her ear. "Thanks to you I think I can do a quickie."

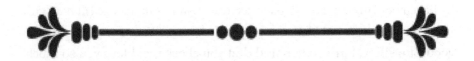

ZANDER walked back into his room in a black robe. A gift bag sat in the center of his bed, opening it he could see that it wasn't from anyone other than Poppi. He touched the Italian silk material and smiled. She knew him so well it made him see how many people didn't, how he was willing to throw his life away for a woman who barely knew his birthday or his favorite color. He never realized how nice it could be to have someone be the things he'd always dreamed of. It was unique and scary.

He was also scared about the magic part. What did it mean for them? Did he have powers? Were they only through Poppi? He wouldn't hammer her with these questions since it all appeared to be new to her too. They would learn this and whatever else came their way together. They spent long enough trying to navigate the world apart. He walked to his closet and started pulling his close out for the night, he looked forward to seeing Keres and Lavender in a spot as a couple, most of the time they acted like lovey-dovey business associates.

"Where the hell have you been?" Carmen stormed out of their in-room bathroom.

"I was taking a shower."

"Why didn't you just come in and join me?"

Because I was taking a shower with my girlfriend.' He wanted to answer but held his tongue. "I didn't know you were in there." He lied.

"Finally, we can spend some alone time together." She wrapped her arms around him. "I'm glad that all the business of today is done and all we get to do is go have fun in the clubs with young people."

"Carmen, we should talk."

She pulled away. "Okay." She sat on their bed. "Let's talk."

"Have you cheated on me? At all."

She looked at him. "Oh my god, not this again Zander! No, I haven't cheated on you." She rolled her eyes. "I can't believe you would–"

"I'll be so fucking glad when she's out of the picture." Zander read from one of the emails the private investigator sent. "I can't live without your juicy cock." He tossed the paper towards her. Then he pulled out another. "I can't wait to see you in Cali babe we're going to have so much fun, I've missed you." He tossed that one on the bed. "Guess what! Z's got the job in Maine so now we'll get to see each other all the time!" He looked up at her "How long have you been fucking him?"

Carmen looked up at him and then back down to the papers. "These aren't mine they could be anybody's!" She screeched.

"I gave Keres Abraxas 25,000 fucking dollars to save you! To prove to myself that you wouldn't do this to me! You were with me for the long haul, but here you are fucking him down the street from my office!" He flung the picture on the bed. "Oh look here's one of you fucking him in a car! And outside of the club, you accused me of cheating at! And here is my golden ticket!" He held up the picture of Carmen and Mitchell watching Poppi get shoved into the back of an ambulance. "You said you got those bruises from an action scene!"

"I did!"

"Stop fucking lying to me, Carmen!" Zander rebutted sternly. "You owe me 25,000 dollars, which you'll have since I negotiated you a nice little ambassadorship from Bone and Beauty today. And I want my fucking ring back! It was a mistake to even assume something like this could work with someone like you."

She looked up at him from the pictures tears streaming down her face. "You loved her first!"

"I didn't know her a year ago! I knew **you**! *I loved you*! And you were fucking her husband and had the nerve the unmitigated gal to tarnish my view of her when you were already causing her damage beyond repair! You were fucking him, Keres, and Silas–"

"I never fucked Silas! He said I wasn't the right person, whatever the fuck that meant!"

"It meant that he has more sense than I or his brother did." He held his hand out and watched her slide the ring from her finger and put it in his hand. He dropped the ring in his pocket. "You can keep this room for the rest of the trip, when we get back I want your shit out of my house. I want you out of my life. I never want to speak to you again Carmen Grace, it's over."

"Zander you don't mean that!" She cried trying to hold on to him as he pulled away. "Zander please give me time to-" He shut the door on his past and walked downstairs. Poppi stood in a yellow backless dress that barely touched her knees. Lavender was dressed in pants and a flowy top giggling as Keres whispered in her ear.

"Finally!" He broke himself away from Lavender to give him dap. "The fourth amigo! Are we ready to paint the town red!"

Zander wrapped his arm around Poppi's waist. "We have so much to celebrate!"

59
Opera

Poppi woke up in Zander's arms her head still pumping from last night. They started at this cute little nightclub and ended up partying on the beach with a bunch of magical creatures. Poppi looked up at the beautiful man sleeping beside her. She sighed, she was never used to being loved out loud. Her mother didn't, her father couldn't, Lydia died because of it, and her husband flat-out refused. Mitchell would love anyone else but her. She was his throwaway, his just in case so that if Paulette didn't leave him in the will he could leech off her inheritance.

Last night Zander was a little drunk, but very loud and proud about who she was to him. He complimented her several times in front of Keres and Lavender's friends Nixia and Maeve calling her things like 'his future wife.' 'His girlfriend.' 'The best thing that had ever happened to him.' Her personal favorite moment of the night was when he pulled her to a dark secluded dock under the boardwalk and fingered her until she came just so he could taste what it was like behind a shot of Tequila. On their way home he whispered to her how jealous he was they wasted more time just to keep them apart. She was sure he didn't mean that, but when they got home, they had sex twice and then he held her telling her how much he loved her and how happy he was for them to be going home together.

"Where are you going princess?" He groaned wrapping his arms around her waist. "We don't have to be up for another hour."

"I know," She giggled snuggling back beside him as he put his head on her chest. "But I couldn't help myself I had to shift."

"What can I do to help you get some much-needed rest gorgeous?"

"Aren't you hung over?" She chuckled. "You went pretty hard last night."

"I'm sorry I couldn't help myself. I was celebrating." He looked up at her. "Did I embarrass you?"

She giggled and kissed him. "Screaming 'Hey everyone I'm finally with my girlfriend.' Was very funny."

"I did say that a lot didn't I?"

Poppi thought about it. Zander called her some sort of name that dealt with commitment. She was 'his lady', 'the most beautiful woman in the world' and to a group of shifters, he called her his soul mate. "You said it over 40 times."

"God Poppi I'm sorry! You just got out of a commitment why on earth did I feel the need to push it so hard." He sighed "I guess I was just so happy to finally get to give you public displays of affection."

"I understand, I guess when you meet someone you love and care about you wanna show them off," She traced her finger up and down his arm. "I'm just not used to it."

"I'm sorry my love I'll try to dial it back." He kissed her cheek. "I will be as opaque as you'd like when it comes to our relationship."

"Just for now, until my divorce is final." She kissed him. "Eventually we will be loud and proud all over the place."

Zander rolled on top of her. "But for now I'm good with being here." He kissed her deeply then her neck and slid her nightgown up. Her naked body expose. "Gods I am the luckiest man on earth." He smiled before going between her legs.

POPPI took her time getting dressed, though she still felt the anxiety of being rushed. It now felt like a ghost haunting the edges of her mind. Instead of having a husband who chastised her for spending too long on her hair and makeup, she had a man who would stop what he was doing just to admire her. She would feel the heat of his gaze while she was filling her smoky cat eye, or undressing her with his eyes as she slid on her black silhouette dress with the silver peekaboo at the lined at the hip. She wasn't used to having someone look at her the way he did, it set her heart on fire.

After she was done being admired by her partner she took a few moments to admire herself in the mirror, she never thought she'd be going to see Esmeray Jacaris in an opera, but she was excited, she was told that she was a jack of all trades, she could sing, dance, and even play the violin. Pearl bragged about her when she gave Poppi the tickets promising her she would enjoy it more than she thought she could ever enjoy something so unique to the experience. She felt cool metal on her neck before she looked in the mirror to see a beautiful sapphire necklace garnishing her neck. "Zander this is beautiful! When did you have time?!"

"I had a meeting, and it was by a jewelry store, and I couldn't resist. You're so beautiful. I know I've said it so many times," He looked at her in the mirror, the necklace bringing out an extra level of beauty. "But sometimes you leave me breathless."

Poppi touched the necklace and looked at the two of them in the mirror. He wore his gift and his tie matched the silver in her dress. He was smiling so brightly at her it made her feel doubt for the first time. What if he realized somewhere down the road that he was being too good to someone who didn't deserve it. "You're being too good to me Zander." She shook her head "I don't know if I deserve it."

He turned her around to face him. "You my darling deserve every-thing the light touches. I'm honestly doing the bare minimum." He shrugged nonchalantly. "I could be doing more."

"Zander the way you treat me is far from the bare minimum and you know it." She poked his chest. "I appreciate everything you're doing for me and I really don't know what else to say."

He kissed her. "You don't have to say anything Poppi," He chuckled "You could just enjoy it."

Zander walked Poppi down the hall and Claudia snapped a picture like they were in prom. "Ma!"

"Oh shush! You never went to your prom! I can at least get a picture of you and this beauty queen. Get close together like you like each other." Claudia winked playfully.

Zander pulled Poppi to him and they posed in the respectable pose with him holding her waist and the two of them smiling at his mother. "If it makes you feel any better I couldn't go to mine either" Poppi smiled up at him.

Frederick put his arm around his wife beautifully dressed in blue. "Sometimes I think she forgets she's going out too. Honey, why don't you take a picture with them?" After several shots with them and the Abraxas family Poppi felt like she was dreaming. The love and togetherness she felt from them for her was such a lovely feeling. Even Lavender partook in the pictures.

"More memories for your wall." She smiled at Zander. They waited until everyone was loading up in the cars and Lavender looked at them "Keres ordered you two your own private car for tonight so when you are ready your bags are packed and I packed you a go bag in the back seat. She looked at both of them. "I'm so excited for you all. If you get the feeling something may go wrong we will be on your back so fast their heads will spin." Lavender looked at both of them. "I don't have to tell you to call me when you land?"

"Of course not," Poppi reassured.

"Great!" She smiled. "Let's get this show on the road."

POPPI sat beside Mitchell during the Oprea. She could feel him staring at her. She knew Zander was on her left, but it didn't make her less uncomfortable. She pretended not to notice. She could feel him getting angrier beside her. She looked at him finally. "Can I help you?" She whispered.

"Come with me right now." Mitchell stood and took her hand. She looked back at Zander begrudgingly but took Mitchell's hand as he led her to the concessions' abandoned hallway.

Poppi watched him stare at her and think about what she was going to say. How she was going to spend her last night in Italy being verbally assaulted by him. "What is it, Mitchell?"

"Did you spend the night with Zander last night?" He asked looking at her.

"You're wasting my time with this! I could ask you something like were you fucking old girl in our bed while I was in the fucking hospital?" She snorted. "Be so fucking serious. Do you see how dumb and a waste of time that is? It's a joke to ask the obvious."

"I am being serious! You've got to be out of your mind if you think that I'm just going to let you go Poppi. You're my wife!" He snapped at her. Grabbing her arm roughly. "I'll kill him Poppi, just like I did that little bitch you wouldn't leave for me! I'll take everything you love, and I'll burn it the fuck down! I'll ruin your entire life. I'll take everything you love, and I'll twist it. I'll ruin it. I'll devour it until you come back to me."

Poppi's eyes blurred with tears. Her jaw clenched. "You did what?"

"I killed Lydia, with insulin." Mitchell smiled as he admitted to the murder of the love of her young adult life. "That's why it looked so natural, I will make sure Zander never sees the light of day ever again. I won't lose you."

She felt the rage and the anger pouring from her heart. She didn't remember what the power of magic felt like but as Mitchell fell to his knees clenching his chest and blood running down his eyes. She'd forgotten what power felt like. She'd forgotten what it was like to be the one standing over another living being praying for mercy. He didn't deserve mercy, not from her, not from anyone he'd hurt, and especially from Lydia. She moved her foot back as he gasped for air and begged her for his life. She felt a hand on her shoulder. "Poppi."

She watched Mitchell writhe and gasp for air like a goldfish who was outside of the tank. A tear fell down her face. Lydia died alone and afraid, she did it to her. It was all her fault for not listening and bringing Mitchell around. He gripped his chest taking wheezing guttural breaths begging for air. She wanted him to die scared and alone the same way Lydia did. "Poppi, it's over sweetpea, you have to let go.." Her concentration broke and he took deep ragged breaths.

Zander wrapped her in his embrace. "C'mon sweetheart." He covered her in his arms "Let's go home. "

60

Blissful Gardens

W hen the plane landed they walked down through customs and
towards the garage, but Zander stopped when he saw a sign.
"Poppi?" He tugged at her hand to pull her back. She turned to where
he was pointing to a man holding a sign with their names on it. "I
think that's for us." She followed behind him as he walked to the man
standing there in a black suit with an earpiece. He looked very official
down to the ray ban sunglasses. Suddenly she felt eyes watching her as
she walked up to the Micheal Clark Duncan look alike.

"Excuse me are you waiting for Poppi Nichols and Zander Bell?" She
asked him adjusting her purse on her shoulder. He looked down at her
and then at Zander. He pulled out his phone and looked back up at them.

"Yes, I am looking for you two, I'm here to drive you home. Ms. Baxter
sent me." His deep gruff voice replied kindly. "I'm Carter, your personal
security."

"Personal security?" Poppi looked at Zander, and then back to him. "I
don't have personal security."

"The moment you stepped on US soil the request for you to have
security came into effect. I'll be your driver and security, and if ever
you need I am a professional chef in my spare time." He cracked a
small smile taking the bags from them. "C'mon let's get you two home."
He turned and walked ahead of them. Poppi was shocked. Why would
Paulette give her round-the-clock security? Was she really that afraid
that Mitchell would do something? Or had her sister insisted on it since
now they were magical royalty according to her and Mrs. Abraxas.

She walked behind him, her head spinning. What did all of this
mean? Was she in danger because she decided to go on a limb and be

happy for once? She thought about Zander, he didn't sign up for this. He didn't sign up to awaken some ancient power put away by her ancestors in fear of another rebellion. She was sure he would be regretting his choice of having a traumatized witch who doesn't understand her powers enough to keep them safe from whatever was marching over the horizon. She was free now, Mitchell was no longer a part of her life. She was hopeful that she would move into a cozy home closer to her office, and her sister she'd had her eye on.

They stopped at a black SUV and Carter started to load their bags. Zander told her he loved her that night and still she was worried he might change his mind. She believed he loved her, but how much baggage was too much baggage for him? Could she really allow herself to be her most authentic self when she was with him, she'd always felt she could, but what if now that the thrill of the chase was over he'd get bored with her? "Your bags are all loaded," Carter spoke cutting through her derailing train of thought. "You can get in the car now. I'll get it started." He walked to the driver's side of the vehicle.

Poppi stared at the open door for a moment. If she wanted this to be her real fresh start, if she wanted this time around to be different than her holding it all in and suppressing herself, she had to start now. Especially since her suppressions could cause far greater damage than they once were able to. She'd never used magic like the kind she was apparently blessed with. She needed to make sure he was in this, really in this, with her.

"Poppi? Are you alright?" Zander asked looking at her with concern.

She looked at Carter. "I need just a minute."

Carter looked at her and nodded. "Let me know when we're ready to take off and we'll be on our way." He turned around and she shut the door.

"Poppi what's wrong?" Zander asked putting a hand on her arm.

She took a deep breath. "We're going back to reality and I need to know if this is really what you want. I don't know what the next few months, who am I kidding, days are going to look like. I may laugh or cry or scream and I don't know if something is gonna catch on fire or explore or if flowers are gonna come raining from the sky. There may be times when I randomly levitate apparently. I've never been on my own without the leash from my mother or husband and I'm not really sure what that will look like. And I don't want to get into this car with you and expect you to be a part of my new normal and then all of a sudden you decide this is too much for this. So I need to know, is this really what you want? Am I really what you want?"

Zander looked at her, a look of shock and hurt was replaced with one of understanding and love. "Starshine, I knew you were going to be my wife when you got me high at my company Christmas party. I don't know what's going to happen with your powers, and honestly, I'm very curious." He placed his hands on her face. "Poppi, I see you're broken and damaged, but what you don't see is that you are the most beautiful mosaic I have ever seen in my life. And I have the honor of loving and caring for you. Through it all Poppi I'm going to be by your side. I have waited so long to be with you, I'm not letting you go. I trust you and I know there may be moments when we both may have to pay for the sins of the past. I won't promise my break from Carmen is as clean as it feels. But as long as we know that we can talk about it and work through it. We are unstoppable." Zander kissed her. "I love you Poppi Nichols, and I'm never giving you up."

The worry she felt melted away and she kissed him back. "I wonder if this car has a partition." She grinned mischievously kissing him again.

"You're being very tempting, Miss Nichols." He booped her nose with his finger. "And kissing me in public no less!"

"I can do that now, I'm a free woman." She kissed him again. "I can kiss you all I want."

"I like the sound of that." He grinned leaning into her reveling in her accent and the sweetness of her kisses. Zander opened the doors. "Let's get home and start this real-world thing you keep telling me about."

THEY were curled together in the backseat having small make-out sessions and mapping what their staying-together schedule would look like. Zander suggested they stay at his place tonight, but check in with Juniper and that's where they told Carter to take them. Poppi was enjoying their drive together, but she was curious about why it was taking them so long to get there. Juniper only lived 10 minutes away from the airport. They'd been driving longer than that. When she sat up to voice her concern they stopped at a tiny home security office with an intercom. Carter pressed the button. "Go ahead?" The guard responded.

"Heiress and Knight entering the garden," Carter replied.

"Copy that." There was a loud buzz and Carter drove to the gates with a large BG in the center, then they heard in his headpiece "Heiress and Knight entering the garden... I repeat... Heiress and Knight entering the garden."

"That isn't my name." Poppi looked at Zander trying not to panic.

"This isn't where you live." Zander looked out of the window as they drove up the gated culdesac. The first two homes were modern cottage homes with a boxed doorway entrance. The one on the left was painted sage green with deep brown trimming The landscaping was clean and the green grass was luscious. Across from that one was a beautiful foxglove cottage with a rustic color scheme. The driveway like the doorway, was framed with cobblestone. The black Audi Jeep looked familiar. "Isn't that Alton's car?"

Poppi squinted. "Yeah, I think it is." Poppi sat up with even more excitement bubbling in her as they drove past another house on the right, which was an English cottage home with sandy brown cobblestone and white trimming around it. Outside there was an electric blue jeep and a Mercedes SUV in the driveway. "That's Kandi and Derrick."

"Don't you think they would have told us they were moving?" Zander asked as they started up the hill. He looked at the state-of-the-art playground that took up a large place of land. The ground was painted bright green and there were so many things to play on he was sure the kids would grow out of most of it before they'd finished exploring it. There was even a picnic area. Zander looked at her. "Wouldn't they?"

"Not if a certain powerful woman told them not to." Poppi saw Alexis and Sara getting into her Mustang and start pulling away from their Modern cottage that was right at 2700 square feet from her estimation. The houses were all so beautifully planned and matched the personalities of the people she loved. Even Alex and Sara's front flower bed with a pride flag of flowers, and one hung outside of their home. She looked up at the upcoming house it looked more European and was very obviously big enough to hold a family. She felt a leap in her heart when she saw the car outside. "Ray and Cris are there!" She pointed looking at Zander. She could see the boys' bikes in the yard. She became giddy with the idea she'd be so close to so many people she'd wanted to spend time with.

She looked at the house beside Alex and Sara, and in an efficient 2 story home that was painted navy blue on the front left side of the house, with a cream color in the middle that stretched to the two-car wooden door garage. The paneling matched the navy color but was for solar power. There was even a stained glass circle window above the door opening. Lavender's new purple Audi rs5 with a forest green 1970 Plymouth Roadrunner. She felt grateful to know Lavender would finally have a place to settle.

The car stopped at a traditional cottage that, to Poppi, looked like three pieces of chocolate cake. On the right side of the house was a sun room with long rectangular windows that had stained glass paneling at the top in an array of colors. She just knew the lighting in that room would be breathtaking. She would make that her fortress of mindfulness. She looked at Zander. "I think we're home."

"Do I carry you over the threshold or... Do we wait til we're actually married?" He joked.

"I mean you can always do it twice. Or every time it's up to you." She grinned as the door opened. "Thank you, Carter."

"Of course ma'am. Welcome home. I'll bring your luggage in for you."
He insisted and walked up to the door of her home unlocked it and
started carrying bags in. Poppi watched him and hugged herself. She
was home. She was in a place surrounded by people she loved. She
looked towards the stunning European home that looked like a modern
castle filled with beautiful rose bushes and other bright vivid flowers
and wind chimes. She assumed that that was Paulette. Making sure
she could keep a watchful and protective eye on her babies.

"Hey, neighbor!" Juniper called from across the street in front of a
two-story home English with stone masonry on the bottom layer and
royal blue paneling on the front. Juniper had a sunroom too. Hers was
more pulled out and her windows had an art piece of the ocean to blur
out her front windows since they were so close to the road. Poppi loved
how her sister thought, and now she'd never have to worry about seeing
Oliver or the girls again, they'd be up under each other like a pride of
lionesses'. She had a kangaroo pouch on and Willow let out a gleeful
squeal.

"Hiya there neighbor!" She waved back. "When do I get the grand
tour?" She asked.

"As soon as you two come up for air!" She giggled "I'll call you later.
Bye, Zander!"

"Good night Juniper." They watched her go back inside.

Carter handed Poppi the keys and looked at Zander. "These belong
to you, Mr. Bell." He handed him another set. "Your home was the
first to the left. And here is your key card. "There are some very nice
things around here. Like if you drive down that way there is a spa and
a market. There are also some nice little shops." He handed her the
envelope with the information.

"How long did it take her to get all of this?"

Carter chuckled. "She's been working on this for a while, she made
sure everyone worked and built their homes together. Rayden's bakery
has moved and so has Roxanna's studio, but I'm sure if you'd like a tour
you can call me or take one of the cars. Paulette said you and Zander
would be able to choose who got what. " He pointed at the new all-black

Lotus Eletre SUV and silver Hyundai Ioniq 5 both of them sat in the driveway with bows on the top. "If you need anything my number is the first on the paper, and Please enjoy the bliss of Blissful Gardens." Carter got in the car and drove back down out of site.

"I thought Paulette was joking when she said one day she was going to make her own gated community." Poppi laughed. "She actually did it." Poppi looked around. "And I don't think I ever want to leave."

"Well Miss Nichols," Zander scooped her into his arm. "With all the christening we'll be doing I doubt we'll have the time to go anywhere." He grinned walking her into their home and closing the door behind them.

61

Settling In

P oppi sat in the sunroom with Willow watching her coo and laugh
as she played with the newest thing Zander had gotten her over
the past week. Poppi had spent the entire week with her nieces and
nephews partly because she wanted their parents to have a well-de-
served break and partly because they flat-out refused to leave, and
when their main ammo was a tiny little baby with chubby cheeks,
ringlet curls, and eyes so deep that they could crack even the coldest
heart, they were almost always victorious. Tonight would their first
night without the children since they found out that their aunt and
uncle were together and all of them could spend the night in one place.
Between Sunday dinners at Paulette and a house full they didn't have
much time together, but they were so happy they barely noticed.

She would deny her excitement to get her alone time with Zander
since Roxanna had a "honeymoon" lounge installed in a secret room of
their fully furnished basement. Complete with a stripper pole. She'd
loved being the favorite aunt, but she missed being with Zander. She
missed having his touch and his kiss. She smiled when Willow looked
up at her. She swiped her finger softly down her nose giving it a small
bop and making her do the hypnotizing giggle that always made Poppi
say "What's a few more hours?"

"There are my favorite girls." Zander walked in and kissed her forehead, "You are the most beautiful woman I have ever seen." He kissed
her deeply wrapping his fingers around her neck when he did. She
started to feel the tingle she had since her first kiss like this with him.
Willow let out a squeal and he turned "You're a sight for sore eyes little
miss." He scooped her up kissing her cheeks and making her laugh.

Zander was marvelous with the children. He was so warm and loving she wanted to jump on him any time he got done reading them a bedtime story. Daisy and Oliver were like totally different children, they were happier, more playful, and free. The change in their lives was causing so much improvement she was glad she could finally add to it, she was glad they could spend time together, even Thea and Sawyer stayed for a few nights.

The doorbell rang "I bet that is Juni and Brant."

"I hope they had a good time." He smothered Willow's cheeks with kisses before looking back at Poppi "Have you heard anything about your divorce?"

"Nothin'." She shook her head, she wanted a speedy divorce, but Mitchell wanted to try everything he could to draw it out until he saw her, and if she could help it, he never would. She even took all the leave she could from her job which was about 3 months. In hopes that this would be over quickly.

"I'll talk to him." Zander's eyebrows creased. "'I'm sick of him trying to drag this out."

"No, I don't want to deal with it. I have lawyers for that and damn good ones, his lawyers just using ignorant tactics to try to make this longer, we have to play the waiting game." She looked at him "Luckily for us, Paulette had a plan."

"Auntie Poppi! Mom and Dad are back." Daisy called running in. "Hi, Uncle Zander!"

"Hey, Daisy! Did you have fun with Thea today?"

"Yeah, she's been working really hard with Auntie though, so we are gonna have a slumber party tonight!"

"Wow, third one in a row."

"Auntie Lavender is teaching us herbology, so we are staying with her."

"Hi, guys!" Juniper made her way to the Willow. "I've missed you tiny!"

"Not as much as me! Save some of those kisses!" Her father joined them.

"You have an announcement to make, don't you?"

"I do," He smiled "I've been saying that a lot lately. We eloped!" Juniper and Brantley held out their newly wedded hands. Brantley kissed her wedding band. "And I'm adopting the children, we're all gonna be one blended and happy family."

RED LIPSTICK by Rihanna played as Poppi sauntered out to the chrome pole. Zander sat in a chair in front of the podium. When the beat dropped she started her newest routine. He watched as her legs danced in the air as she slid upstairs. Her honey bronze hair fanning out as she waved her arms and waist in opposite directions. Poppi felt alive dancing again, and it felt even better to dance for Zander out in the open in the privacy of their own home. She could feel his eyes watching her as she slid into the split and rolled onto her stomach.

Her body slid into a crawl and she slid into his lap. His hands were tied behind his back, his idea, to see how long he could resist not touching her when she was like this. Her ass whined in a circle on his hardening dick. She heard him growl when she turned around and flipped her head down to his crotch. "You don't know how bad I want you to put it in your mouth you fucking goddess." He hissed.

She felt a chill shiver down her spine and between her legs. She stepped out of the red silk panties she wore and slid them into his mouth. He growled, his blue eyes blazing with lust. She grinned playfully as she tossed her bra to him too. She twirled around the pole again and one more flip upside down letting him see her womanhood glistening with desire for him. His nostrils flared and his eyes narrowed. She put her feet on the floor and shook her ass in his face. She knew she would regret teasing him, but she wanted to see what else lay in store for their lovemaking.

She walked behind him and planted a kiss on the back of his neck as Anywhere by 112 filled the air and the lights' rhythm changed from the deep red they were pulsating. She tugged at the restraints and they fell to the ground with a soft clatter against the chair. He stood up and tossed her over his shoulder making her laugh out loud when he smacked her ass with a loud thwack. Poppi never felt overjoyed being with a man like this. She never felt giddy excitement with Mitchell. She always felt like she was doing a service. Like she was a sex worker and not a partner, but she was sure some sex workers probably got more enjoyment out of it than she had.

Zander tossed her on the bed and was immediately between her legs licking and sucking like he was starving for her. Her body melted into black satin sheets and an overstuffed matching comforter. He wrote love letters between her thighs. Words of affirmation that only her soul could hear, and each time he wrote them, she listened. They made her stronger. They made her feel the power she thought she wouldn't ever find. His fingers teased the core of her as her back arched. "That's right my pretty flower, give it to me." He cooed.

Her body tensed from her orgasm her hands clenching the sheets as she did. His hands grabbed hers tightly as he kissed her clit and then up to each of her breasts. He got to her neck and let a warm breath along her wet neck make her audibly moan. "You teased me so badly I thought I was going to explode Starshine." He rubbed his cock against her. "I have never been this hard for any other woman, even my dick knew we belonged to you from the first time I met you." He slid into her and her gasp was deep as he put her legs on his shoulder.

His thumb rubbed her clit watching her. She loved being looked at by him. She wondered what he thought when he stared down at her like this. He slid out of her and pinched her clit with enough pressure on the build-up to make her bite her lip and draw blood. He slowly slid back in releasing the pressure with each inch. By the time he was touching her G-spot, he'd made her cum again.

Zander started grooving his hips in the perfect stroke for her. He'd worked so hard to do things with her in mind, every time they slept together he'd ask her what she wanted, and then he would do them until she cried in the most mindblowing pleasure. "Did that bring you pleasure, my love?" He asked bringing her legs to her ribs. She moaned loudly. "Do you like this?" He asked kissing her collarbone.

The pleasure from the stretch and the penetration made her white hot. She nodded frantically unable to find the words to tell him to give her every stroke he could like this. He started stroking deeply making her mouth dry and her hands claw his back. He let out a primal rough growl and the strokes became harder and rougher. Paradise. He kissed her hard shoving his tongue in her mouth and she nipped at his kissing him just as frantically. His pace finally slowed and he let out a gurgled growl as his release made him hold her tighter.

"Thank you, darling. You wait here." Zander kissed her once more before pulling out of her and walking to the bathroom. Poppi heard the water running and smiled to herself, she was going to be spoiled by the end of this. She rolled out of bed and walk past her her window and stopped. A large oak tree sprouted in front of her picture window. Zander walked out of the bathroom "What are you looking at?" He asked wrapping his arms around her.

She pointed to the large oak that had a few woodland creatures running through it. "That. That shouldn't be there right?"

Zander kissed the top of her head. "Right. Maybe it's one of the entrances to that realm of fae Lav mentioned."

"I'm confused as to why you're so calm." She looked at him.

"You're a witch who makes things grow after we haven't had sex in a while. It happened in Italy for the first time and it now it's happening now. After a week of having to be saints in front of the children." He kissed her neck. "Just means I have to keep your toes curled and eyes rolling back and we shouldn't have any problems."

"Is keeping me satisfied your solution for everything?" She chuckled as he lead her into the bathroom. He ran her a bubble bath and turned on her jets.

"No," He helped her in, kissing her hand. "But it is my life's mission."

62

9 ½ Weeks

Zander hated every minute of being back in the office. He'd worked from home, his home, mostly and then he'd spend his evenings with Poppi. Their life had become routine in their two months together. On Fridays, they'd take their nieces and nephews out on the town to do something fun or have a movie night. Saturdays they'd go on dates, and on Sundays, they would have family dinner with Paulette and the rest of their families. On the quieter nights of their life, they took turns cooking, but Zander always washed the dishes and took out the trash.

They would take bubble baths together and they'd made love every other day. Zander was in a euphoric paradise, but he knew that when he walked into the office. Poppi couldn't come to the office, because Mitchell still worked there, she refused to take his job from him. Even if he still refused to sign the papers. She did, however, pack his lunch and gave him a blow job goodbye.

She was liberated with him, she told him herself. She'd been asking him to let loose with her, so that she could explore the kinks and wants that he had. And so far they'd been compatible and the amount of orgasms shared between them had almost become a sport. He couldn't keep his hands off of her. She was addictive, every part of her tasted like his favorite flavor.

He missed her while he sat there staring at his screen. He wanted to go home, but there were meetings today that he had to be a part of. He had an hour before his next one and he thought that he could spend it trying to find the best anniversary gift for his Poppi, who was much more than a girlfriend, and when they finally got the okay. He'd show her that.

There was a knock at the door. "C'mon in." He sounded cheerful despite his attachment misery.

"Mr. Bell. You have a delivery." A southern voice filled his ears and the tingle down his spine made him stand at attention. He heard the door shut and curtains draw. He stared at his screen. He knew that this was his mind playing tricks on him. Until the package was put on his desk. He looked up and she stood there in a UPS outfit with the buttons coming down to her red lacy bra, and she even wore the boots with knee-high brown socks.

Poppi wore a yellow wing with pigtails and her make-up was very urban 90's. He was all but drooling when he stood. "Are you going to open it?" She asked as he walked over to her.

"Yes, I am." He grinned pulling off the jumper to watch it fall to the floor. "I love this set Peanut where did you get it." He asked leading her to the couch.

"I brought it at that store you liked when we went shopping last week." She laid back "You said you wanted to see me in it."

"You picked the right day." He smiled sliding down the panties and lifting her legs onto his shoulders. "I have been thinking about this all day."

"Are you afraid that-"

"I don't care." He shook his head and dove into his favorite place. He began licking her sweetness and all the aggravation had gone away. He sucked on her clit as she bit her lip. He took his tongue and started to slowly stroke up and down. He knew she loved this pace, and he loved taking his time.

She leaned back and he sunk his fingers into the wetness wishing already it was him. She was warm and inviting. He was starving for her. He showed it with each passionate stroke of his tongue on her pink walls. She held the back of his head, and he gripped her thighs. "I love it when you eat it." She moaned as she bucked her hips to set the tone. "But I want you to fuck me on your desk. Like you've always wanted." She grinned.

"Is this my anniversary present? I haven't gotten you anything!" He pulled away.

"Fuck me on your desk." She pointed. "Then maybe you can give me a pearl necklace tonight."

"You're a filthy-minded beautiful little princess do you know that." He grinned. He lifted her up and carried her on his side of the desk sitting her down. Then he pulled it out "Spit on it for daddy."

She grinned and put it in her mouth for a few strokes and then let a long line of saliva touch the tip of his dick.

"You are such a good girl." He turned her around. "But now I want you to be my good little secretary."

She took her hands and spread them across his desk. She bent until her lacy black bra was touching his papers, her womanhood exposed to him.

"Look at my perfect little flower being so good to her Mister." He gave her ass a nice smack and she whimpered. "Would you like a gag angel?"

"Yes please."

He took his tie from around his neck and tied it across her mouth her lipstick leaving a glossy stain on the material. He slid into the wet pool between her legs. "Oh thank you, baby. I needed this." He released his tense sigh. He put his hands on her hips and slowly started to long stroke her. His eyes rolled back from the high he got from entering her. It felt just as good as the first time.

She whimpered in pleasure and followed his rhythm with her body. Bouncing her soft juicy ass back against his thighs. He knew this was supposed to be a quickie, but he was almost positive that he would have to give up his meeting to enjoy this. He wanted pictures of her like this. Hazed with lust his tie wrapped around her lips.

"Have I told you I loved you today?" He moaned trying to keep himself steady. "Have I told you I missed you?"

"MMmmhmm." She nodded.

"I love you. I will always love you. I'm so glad I get to be the one who does this with you." His speed began to quicken. "Oh, baby you're so good to me." He pulled her head back with his tie. "I love how much thought

you put into this. You're so good to me. I can't wait to be good to you."
He'd never had a woman dress up and come to his anything. To have
this was so special. He understood the value. He was a lucky man.

As his climax quickly approached with her help. He hunched over her
allowing all of his semen to spill into her. She was the only woman he'd
even been with without protection. The only one he trusted to bare his
children if it was to come to it. He kissed her back and neck as he untied
her gag. "You're really too good to me."

"It's our anniversary. I wanted to do something special." She kissed
him. She handed him her panties. "Keep these until I see you tomorrow.
Since the bachelor party is tonight."

"I don't even wanna go, just gonna be a room of men complaining
about how much they'd prefer to be with their either soon-to-be or
already wives. Brant is being dragged out by his ankles at this point,
and Alton has asked if we can invite you guys seven times. Since most
of you are already or have been strippers."

"It'll be fun. I promise." She laughed kissing him again until she
heard her alarm. "Shit. I'd better go. Before you know who sees me." She
slid on the jumper with no panties and Zander's erection found him yet
again. She looked at him. "Don't look so sad, you'll be back." She kissed
him and "Open your present." She winked.

Zander watched her walk out of the open door and bump right into
Mitchell. He tensed but with the hat, she was barely recognizable.
Mitchell looked at her and then shook his head as he headed towards
his office.

"When did they make delivery girls like that?"

"They don't." He watched her turn around and wave at him with a
smile. "She's special."

ZANDER looked down at his desk and a pair of her lacy green boy shorts hang on the side. He quickly hid them in his pocket annoyed to be in the presence of the scum in front of him. He was glad she was working with her sisters on her magic, Zander assumed that was the reason he didn't notice her.

"A little afternoon delights?" Mitchell looked at him. "So you're not with my wife anymore. Where is she?"

"You wouldn't believe me if I told you," Zander muttered annoyed flipping through his papers. He had the urge to tell him that he just bumped into him in hopes to make him feel a little crazy. He handed him a file.

"She needs to come home." Mitchell snatched the file from him. His face looked like a child watching someone play with a toy they disregarded and now want back. "I'm tired of being with Carmen, she doesn't cook or clean. She's not very helpful at all, and her damn ash habit is costly."

"World's smallest violin Mitchell." Zander gathered his forms. "Maybe you should have treated her better and she wouldn't have fallen off the face of the earth, but seeing as how you almost killed her, I guess she had other plans than to stick around."

"My own mother won't talk to me; she says it's my fault. My Grandmother has disowned me because of it."

"She's not wrong."

"My wife was having an emotional affair with my boss; everyone was in on it and I'm the bad guy." He scoffed. "You're just as responsible for the failure of my marriage as I am! She didn't discover she was unhappy with me until she was around you!"

"Are you sure about that?" Zander folded his arms "You were fucking your boss's girlfriend and your now ex-sister-in-law. And not to mention the countless verbal and physical attacks. You should be in jail you ain't shit mother fucker, but instead that saint of an ex-wife of yours is letting you walk the earth. You need to let her go."

"She's not my ex-wife."

"Oh, she very much is." He looked at Mitchell sternly. He knew she didn't want him involved, but he was tired of the antagonization. "And I suggest you sign those papers before the legal action causes Carmen to have an attitude about you not being able to foot the bill."

"You don't know a damn thing about Carmen."

"And you do? Is that why you're desperate to hold off on your divorce? Because you know no one can hold a fucking light to the woman you married, and now lost. Shame. I bet she's making another man or woman so happy right now... Finding herself and what it means to be truly happy and not miserable with someone like you."

"You know she played you too. She used you to get out of this." He smirked. "She's not making you happy, is she?"

Zander looked him up and down. "Listen you incompetent pig. If Poppi used me to get you of your bitter dark loveless marriage then so be it. I've more than been repaid for that, and I'm sure she's making some man or woman the happiest person in the universe. I envy them for enjoying the best of her and I pity you for having the best and losing it because you're too much of a fucking idiot to see the treasure you had and lost because you couldn't seem to leave another man's woman alone. Now you're reaping the consequences of your actions and you're stuck without Poppi to come and forcibly clean your mess up. You're worthless to her Mitch, you'll never ever have another chance to do anything to her other than divorce her. And I suggest you do that quickly." He walked with him to the door and opened it. "Oh, and one more thing Mitch,"

"What?!" He spat. "What else does the great and wonderful fucking Zander have to say to me?!"

He took one more step to him. "If you say one more fucking word about her, I will make sure that you go missing."

"You boys ready for this meeting?" Frederick met them outside of the office.

"Always." Zander smiled and slapped Mitchell's shoulder as if he hadn't said anything but a friendly word. "Right Mitch?"

Mitch forced his face to find a smile. "Right."

63

Bachelorette

"**T**ake a shot bitch! You've texted him seven times since we've been here." Roxanna laughed dressed up as a Hex girl from Scooby Doo. Kandi and Derrick wanted a Halloween wedding, and they were doing a great job keeping the theme. Kandi even had a costume party-themed Bachelorette party.

Poppi and her sisters dressed as Huey Duey and Luie. Kandi dressed up as Queen Candy from Candy Land and her sister matched her dressing as Lady Licorice. All of them were lovesick women missing their partners, but they were having the best time. Poppi put her phone on do not disturb so she'd resist having to take a shot every time she looked at her phone and texted Zander.

"I'm going to get alcohol poisoning." Kandi groaned taking a tequila shot with pickle juice. "I hate all of you for this."

"You're going to be fine future Mrs. Hallbrick." Lavender smiled. "You're getting hitched to a hot writer guy, my sisters are finally getting their backs blown out properly, and magic has been restored I don't think things could be any better."

"My divorce could be final." Poppi took a shot. She didn't want to bring up anything that happened at Zander's office, but she couldn't help herself. She was happy for all the good, but she wanted the dark cloud hanging over her to be far away.

"It will be honey, and then we'll get even more drunk. And twerk on all the tables. Like Kandi has been." Juniper squeezed her shoulders.

"I like the song I can't help it." She laughed. "C'mon, we should dance these blues away I'm getting married in fifteen hours!" She cheered pulling them to the dance floor to the latest Lina J song.

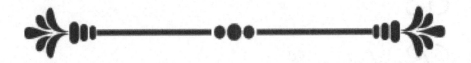

AFTER dancing her heart out with the bridal party she slid to the bathroom to relieve her bladder and sneak a quick text to Zander the same way the rest of the girls had cheated all night. She was applying her lip gloss and checked her phone. *'You're so going to wear that costume later Starshine XX'* She smiled at the text and froze looking at herself smiling in the mirror, she was surprised about how foreign it still looked to her. How the brightness in her face still made her look like a stranger. And she liked it, she loved it, she never thought in a million years and it was all because of him.

"How's Zander?" Poppi looked up from her reflection and Carmen was leaning against the wall in a white dress with floral patterns sewn into it. She stepped towards her. "I went by his condo, but he wasn't there."

"He doesn't live there anymore, at least I don't think so, it's still open if you need it since you have a key."

"Where is he?" She looked at her. "Is he here with you? I need to talk to him."

"He isn't and I doubt he wants to talk to you." She looked at her. "If he hasn't reached out by now. I don't think he could be any clearer."

"I think he needs to say something to me I'm owed that; I'm owed an explanation."

"For what?"

"Why he thought that you are some sort of fucking upgrade! I mean look at you, you're as common as well...a can of paint. And I'm a fucking TV and Movie star. Even Mitchell knows!" She snapped. "That's why he left you!"

"I don't think you need to know the answer to something you already know. You told him marrying him would be the biggest mistake of your life and then you used him for a hiding place after stealing money and drugs from a really powerful family. He paid that debt back and gave you his all and you still chose an abusive asshole who will *always* put you last. I'll never understand what you see in Mitchell." Her golden eyes zeroed in on her trying to find her reasoning for leaving Heaven for an extended stay in hell. "He must be holding that prince charming act on real hard, so you believe it, but he hates not having me under his thumb it's killing him to see me happy."

"If you're so fucking happy, why don't you sign the papers?!"

"What papers? My divorce papers. I did, he's got them and probably hiding them because he's feeding you bullshit Carmen. You're mad at the wrong person; he doesn't want to be with you because you're hollow. No offense, but let's be honest you're a maid service personal chef kind of girl. He's a dinner on the table by five, martini by six, be seen and not heard kind of man. I was the meat that made his life good, and now he will starve. If you're smart, you'll get the hell off the boat." She sighed tossing up her hands and putting her lipgloss back in her bag. "But you're spiteful, you'll stay with him in hopes that you prove someone who doesn't give a damn wrong. And you'll make yourself miserable doing it. You'll be abused, cheated on, and lied to. Do you think I want that for you? I don't like you, which doesn't mean I want you to be in my position. I'm not totally heartless, I wouldn't wish that on my worst enemy, I certainly wouldn't wish it on the woman who literally fumbled the best thing that ever happened to her. "

She walked past Carmen and she grabbed her arms. "You don't know what you're talking about bitch. Mitchell loves me. He loves me more than he's ever loved anyone else."

Poppi knew that line by heart. "And he's never been as happy with you as he has with me. You give him life whereas I made him feel dead inside right?" She snatched her arm away from Carmen. "You will never believe how many women came to say that exact same thing to me. They were smart enough to leave, I'm sorry I can't say the same to you. Have a nice life Carmen, best of luck." Poppi walked back to the table where her friends were sharing a shot. She felt an impending sense of dread and by the look on Lavender's face, she could feel it too.

"Are you okay?" She asked looking at her.

Poppi nodded taking a deep breath and another shot. "Whatever it is. We can worry about tomorrow, tonight, we celebrate."

64
A Wedding

K andi walked out of her dressing room with her black corset gown with a Victorian skirt that had a gossamer rainbow train down the middle. The iridescent crystals on her bodice made her extra dazzling. She wore a handmade tiara in her extravagantly pinned up hair with small curls falling around her perfectly made-up face. "Well?" She asked.

"Thea did a lovely job." Juniper looked at her. "You look absolutely stunning, and for her to just be nine with very little help, she did a great job."

"Thank you two so much! I am in love I feel just like I always wanted to on my wedding day. So beautiful and happy! I'd cry, but Lav would kill me if I ruined her makeup."

"Everything is waterproof. But I worked my ass off trying to get those rhinestones the way you wanted them." Lavender put eyeliner on looking over at Poppi. "Do You know how hard it is to bedazzle a jittery bride?"

"You did beautifully. A room full of talent!" Roxanna reassured.

Poppi stood in her black satin gown "Here, these are from Paulette, they were carved from sapphires her father found on Safari in 1928, she wore them at her wedding to the love of her life, and they were married for the good 20 years. That was after her first marriage, but she married for money when she found love. Her mother gave these to her, and I thought you could wear something old, borrowed, and blue."

"Are you fucking serious?! Poppi these are beautiful." Kandi looked at the box she held in her perfectly coffin-manicured fingers. She put them to her ear smiling widely "Do you think she'd mind?"

"If she wasn't fawning over Willow, I'm sure she'd tell you how much she wants you to wear them, but she is always with the babies. When she isn't trying to convince Daisy to take over the company, or showing Jarren her mad hops in one on one, she's crawling on the floor like she isn't in the age range of 70–80." Poppi laughed along with the rest of them.

"Her house is literally built for them." Juniper laughed sipping champagne. "Down to childproof sockets."

"Take the earrings, babes, they'll make you look even more breathtaking than you already do. You deserve to be spoiled on your wedding day!"

"I never had a big sister, but gods am I lucky I found you." She hugged her tightly. There was a flash of photography. Kandi put on the earrings. "You mean the world to me Poppi Nichols and don't you fucking forget it."

POPPI watched as Derrick fell into a crying heap when Kandi and her also teary-eyed father walked down the aisle together. Kandi always said she'd marry a man who loved her on a molecular level, and watching Zander smiling as Derrick cried "That's my wife!" showed she got exactly what she manifested. He took her by the hand after shaking her father's hand and thanking him for trusting him with his daughter. After they got to the altar Derrick stopped the ceremony and told the audience, "This is my wife y'all! She said she was gonna marry me." The entire audience erupted in laughter and applause.

Kandi's vows to Derrick were simple and full of love. She promised to love and cherish him through the best and the not-so-best times of their life, because anytime they were together it would be the best. Derrick told her how lucky he was and how much he loved her. He dedicated his entire life to being her husband. Poppi watched everyone occasionally dab a tear from their eye including her. She was happy, and a bit envious if she was honest, that Kandi got it right the first time. She looked at Zander and wondered what her life would look like if he was her first.

Her wedding was a nightmare. Her mother picked her dress, she was drugged for most of the planning, and Mitchell was late to their wedding. He was most likely fucking Patricia, since they were the ones dancing and laughing all night and she was catering to everyone at their reception with Paulette asking her to annul. Sometimes, she wished she would have just taken the advice. She wouldn't be having to suffer the way she was.

If she ever got to have another wedding she and Zander would be surrounded by love and understanding just like Kandi and Derrick. She smiled as they kissed to unify their marriage and the crowd applauded. Kandi held up her hand and in true tradition shouted "I's Married nah!" All of her bridesmaids laughed in unison. As she kissed Derrick again. Poppi and Zander carried the broom decorated by Kandi's generational line across the threshold. Kandi and Derrick clasped their hands together and jumped the broom.

AFTER an hour of faking a smile for Kandi's bridal pictures Poppi sat by herself in the dressing room while everyone else busied themselves getting ready for the reception. She sat in her red silk dress with the slit that touched her thigh staring at her open-toe black strappy heels in the mirror. She was trying to distract herself from the need to throw up rising in her. Her body had felt like it was running on high adrenaline since the club and she couldn't focus on it with all of the events that built up to it. Now she was alone and filled with even more worry and angst than before.

"Alright woman." Juniper handed her a glass of ginger ale. "Spill."

She looked up at her sister. "What are you talking about?" She took the glass.

"She's talking about why you have looked like you've had to vomit since we wrapped for wedding party pictures." Lavender rubbed her bare back, her hands sending a cool relaxing wave through her and causing her to let out a deep sigh. The need to vomit teetering between urgent and not-so-bad.

She took a long sip of the cold soda and looked up at Juniper. "Do you ever get the feeling something awful is about to happen and you don't know what it is? Like someone has cut the rope while you're rock climbing and now you're freefalling in absolute terror?"

Juniper blinked. "That's not a feeling to have on the happiest day of your adopted baby sister's life." She looked at Lavender. "Everything is good right?"

"Babe we got detail all over this shebang if that motherfucker stepped a toe in this bitch he'd be handled." Lavender waved her hand. "So it can't be that. When did you feel it first."

"After seeing Carmen at the bachelorette party, she was angry with me about my divorce not being handled."

"Well, that's not your fault now is it?" Juniper put her hands on her hips.

Roxanna walked in and looked at her. "Are you pregnant?"

"No!"

"Okay good! Cause it's time to go get drunk on rich people's liquor." Roxanna danced out of the room.

"Don't worry Poptart. We will handle whatever this is." Lavender rubbed her shoulder. "I promise."

"ALRIGHT, Ladies let's see who's next!" Kandi tossed her bouquet into a crowd of her friends and it fell into Poppi's outstretched hand. Everyone clapped for her. "Oooh Zander it's time to go ring shopping!"

Zander stood beside her wrapping his hand around her waist. "You don't have to tell me twice." He kissed her cheek as 'All My Life.' By KC and JoJo started playing. He started to dance with her and smiled. "I guess now you know this is real. You didn't even try to catch it and it just fell into your hands." He kissed her.

"Well if you catch the guarder I know that this is obvious fate." She chuckled laying her head on his chest. "I love you, Zander. I wish it didn't take this long for us to find each other, but I'm glad that it's here."

"You know it's almost been a year since we met." He looked down at her. "And I still can't believe this much happiness exists. You are the light of my life Poppi Celeste Nichols. I love you more than I can explain, and I can't wait to marry you."

Poppi kissed him deeply. Until someone cleared their throat behind them. "Excuse me, Mrs. Baxter." A deep voice addressed her making her turn around. There was a tall man in a black suit and a matching button-down. Beside him was a fair-skinned woman with curly black hair and thick red glasses. Her suit was also black, but she had a silk white blouse under it.

"That's not my name." She looked at him. "Not anymore at least."

"I'm sorry ma'am." The woman spoke. "It's the name we have on file. Poppi Baxter."

"It's Poppi Nichols. And what file are you talking about?" She looked at him folding her arms.

"The next of kin file ma'am." He replied.

"Who are you?! My kin is here other than my father and stepmother."

"I'm Detective Hall and this is Detective Nevil. We are so sorry to have to do this here ma'am but your husband, Mitchell Baxter, has been killed in a fatal shooting." Detective Hall looked at her. "We need you to come and identify the body."

65

Monster

Mitchell Baxter lay on a steel slab with a white sheet up to his shoulders hiding two of the three bullet wounds he'd received in the shooting. The one in his throat was there a gaping hole in his lifeless olive skin. His handsome face was still. The eyes that used to hold such hate for her were closed his long eyelashes were curled to perfection. The lips that cursed her and told her she'd never be good enough for anything were in a line. She stared at him. He was so still. A man she knew to be full of life, who scared her to death some days was finally still.

Poppi felt shocked seeing him. Seeing the man who promised her that he would kill her and have her sisters standing in her position laying on a slab was oddly satisfying. She leaned down to him and whispered. "Funny how life works isn't it? I hope Javid weighs your heart with mercy." She wiped a hot tear away from her cheek. She was thankful for Brantley being at the wedding. She and he came ahead of Juniper and Zander, she wanted to have someone there who could witness this and tell Sabrina with sympathy that her son died in the same way as her husband did. Death by mistress. Only his father at least got to enjoy a happy ending as his plane crashed.

"All of those times he threatened to put you in the ground and look where it got him." Brantley put his hand on her shoulder. "Exactly what he deserved. I know Grams is watching the news right now with a smirk on her face."

"She'd never laugh at one of you three dying." Poppi touched his hand. "Deep down she just wanted Mitchell to be a good man."

"I don't know Pop; this is biblical justice. The meek shall inherit the earth. Look. You went through years of meekness. He made you feel less than and now he's dead. Now he'll never hurt you again. You're really free Poppi."

"The DA would like to know if you would like to proceed with further charges." Detective Nevil spoke to them after they identified him. "Since the DA thinks that this was, in fact, self-defense they are asking if you'd like to press the charges for Miss Grace. She is in critical condition from the stab wound."

"No, I don't, I know exactly what she went through, and she wasn't the best, but she didn't deserve to almost die." Poppi shook her head. "I want her to have a good life, I don't want her career tarnished because of this."

"Also, Miss. Nichols. Do you know a young woman by the name of Lydia Hart?" Detective Hall asked.

"Yes, yes I do." She shook her head. "I mean I did, she was my fiance."

Detective Hall and Nevil exchanged looks. "Was your husband close to her?"

Poppi shook her head. "No, Lyds hated him. We didn't even start dating until after she died, and I was under a conservatorship then." She looked up at them. "Her death wasn't exactly the happiest time of my life. I'm sure I don't have to say that."

"We run DNA of all of our homicide victims and his hit on a rape kit that was done on Lydia the day she was found. We have reason to believe he may've had something to do with her death do you know anything about that?"

Poppi nodded and closed her eyes tears were flowing now, not for Mitchell, but for Lydia. The fact that she didn't protect her from him, she didn't listen to her warnings as well as she should have. "Before I left him for my own safety he told me he'd kill me just like he did Lydia, and I didn't have any proof, and with the records you all could have pulled I wouldn't have been believed so I just.... Held on to it."

"Are you saying my brother is a murderer?" Brantley asked Poppi and then the detectives. "Do you think that?"

"Her hymen was broken and he was the only specimen we found. Not to mention according to the autopsy said there was some violence to her vaginal area. I guess college woman, and because of that they didn't really consider her sexuality." Hall shrugged. "I'm sorry to have to tell you all of this Miss Nichols." She looked sympathetic.

"Mr. Holden do you also not want to press charges? You are family we can take that to the DA if you feel it's necessary." Detective Nevil looked at Brantley with a look that prayed he said the same thing.

"No, I don't find it necessary, if my brother did what you believe he did. What my sister said he did. Then that young woman deserves a fresh start."

"Then this is where it ends." The officer shook their hands. "I'm sorry for your loss ma'am."

Poppi watched the officer walk away. Poppi didn't feel a loss, she felt dread. She was going to have to plan a funeral and call her mother to inform her that her baby has passed on. She was going to have to explain to Sabrina how sorry she was for not being able to help her son. She just wanted all of this to be over. She wanted to crawl back into her bubble and pretend that she never even knew the monster named Mitchell Baxter.

66

They both reached...

Z ander stood beside Poppi as she delivered the news to Sabrina. Sabrina held Willow tightly in her arms. Her eyes glazed over as she listened to Poppi repeat the speech that she rehearsed all the way home. "Sabrina, I am so sorry. I... I don't know what to say other than I'm sorry." She stood there staring at her. "He stabbed Carmen and she shot him, that's what the detective said. He died before they got to the hospital, he choked on his blood."

Sabrina blinked and a tear fell down her soft cheek as she kissed Willow's forehead and handed her back to Brantley. She looked up at Poppi her eyes desperate to find meaning in what Poppi just told her. "You're telling me that my son is dead." She bit her bottom lip covering her face and taking a breath. "You're telling me the bitch who ruined your marriage killed my son! That's what you're telling me?! You're telling me you refused to press charges on the woman who killed my son! That's what you're telling me."

Zander felt Poppi's arm tighten around him, bracing for the impact. "Sabrina, I wish there was something else I could say. I wish I could tell you that this is all a joke and they got it wrong, but–"

"But nothing Poppi my son is dead! There's no going back there is no fixing this! I get you out of there! I convince myself that I will break the cycle and I will fix this one. Mitchell will see the error of his ways after losing her. And he dies Poppi! He dies and I'm just supposed to what?! Accept it."

Poppi swallowed. Zander held her tightly. He loved Sabrina like family, but this was a different situation, there was no guarantee the woman who loved Poppi could become bitter because of the loss of her child.

Poppi was a surrogate for her. Zander could see her having to choose between blinding herself to the man Mitchell was out of grief and blaming Poppi for leaving or accepting the fact her son was a monster. Poppi opened her mouth but Brantley interrupted.

"She's sparing you, mama." Brantley stepped up to her. "You wouldn't be acting like this if you knew half of what Poppi does about that man. Mitchell was served his Karma today. It's as plain as that."

"Brantley!" Randall looked at his son. "That's your brother boy!"

"And? I don't feel bad for him and neither should you! Or you." He looked at his mother. "He's a killer Mama. He killed Lydia Hart."

"Wait, what?!" Juniper looked at Poppi. "What is he talking about?!"

Poppi looked at Zander pleading for him to help her. Zander looked at them. "His DNA was a hit in her kit. Her parents asked them to do a lot of tests before she was buried and a rape kit was one of them, it was him. He assaulted and killed Lydia."

Sabrina let out a sob. "He was wretched to you from the beginning! Oh, Poppi I'm so sorry." She reached for her. Poppi walked over and Sabrina wrapped her arms around her. "I am so so so sorry you had to go through this! But he was my son, you have to understand-"

"You don't have to explain Sabrina, I wouldn't expect you to be anything but upset over losing Mitchell, he was your baby." Poppi comforted. "I'll take care of everything. I want you to be able to take care of yourself and Randall. You need each other right now." The doorbell rang.

"I'll get it." Zander walked to the door and his parents stood there. "Hi, guys."

"Where is Sabrina?" She asked. "I am sure she's not taking this well."

"I mean as well as a mother can."

"To lose the father and the son to the mistress is a odd fate." Claudia shook her head. "Mitchell's father died in a plane crash while his mistress was... Well, I don't have to give graphic detail, but they found her head in his lap and her body six feet in the opposite direction. I just hate this for her."

"Maybe lead with a hug mom, I don't think the statistics will be a helpful idea." Zander grinned as his mother playfully swatted him. She wrapped him in a hug.

"You take care of her Zander, No matter how it ended, that was still her husband." She kissed his cheek and walked into the living room.

Zander answered his ringing phone in his phone. "Zander Bell."

"Hello, Mr. Bell, This is Docotr Corneilious Faltori, and I'm calling on behalf of Carmen Grace."

"Is everything okay?"

"Yes, she wants to see you."

Zander sighed, It had to come sometime, he had to say something to her. He couldn't believe that it was like this. He walked back into the living room. "Tell her I'll be there."

"Who was that?" Poppi asked

"Carmen's doctor, she uh... She wants to see me."

Poppi nodded. "I understand, You go I got it for a bit."

"Are you sure?"

"She almost died, and she's asking for you, I think you can go and see her. She deserves to be checked on." Poppi kissed his cheek and walked to the kitchen. Zander watched her go and wondered where she was in her mind. How could she be so clear-headed and rational? He would have to talk to her about it all one day. He would have to ask her why she was so calm about this. Why wasn't she crying? Why didn't she fall apart? She loved him, he knew she did, he watched her hold out hope that he would change for her. And now he was gone. No redemption. No resolution. Poppi was a widow, and she'd barely shed a tear.

ZANDER wasn't a fan of hospitals. He never enjoyed the sterile smells and loud beeping. He wondered what she looked like. He wondered what happened. Part of him wished Poppi would have come with him. He needed to feel grounded. He was feeling jittery and a sense of warning radiating around him. He decided that it was just his feelings for hospitals. Something about them just screamed unwell. He shook it off as he walked down the hall to find her room, but the hairs standing up on his neck made him even more weary. He should have asked Poppi to come, even if it was just to sit in the car at least he would know she was close and she was fine.

He made it to the hall where her room was and bumped into a man in a tan suit with aviators on. His head was bald and he wore a tailored tan suit and a sky blue shirt with a matching trilby hat cocked to the side. Something ran through Zander and he stopped. The man took off his glasses and his eyes were white. and something behind them told Zander he wasn't exactly trustworthy. His skin was turning into a deep gray like a thunderstorm cloud. He squinted."Do I know you son? You look familiar."

Zander shook his head. "I'm sorry I'm afraid I don't know you, sir." He blinked twice and the man was back to normal, his eyes just a light gray and playful. "But Carmen and I were friends, I'm sure there may've been parties or something we both attended."

He nodded still studying him. "Yeah, I guess so, Well nice to meet you blue eyes." He slid his glasses back on and walked out of the door. Two guards walked behind him. Zander didn't like that at all. He should have brought Lavender. She could have told him who that was, and why he made him feel like trouble was coming.

He walked into her room and she was staring at herself in the mirror. For someone who was near death, she looked beautiful. Her hair was soft and black in a ponytail at the top of her head. She was in a white hospital gown and she was looking at the small scar over her eyebrow in a mirror. She was smiling from ear to ear until she saw him. Then it fell and she looked miserable like it was a switch. "Hi, Carmen." He handed her a dozen white roses. "These are for you."

"Thank you, Zander. Have a seat." She patted the seat beside her. Zander sat beside her. She looked at him for a long time searching for something in his face she didn't see. "Thank you for coming." She looked down at the flowers. "These are lovely."

"You're welcome. Are you alright?"

She looked at him. "No, but I will be, if you spent twenty-four hours being fucked, screamed at, and tortured you wouldn't feel your best either." She looked at him. "It was awful Zander, It was all because I asked him why he was lying to me about the divorce. I told him I saw Poppi at some Halloween bash and I asked her what was taking so long and she...." Carmen stared out of the window her tongue going over her teeth. "How did she do it? How did she go home every day knowing that's who waited for her?"

"It wasn't exactly easy I'm sure."

"She's so fucking nice, you'd think she pissed sunshine. She does nice shit for people and she never acts like this man was beating her ass and killing people off for her. While he was choking me one night he told me that I didn't deserve to be anything other than a whore he fucked and partied with. He told me that if he got me out of the way like he did Lydia, she'd take him back and all would be well. I told him he was fucking nuts and that's when he pushed me down the stairs and dragged me by my hair. Then he grabbed a knife and stabbed me with it. I wiggled away and ran upstairs. I grabbed the gun and I shot it three times. I thought I missed."

Zander listened to the way she told the story, it almost felt robotic. Like she was trying to recite a script. Zander didn't want to think the worst of her, but she was sitting up and talking as if nothing happened. The face wound that the detective told Brantley and Poppi she'd suffered from when they were going over the gory details was barely scratched. She didn't even seem phased by what she was saying.

"I could have been better to her, you know, Poppi?" She looked over at him. "He tried to kill her when she found out about Patricia in college, and then he hit her in front of me, he threw her down the steps and I kicked her in the face. He told me she was crazy, I watched them carry her out handcuffed to the bed Zander. He told me this was different. He told me he loved me, he needed me, and then suddenly I was the only thing standing in the way of Poppi coming home to fix everything he'd broken. When he got angry like that he said it was because of the divorce papers or you toying with him about the whereabouts of his wife."

"Poppi signed those divorce papers, Mitchell refused to. I'm sorry it had to be this way for you Carmen, I wanted better for you."

"Then why didn't you try fighting for me?!"

"Because you told me that being married to me was literally the worst thing you could do. It would kill your career it would ruin propositions. And you couldn't do it. You didn't love me Carmen, you loved this idea that I'd always be waiting around for when you were ready to come home. But I couldn't wait forever and I knew I was just a placeholder til something better came along, I'm just sorry you thought it was Mitchell Baxter." He stood. "Listen, I have to go, but... Be careful out there Carmen, you never know who someone is."

"That's what Sepehr said."

"Who? The guy who left before I got in here?"

"Yeah Sepehr Favionni? He's that hotshot attorney turned Politician. I think he's like the Mayor of some city now. But Taryn called in a favor in case Poppi pressed charges."

"And she didn't?"

"Aren't we lucky she wanted him dead too?" Carmen smiled and went back to examining her face in the mirror.

67

A Funeral

'Speak from your heart Poppi, You won't say the wrong thing, you never have.' Lydia told her that for her public speaking class, but the statement held strong. Poppi couldn't find good words for her husband, and she'd rehearsed with Zander all night. All she could come up with was that she hoped Maniae was serving him to Lydia on a silver platter for what he did to her.

She looked at the sea of black ahead of her, she felt sick even standing there. She looked at Sabrina in the front row. Randall wrapped his arm around her, She was completely still, and not even a tear rolled down her perfect cheeks. She just stared at the sleek black coffin that her son laid in. Patricia was wailing in the back. She must have never suffered from him. They must have shared true and deep love. The kind he was supposed to have for her. She saw the bright blue iris' that was her anchor.

Poppi couldn't find good words for her own husband. She wanted to tell the truth, but she knew Sabrina would be devastated. The last thing anything knew about her son was that he was a horrible man. She took a deep breath. She wanted to tell a good story. A story that made sense but didn't diminish how turbulent Mitchell was to her or his family. "Mitchell was a complicated person; his life was a complex in and out of hurt and anger." She began praying that it made sense.

" His mother and stepfather tried to make that painless, but losing a parent isn't ever something that you just recover from in the way they thought he would. Some nights he would tell me how hard he wished that his father could tell him that he was proud of him. I think that he wanted that so much that he turned into the dedicated hard-working man that his father was, and he also took his demons. I wish I could have gotten him to see that there was peace beyond the pain, but he never wanted to see it. He wanted to forge his own path from his father's ashes, and they both burned out in the same amount of time.

Mitchell taught me so much, but mostly he taught me the value of life, how easy it was for it to be taken in a moment, or for it be given in months. He made me realize how much the mundane things in the world matter. How beautiful it is to sit across from the person that you love and have a cup of tea or play with your favorite five in a playground.

He gave me a family when most of mine rejected me for being a bisexual woman who was grieving the loss of their fiancé, he gave me a family that allowed me to weep. To feel. And I have never been able to thank him enough for the constant out-pour of love his family has and continues to give me. Without him, I never would have met Paulette, and no offense to any of my friends, but she's my soulmate. My best friend. My kindred spirit. And despite his bitterness, she still tried to combat that with love. I wish he could have felt that love, not just from her, but from his brother and his sister. From their families. From everyone who was willing to give it to him.

I wish he would have seen them more, valued his time, and knew that work would be there in the morning. I wish he would have seen that love..." She choked on a sob. "I'm sorry, that love, was always there. I hope he didn't meet his creator thinking that he wasn't loved because he was. Look at all of the people here. That is love." She looked at the coffin. "Rest now Mitchell, we love you."

AS the five of them sat there watching the coffin sink into the ground Poppi wiped her eyes. She couldn't stop crying when the descent began. This was it, he and all the pain and hurt he caused would be buried in this hole. She went over the eulogy she gave in her head several times and each time she tried to make sure she didn't hurt Sabrina, Brant, Sara, or even Randall. Paulette decided it would be best if she watched the children. She didn't want to see her grandson in a coffin even if he did deserve to be there, her words, but still, she wondered as they sat there in silence if she had done the right thing.

"Thank you, Poppi," Sabrina whispered finally as his coffin went out of view. "Thank you for not being the person I would have been if my mother-in-law asked me to speak at his father's funeral. Thank you for giving my son your love til the end."

"I love you, Sabrina, Brantley is my brother-in-law, I couldn't be terrible to you all. You're family."

"Always." She patted her hand. "Where is Zander?"

"Preparing the repast with Claudia."

"You really took care of everything didn't you?" She sighed. "We never deserved you."

"You got me, and you're stuck with me Ma." She laid her head on her shoulder.

"Did you mean what you said about Mom loving Mitchell?"

"Paulette loved Mitchell so much, what he said Christmas Eve really hurt her. She always hoped they could sit down and figure out why they didn't click. But after the accident and when he came with Patricia, they never really got there. She was angry she had to watch yet another woman she loved suffer."

"Wow, that breaks my heart. Mom never even mentioned it. She's been distracting herself with the children of course." She jumped when the wrench stopped with a loud click. "That's it, isn't it? He's in his final resting place."

"That's all. I've watched enough of these to know watching them fill the dirt makes you feel really empty. Why don't we go?" Poppi wrapped her arms around her. "It's freezing and Randall will kill me if you catch a cold out here."

She looked down at the hole. "You be good down there Mitchell. You be good wherever you are." She looked at Poppi and wiped another tear from her red eyes. "I couldn't have done this without you Poppi. I love you more than words. I'm grateful my son brought you into my life."

"Me too." She hugged her. Poppi watched her walk away. She pulled a purple mesh bag from her trenchcoat and opened it to make sure everything was there. Two gold coins, one bottle of his favorite liquor, and two twigs of Lavender since Hestheia, the goddess of eternal resting places, and Javid's wife, loved lavender. "Safe travels Mitchell." She tossed the bag into the deep hole.

68
Showdown

"Honey you were amazing today. I'm so proud of you." Lavender hugged her. "I would have spit on him. Then maybe caught him on fire, not in the cremation way, but you, you handled it with class and beauty."

"As if you expected anything else from our girl." Zander smiled squeezing her shoulders into him. "I'm proud of you baby cakes."

"Thanks for being here for me stud muffin." She giggled. Lavender made a gagging noise. "Oh come on Lavender I deserve a little sap."

"Yes, but without me in the room." She rolled her eyes with a grin.

"Glad to see that you can be so cheerful when you just buried your husband, Poppi." Her mother spat looking at her and Zander. "Is this the man you were cheating on my Mitchell with?"

"Mother he wasn't your anything and your emotional attachment to your son in laws is very disturbing." Lavender rolled her eyes.

"I don't remember asking you for anything you ungrateful heathen." She hissed looking at Poppi. "You've been parading around cheating on your husband and it's your fault he's dead. You know that don't you! Your fault that your mother-in-law doesn't have her son! Your fault that you will never bare his children, or he'll never grow old because of you!"

Poppi felt small, she wanted to cower behind her sister like they did when they were children. But Juniper was upstairs changing Willow, and Lavender was gripping her steak knife a little too hard for Poppi to give her a reason.

"You know no one would ever love you again. No one wants a used-up cheating whore!"

Poppi began to sob and Zander stood in front of her. "Alright now that's quite enough ma'am!" He spoke sternly.

"Excuse me?! Who the hell do you tink you're talking to?!"

"I will have you know your daughter is one of the kindest, bravest, strongest, and loving women I have ever met. Her love for Mrs. Holden's son knew no bounds! Not one ounce. She loved, honored, protected for better or for worse and if you think for one damn second, I'll sit here and let you disrespect the woman I love for man who didn't deserve your daughter let alone the kind and wonderful things she said about him today. Or her sisters you're sadly mistaken, and I don't give a good goddamn who you are! Now if I were you, I'd stop disrespecting my daughter's home with my presence and go."

Her mother looked at her. "Poppi Michelle Nichols-Baxter are you going to let this... Oaf talk to me like this?! I am your mother! You better respect me! Don't you know that's in the bible!"

"You're not her mother." Sabrina stood beside Zander. "Not one child in this room belongs to you."

"Sabrina, you know we've been close, and you know I'm right." She wiped a tear from her eye. "She is the reason your son is dead. "

"My son being a liar, cheater, and domestic abuser is the reason why he is dead. I have no idea why you would feel we were close. You and I don't see eye to eye about anything, and the only reason why I feel any god put you in my path was so that I could have my granddaughter. And as much as I love her, I hate that it came in the wake of Poppi's misery. You put your daughter in a conversion asylum where she was mentally tortured by fanatics. You knew about my sons abuse and did nothing! You did nothing! You encouraged him!You said It would change her attitude!"

"Sabrina it wasn't-"

"Do you know that's what she told him on your trip to Italy?" Sabrina looked at Zander "I found his phone, and there was email after email of you encouraging him to abuse her! I was hoping you wouldn't come today. I was hoping you'd give her peace and let this entire thing die with my son, but instead you come in here and you accuse your own daughter of murder! You need to go to hell. And very quickly."

"I believe you heard the mama, Marigold." Lavender snarked. "Get ta steppin'."

. "You've always been ruined. And you'll ruin this man too, I feel sorry for any child that is bore from the womb of a killer." She spat and sauntered out of the house.

"Are you alright?" Zander wrapped his arms around her. "I am so sorry I thought she was speaking with Juniper."

"She was and she saw her opportunity and took it. Juniper will be pleased to know you will never see her again after today."

"God one can only hope." Poppi folded her arms. "You didn't have to defend me Sabrina, I know this was very uncomfortable."

"When your cub is in danger uncomfortable or not you come to the rescue." She looked at Zander. "Not that you really needed it."

"Right?" Lavender snapped her fingers twice. "Where were you when they locked her up?"

"Obviously in the wrong place at the wrong time." He looked at Poppi who was doing deep breathing. "Come on Lolli Pop let's get you a drink."

"If you guys get any grosser, I'm gonna barf." Lavender looked at Sabrina. "How about a smoke?"

"Sounds damn good to me." She looped arms with Lavender and walked out to the balcony.

69

648 Days

Life had changed drastically for Poppi in the short time she'd met Zander. Love had never been a thing she'd been realistic about finding, but now she had it. She had the man of her dreams who loved her more than anyone could have. She knew Lydia sent him to her, and she was thankful for that every single day. Now that she could grieve and talk about Lydia freely there was a weight lifted from her she didn't even know she carried. Each time she'd been able to laugh at a memory or put a picture of Lydia in her home, even have her family over, she was one step in the right direction.

Zander had the tree that had magically appeared during one of their first times making love moved to the backyard in a safer place for one of their anniversaries. He was sure that it would be better out of view and Poppi was overjoyed. They loved looking at the reminder of what their love could do when the right moment struck. He loved being with her, being her person. She felt like home to him. Everything good in his life other than Thea, Jarren, and his job came from her. He never stopped reminding her how lucky he was, which was new and unusual for Poppi, but with therapy and support it all became a new normal.

On her birthday Zander asked her to spin the globe and where it landed would be where they had her birthday party. Lavender, Keres, Kandi, Derrick, Roxanna, Alton, Juniper, and Brantley all joined her as they had dinner inside the Eiffel Tower. The world beneath them glimmering with life and beauty. Zander pulled got down on his knee and pulled out an exact recreation of Paulette's ring from her first marriage. A Haydee oval halo engagement ring with a shining emerald in the center. Around the emerald was the birthstone of everyone she loved, he added his birthstones Opal at the top and Torumaline at the bottom to show she was his balance. She was a sobbing mess before she could even answer, and of course, she said yes.

When they were celebrating their engagement together for the thousandth time Zander tied Poppi to their oak. Entangled in passion and feeling neither of them noticed their tree glowing behind Poppi until the thick wood on her back was cold wet grass in a new and uncharted place. Poppi was greeted as the Queen of the Realm of Oryn, the realm of the fae of earth wind, and sea. Poppi looked around at the magical creatures that in no way could walk around the city of Cole Harbor Maine. The ripples of the great awakening slowly ripple through the earth.

Zander stood with her as King of the Mortal Ones. Zander stood beside Poppi hand in hand at her coronation. Lavender, the warrior witch, took to building an army in case the immortals decided to declare war against her in case she would try to diminish their newfound powers. Keres stood beside her and helped her build. Daisy, Jarren, and Oliver all took to sword fighting, but Thea took to potions with Poppi and Juniper. Rayden and Crispin were glad their children were able to be a part of something that hadn't happened in several centuries. They were a family united in secret royalty.

Pearl, Keres, and Silas Abraxas gave their alliance to Poppi and Zander promising them their safety. Although, Silas preferred to keep his distance from them, Pearl and Keres offered to plan and pay for the wedding with all of their input as a gift for them. Keres even had Esmeray Jacaris, the classical performer, and her brother Enzo sing 'At Last' as Poppi walked down the aisle. It was Zander's time to cry on Dereck's shoulder as she walked down in her powder blue off-the-shoulder gown where her sleeves met her trail. She even wore a silver tiara with opals in her hair. She looked absolutely perfect.

Now they were together on their honeymoon. Speaking words of meaning and deep love to each other as he made love to her in the waterfall outside of their castle. It was their second favorite getaway place. Poppi loved the beige stone that made the columns and the foundation.

She loved the black marble that made the roofs. Vines grew around the archways and flowers wound around the door frames and staircases. He told her tonight she had to count how many orgasms she had. She loved how he was just the right amount of dominant to her. He protected her limits and opened her mind to so many other ideas.

This was it, this was Poppi's happily ever after. She never thought she'd make it to the part of her story where she'd get to say that. Where she could finally engulf herself in joy and allow herself to feel happiness that she never thought she could. She never knew much else other than surviving and now she was in a place she couldn't have imagined years ago. Now she was here where the water kissed her already electrified skin sending her on a world of sensory pleasures. Her body released another orgasm as she clawed into Zander's back. She kissed him on the ear. "Five."

70

Epilogue

They start the same way. They always start the same way.
Wrapped in his arms she feels bliss. In her heart, she knows this is
where she belongs. He kisses her. "I am lucky to have you light bringer."
You are all that I have ever wanted in my world. One day I shall create
a place for us. I will find a way for us to enjoy being like this forever."
"You're just talking Oryn, your words are sweet but both know why we
cannot." She rejects him. The pain in her heart burning for him, but
her logic not allowing it to blind her. "Kenye doesn't approve, and he will
tell the creator, we will be banished if we go against him. We have just
gotten the humans settled. Look at them." She points down at the land
below them. Humans tilled and worked the land so they could have
liveable crops. "After we have the immortals, we will leave this place,
we will go back to the land of the creator and there we can be together.
You and I."
He kisses her again. Deeper this time as if this will be the last kiss they
share for some time. "You protect Mecara, she is my vessel, she will
bring my immortal into the world. She will bring my girl to life. She
will do me proud." He stands. "I will always be with you light bringer."
He kisses her hand. "Always."
In the temple, he hears her voice. "My love." She beckons
. His smile widens. Mecara has given birth to her. To his Pearl! Since
the day the creator left them here to prepare this marble for his next
batch of creations. He turns to her and the world goes black.
She is terror. The woman with Obsidian skin and flaming hair
screaming for death and destruction. Begging the creator to take her
back to where she belonged. Where he was. The smell of smoke and

fire choke him. Make him claw for breath and she looks at him. The fire wrapped around her pupil looks at him. She points her sword at him. "It is you! You know the truth!"

Silas jolted awake. He rubbed his face with his hands. He'd cried the same way he had since the first time he had the dream. Who was she? What truth was she talking about and why was it that he had to know it? Ever since he'd met Poppi Bell she had this effect on him, no surprise now, she was a fertility witch. She'd woken some ancient power that hadn't been real since his mother was a child. It was why they decided to go to witches to create serums to make their heirs. Just in case they died and were unable to return. But an immortal hadn't been killed in 50 years. And the one who was it was an accident.

His phone started to buzz on his nightstand and he pulled it off the chord. "Go for Abraxas."

"Silas, it's me, you need to come home."

"Ma? Are you okay?"

"Your father and brother were killed in an explosion tonight, you need to come home." Pearl hung up. Silas got up and walked to his mirror. He splashed water on his face and looked at his mirror. The man from his nightmares stood in front of him

"It's time Silas." He spoke in a voice that could have commanded the weakest seed to grow. "You must find the light-bringer."

71

ABOUT THE AUTHOR

M any words can describe J. F. Ruffin.

Mother, partner, daughter, and friend are a few. When she's not creating worlds from small specks of ideas she grasps from anywhere. You can find her with her nose in a new craft, laughing about the small things, and breaking the generational curses that her ancestors thought she was strong enough to break.

COMING
Soon

IMPROPER
Arrangements

J.F.
Ruffin

Made in the USA
Middletown, DE
12 September 2023

38399442R00179